ENTANGLED
IN THE
WOODS

EVI JAMES

ISBN: 979-8-9911988-0-6 (Paperback)

ISBN: 979-8-9911988-1-3 (e-book)

Library of Congress Control Number: 2024918106

Cover Art by Miblart

Editing by Mandi Andrejka, Inky Pen Editorial Services

Visit evijamesauthor.com for more information.

AUTHOR'S NOTE

Entangled in the Woods contains adult themes that may be difficult for some readers.

Please read the content warnings on my website for more information.

www.evijamesauthor.com

For the risk takers.
Jump.
I can't wait to see you fly.

CHAPTER ONE

"Oh, this is going to be an adventure!" Mom said as we passed the road sign that read 20 *Miles to America's Best Small Town!* We'd spent ten hours in the car today, and it was getting dark. Even after ten hours, Mom was still buzzing with excitement. Her energy made me, thirty years younger than her, jealous. I was tired. For the last three days, my parents and I had been driving, only stopping for the occasional bathroom break—in which Mom timed us, threatening to leave us at the shady rest stops with the long-haul truckers if we didn't make it back to the car in time.

Now I was in the car, in the back seat, sitting next to our family cat like I was seven years old. Only twenty more miles. We had driven from a small town along the Atlantic Ocean to the northernmost part of Minnesota, almost in Canada. The trees up here grew thicker and taller. The roads winded through thickets and along the edges of lakes. After all the sing-alongs and ridiculous road trip games my mother came up with to pass the time, we were twenty miles away from dropping off my parents at their new house in the small town of Fenrirton and one hundred miles away from *my* new house, which was a research cabin nestled deep in the woods along the Canadian border that I would share with two other graduate students.

The thought of living in such close quarters with these new people still made my heart pound. Even as a kid, I'd preferred wandering wooded trails alone to playdates or a quiet spot in the library to a Friday-night football game. My interests usually meant I was never up on the latest gossip or fashion. It had been lonely being the outcast throughout secondary school, dressed in what my mom considered "cute" clothes. Usually I'd been stuck with overalls, complete with homemade patches sewn to the knees. I had hoped that after I'd left high school and majored in ecology, I would be surrounded by like-minded people. And I had been. There'd been a few girls from class who I'd spent a lot of time studying with and completing capstone projects. But as our fourth year had approached, one had gotten engaged and the others had found jobs and moved away.

Now I felt like I had at the end of high school. Lonely but hopeful that I would find *my* people. This summer was my best bet. Maybe I would make good friends? Ones who stuck around. Ones who didn't think my interests were weird. The people the university had accepted for this graduate program had had to submit previous research and write several essays to get an invitation to the cabin. Someone who was looking for a vacation here wouldn't bother to do all that.

I hoped my new roommates would be like me in the sense that they loved what they were studying, experienced the same rush when they discovered something unexpected. We were going to be out in the woods without cell service for the entire summer. They had to be similar. No one who wasn't passionate about their research would subject themselves to an entire summer so secluded.

"I'm so excited to see the house your uncle left us," Mom said, drawing me from my thoughts. "I'm sure it's going to be just as charming as I hear the town is. Let's just hope it has some studio space."

I could sense my dad rolling his eyes even from my vantage point in the back seat. Mom would make room for her sculpting anywhere. I grew up with her work strewn throughout the house.

"I'm sure it's nothing fancy, Deb. If it has a kitchen and a bathroom, we'll make it work. We don't have much of a choice." Though he was always the quiet to my mom's loud, opposites in every way, today my father sounded more exhausted and subdued than usual. I chewed on my lip to keep from asking if he needed anything, since he'd been asked that plenty already by Mom on this entire trip.

"Oh, Roger." Mom sighed. "Let's look at this as a fresh start. We have each other and dear Bessie." A loud "meow" came from the beige plastic kennel sitting in the seat next to me. "Elise won't be too far away either, right, dear?"

"Just over two hours away," I said from the back seat.

"See—closer than before. I'm sure she'll visit on weekends?" she asked, looking expectantly in the rearview mirror at me.

"I'm going to be busy, Mom. I have a thesis to start, and I need to explore the forest. I can try to be back to visit, but I also have to work." Though if everything went according to plan, I wouldn't have to resort to visiting my parents at all this summer. My research would keep me busy, and if my roommates were as awesome as I hoped they'd be, I'd spend the weekends with them.

Mom just looked forward and hummed the song on the radio. I leaned back against the cloth headrest of our old Subaru. It would soon be mine to use. The town my parents were moving to claimed to be "America's Best Small Town" because of the ability to walk to everything you needed. The grocery store was a couple blocks away, as were the pharmacy and movie theater. Mom and Dad would have no need for a car, and they wanted to make sure I could make it back to see them and help if necessary.

The car swayed as the wind hit the side, the small trailer we pulled behind exaggerating the movement. The sky was getting dark, and there were visible stars here, unlike the bigger city where we'd come from. I closed my eyes and tried to zone out for the next fifteen minutes until we arrived. During this three-day trip, I had been constantly alternating between road sickness and boredom. I couldn't listen to music on my headphones during the entire ride because of my mom's constant need for conversation. My dad, in the front seat, was a good listening ear but rarely added much to the dialogue.

"I've got you, Roger," my mom said between song verses as she grabbed on to his jacket to keep him upright as we curved right on the road. My dad grumbled that he was fine, even though I saw the way he clung to her arm to hold himself up.

I was about to finally let myself ask how Dad was doing when I noticed something standing twenty feet in front of us in the middle of the road.

"*Mom!*"

The smell of rubber entered my nose as the tires skidded on the dry pavement. I could hear my mother let out a litany of curse words as she white-knuckled the steering wheel, willing the car to stop. From the back seat, my eyes locked with the animal's. It had come out of nowhere. Our headlights illuminated the two irises that looked as if depthless golden pools dwelled within them.

As the car slid toward the creature, our eye contact never wavered. I couldn't look away, and it seemed as if the being couldn't either. It didn't seem scared by a ton of metal barreling toward it. It stood calm and collected, just staring into my eyes.

I froze, pitching forward as the car finally came to a stop. We were ten feet away from the animal. It looked like a wolf, but it was much larger than any wolf that I had seen in captivity. Maybe the wolves ate well out here. The wolf had the darkest black coat, almost iridescent in the headlights of our car. I broke eye contact as my gaze traveled down the wolf's body to its giant paws. Fluffy mounds of fur covered its toes, and shiny black claws gripped the ground, ready to run at a moment's notice.

As my head lifted back up to make eye contact once again, the wolf blinked. It turned and ran, disappearing as fast as it had appeared in front of our car. That was the biggest wolf I had ever seen in my life. I shook my head, trying to get out the image of its golden eyes that had sucked me in—whirlpools of glittering gold that I couldn't stop seeing in my mind. Having read about the wildlife and foliage in this area, I'd known there were wolves and other wild predators like bears that lived up here. I just hadn't thought I would see one so soon—and so up close and personal. I also hadn't known that wolves had eyes like that. Eyes which seemed all too easy to fall into.

"Are you okay back there, Elise? How about Bessie? Is Bessie okay?" Of course Mom would confirm the cat was okay in the same breath as her own daughter.

"Yep, we're fine," I said, peeking in on Bessie, our orange elderly cat. Rearranging myself in the back seat behind my father, I nodded at my mom as she locked eyes with me, getting permission to continue. Dad's seat belt had prevented him from flying through the windshield, but his body lay in the seat at an odd angle, his head resting against the passenger window. Mom re-situated him in his seat the best she could.

"Let's keep going! Hopefully no more wild animals will run into the road before we get to our new lives."

I rolled my eyes at my mom's characterization of what had just happened. She hadn't stopped talking about our "new lives" since we'd left my childhood home. It seemed like a coping mechanism, to always be looking forward, purposefully forgetting the past.

We weren't strangers to a scare. The last weeks had been full of hardship, one thing after another falling apart. A car wreck would have been a cherry on top of an already disastrous month.

I looked around the car, watching my family pick themselves up and brush themselves off like we always did, well-practiced in taking whatever hits life decided to throw at us.

CHAPTER TWO

When I had received the hysterical call from my mother during my last year of undergraduate school telling me that my father had fallen, I'd been shocked. They had kept my father's failing health from me while I'd been away.

Sitting in the emergency room while the back of my father's head had been stitched up by a doctor, my mother and father had begrudgingly explained to me how he'd been getting weaker over the last couple of years. They'd kept this from me during my holiday visits home, as his weaknesses hadn't been as visible as they were now. He'd gone from occasionally stumbling or tripping to having trouble with stairs and sometimes suffering from such bad vertigo he had trouble staying seated upright in a chair.

Dad had been to two different doctors, both of whom could not find the reason for his sudden health failings. Even though his health continued to deteriorate, there was no money for expensive specialists or extensive testing. His body was weak—Mom had to help him use the bathroom every couple of hours and assist him in the shower. He spent most of the day on the couch with Bessie on his lap, trying not to be a burden. Mom never made much money as a sculptor. The few people who bought her art we knew or had taken pity on my family after news had spread about Dad's health.

My dad had worked in road construction since I'd been born. He had made decent money—enough for us to afford a place to live and food to eat, but nothing special or extraneous. As his health had failed and he couldn't physically do the manual-labor part of the job anymore, he'd had to quit. Neighbors and friends had given him the odd job here and there as a handyman to keep my parents afloat for the last couple of years. Then they'd received a letter from a lawyer up in the northern part of the country. When I'd first read it, I'd thought they were being conned. It seemed too good to be true—my father's great uncle had left him a house. A small house in a small town, but a free home nonetheless.

Seeing my doubt, my father had explained that this great uncle had been, in fact, a real person from the Wilson side of the family he had met a handful of times growing up. He hadn't seen him in over thirty years and hadn't even known that he'd passed. But this seemed to be a miracle—one my parents had greatly needed. With no other choice, they'd signed the papers and the deed to the house in the hospital room. The house was theirs, and the one that I'd grown up in was now the property of the bank.

Several weeks later, I'd graduated with my undergraduate degree and helped my parents pack up what little belongings they had. We couldn't fit much in the compact car and trailer we were taking to the new cabin. Mom had jammed most of the trailer with her sculpting supplies, and we'd filled the car with clothing and miscellaneous items from the house. I had all my clothing and personal items in a single duffle bag and laptop bag that contained my computer and research I had completed over my undergraduate studies. My small plant collection I'd tucked into the rear deck, hoping it would get some sunshine on the drive.

I collected plants with healing properties, like aloe and yarrow. There was something about the ability to heal your body with nature that had always intrigued me. Before we'd left, I'd rescued a few plants from the garden I'd tried to maintain in the backyard. My mom wasn't a gardener, but she had kept it watered for me when I'd been at school. I hoped to expand my collection of plants with ones I found during my research this summer. Pushed close to me in the back seat, these were all the items I had to my name.

A squeal from the front seat of the car made me lift my head and open my eyes.

"Well, isn't this the most darling town you have ever seen? It looks like a movie set!" My mom was practically beaming sunshine, poking at my dad as if he couldn't see what she could. I couldn't argue with her.

The town had a long main street that was lined with shops and a couple of restaurants. Each shop had its own personality. Different-colored shops selling handmade items or homemade foods lined each side of the street. Every several feet there was a black lamp post with a large basket of multicolored petunias hanging from it. Tilting my head up, I noticed string lighting that hung across the street between the lampposts in a zigzag pattern. The street would look nothing but magical in about an hour when the sun set.

As we neared the end of the street, there was more space between the buildings. Small homes with white mailboxes replaced the businesses that lined both sides of the street. Dad carefully lifted his hand, and his index finger pointed to a house on the right side of the road.

"Oh, look at it! East-facing to get all that morning sunshine. It'll be so wonderful to work in the morning light," Mom said.

The Subaru groaned up the short gravel driveway, parking in front of the two-car garage. Even the car seemed to be happy our trip was over.

Stepping out of the car, I stood holding the door open while the blood rushed back into my legs. A low "meow" had me glancing back into the car. Grumbling, I grabbed Bessie's kennel. That cat always made sure not to be left behind. Holding the kennel, I made my way up to the house.

Typical of the town, the house was a cute little rambler with a wide front porch. The wood siding could use a fresh coat of paint, but other than that, the house seemed to be in good condition. Scrambling by me, my mother ran to the front door, holding the key. With a quick push, she was in the house.

"Roger! You have to come see it!" Mom said from inside the house.

"Well, I need a bit of help," my father mumbled, still inside the car.

She flittered down the steps and past me, helping my dad out of the car. With one arm wrapped around my mom and the other holding his cane, Dad slowly made his way down the sidewalk and up the two steps onto the porch.

With fresh energy, I stood ready to help my mom unpack the car. The sooner we unloaded and I got my parents settled, the sooner I would be on my way to *my* new life. I sounded like my mother.

There weren't many boxes to carry in. Two or three were clothes, a couple were home decor, and the rest were my mom's sculpting supplies. Mom directed her sculpting boxes to be put in the garage, where she would set up her new studio. We put the clothing in the primary bedroom and placed the decor boxes in the living room.

"Elise, come help me hang the clothes in the closet before you leave us," Mom said. "Who knows when we'll see you next." I followed her into their bedroom, rolling my eyes. My eyeballs were going to be sore after spending this much time with her. My father smirked at me as he pet the purring orange cat on his lap.

"I know you want to get on the road, but I just wanted to talk to you." As she handed me a plastic hanger, Mom's eyes tried to look into my soul, and I just knew what was coming. "We're so proud of you, Elise. You went to college all by your-self and did so well. And now a full ride to graduate school? It's just amazing. I know you want to get on with the next part of your life, but just know that we're a couple hours away if you need anything."

"I know, Mom," I replied, slipping a T-shirt onto a hanger. "Just make sure you keep me updated on Dad. I don't want to be surprised again."

She got a serious look on her face and said, "We won't do that again."

We continued hanging clothes in silence, getting closer and closer to the bottom of the cardboard box. Lifting a small wooden box with a hinged lid from the bottom, Mom sighed. "Oh good, I'm glad your father's junk has followed us here," she said sarcastically. "I'm going to put it up on the highest shelf in the closet so that it can collect dust until the next time we move. Your father's so sentimental."

"My ears are burning out here on the couch," my father called out from the living room.

"Yes, well, I've moved that darn box from house to house since we met. A dust collector is about all that it's good for."

As Mom finished hanging the last of the clothing, I opened the wooden box that held a few baseball cards, a stone the size of my fist, a bag of my baby teeth, and a plant journal I had made in third grade. I picked up the rock and passed it between my hands as I paged through the journal. I had spent so much time on the journal, carefully taping the flowers inside the pages after I had pressed them flat. Some of the nectar had soaked through the printer paper I'd used, staining the paper. I used better paper for collecting samples now. My handwriting had also been terrible. I could barely make out what I had written. It was sweet that my dad had kept it.

Sighing, I closed the journal. I put all the contents back into the wooden box and put it up on the highest shelf in the closet for my mom to find, covered in dust, years later. Following Mom back into the living room, I switched on the lamp that sat on one of the end tables. It was almost dark out, and I still had a two-hour drive ahead of me.

"I need to get going," I said as I gathered the car keys from the table. "Please let me know if you need anything. I'm planning on coming back at the end of the summer once the semester ends, but if you need anything before that, I want you to call me."

"Of course we will." My mom walked across the room and gave me a big hug. "I have the number for the satellite phone at the cabin already in my cell phone. Are you sure it's safe up there with no cell service? I don't want you to get into any trouble and not have a way to contact help."

"I'll be fine, Mom. People got along just fine without cell phones back in your day." It was my mom's turn to roll her eyes as she let me escape her embrace.

To be honest, I was looking forward to the lack of cell service deep in the woods where I was going. There was something about being disconnected from the world and getting connected with nature that had always brought me peace. I wouldn't miss my phone at all. I didn't have anyone that I texted with daily anyway.

As I sat on the couch to say goodbye to my dad, Bessie gave me the stink eye. "I'll miss you too, old lady," I said as I scratched under her chin. She submitted to my attention, lifting her head to deepen the scratch.

"Be safe out there, Elise," my dad said with teary eyes.

"Don't get all emotional now," I said, giving him a big hug. "Take care of yourself. Don't be afraid to call if you need anything." His nod told me he had agreed.

Mom opened the door and walked me out to the Subaru that was now mine. I made quick work of detaching the trailer.

"Drive safe! Watch out for wildlife!" Mom said.

Now that it was dark, she had a good point. I would have to be extra cautious if I didn't want to end up in a wreck like we almost had earlier today.

I waved at my mom standing on the porch as I backed down the driveway and into the road. Thinking ahead, I had printed out turn-by-turn directions from my parents' new house to the cabin I would be living in. About an hour into the drive, I would lose all service and my GPS would be useless.

As I turned out of Fenrirton and onto the winding highway headed north, I let out a huge exhale. Letting my hair down from the clip that had been holding it up, I took a moment to breathe and settle into the freedom that was now mine. I had taken care of my parents and was now on my own journey toward "the next part of my life," as my mother had referred to it. After the hospital visit and the chaos of moving, it was nice to be on my own again.

Tucking my long brown hair behind my ear, I turned on the radio to listen to some music before I lost signal. I let myself fall victim to highway hypnosis as my car traveled deeper and deeper into the forest.

CHAPTER THREE

AFTER ONE MISSED turn and the constant dodging of critters that scurried right in front of my moving car, the Subaru pulled up in front of a simple log-style cabin. This was just about as remote as you could get. My headlights illuminated a generator that sat beside the structure and a basin that collected rainwater for the cabin. Luckily we'd have toilets that flushed into a septic tank, but that was it for modern conveniences. For years now, Northwind University had managed this cabin that served as the research base for graduate students studying the forest, and judging by the state of things, it had seen its fair share of students. Grabbing my two bags, I made my way up the gravel sidewalk to the front door of the cabin.

Surrounded by evergreens, the air had the scent of pine. I took a deep breath before climbing the stairs that led to an oversized porch with two rocking chairs. Overgrown plants climbed up the porch, covering the railings and some of the wood planks in purple flowers. As I lifted my hand to grab the door, someone flung it wide open, letting a musty smell out of the cabin. The screech of a small female as she grabbed me in an embrace bombarded my senses. Unable to use my arms because of the bags I was holding, I awkwardly stood there, my face smothered by her curly blonde hair.

"Oh my gosh, oh my gosh! I'm so glad you're here! I'm so glad you're a girl! There's a guy here already, and I was so worried that I'd be the only girl. Can you imagine? The bathroom would be a war zone." The woman let go of me, and I finally got a look at her face. She was a petite girl with petite features. Her curly blonde hair framed her face and fell just past her shoulders. Her blue designer sweat suit matched her eyes, although her eyes were lighter.

"I'm Jenny. Leo, the guy, is in his room unpacking. I think he said he was from Canada? I don't know," she said, barely pausing to take a breath. "I've just been so excited since I got here. I'm having trouble focusing."

Setting my bags down, I looked around the interior of the cabin. Simply constructed, it was the epitome of *rustic*. A small kitchen with a stove, oven, and refrigerator opened to a cozy living room with a fireplace. The living room had minimal furniture, only two couches, and a coffee table. Shelves stuffed with books lined the walls on either side of the fireplace. I walked over and ran my fingers along the spines. Most were local topics ranging from flora and fauna to tourist destinations. Jenny vibrated in the small space with a smile on her face as she watched me explore.

The light in the cabin came from the fireplace and the few electric lanterns scattered around the room. A small round table had been placed between the kitchen and the living room, surrounded by four wooden chairs. I could see myself having my breakfast at the table before setting out to explore for the day. Instead of art on the walls, pieces of iron hung as decoration. Some were twisted and manipulated into artistic swirls. Others looked like rudimentary weapons with points that had once been sharp and blades that would have been deadly had orange rust not formed on them.

Stepping back—and feeling thankful for my mother's insistence that I keep up to date on my tetanus shots—I turned to the only part I had yet to explore, a narrow hallway in the back.

"Sorry, but you get the last room," Jenny said, following my eyeline. I picked up my bags and followed the bouncing blonde through the living room and down the hallway. The first room to my right had the door open and was already decorated with pink bedding, and the closet was already full of mostly pink clothes.

"My friends all say I'm obsessed with pink, but I just like to wear what makes me happy!" Motioning to her blue sweat suit, she said, "This is about the only thing I have that doesn't have the color pink somewhere on it."

Across the hall was a small bathroom with a simple sink, toilet, and shower.

A couple of steps later, we paused at another room on the left side of the hallway. The door stood cracked open, and I could hear music coming from the room.

Jenny knocked on the door and stuck her head in. "The last roommate has arrived!" she announced, swinging the door open.

A man wearing a T-shirt and jeans turned around quickly, surprised at the loud intrusion. His shoulder-length brown hair that had been tied back came loose with the sudden movement. A sly smile crossed his lips as he walked over to us. Deep brown eyes glanced between Jenny and me. He was good-looking in a *nature, folk, granola* kind of way. Not my type, but I could appreciate an attractive man when I saw one.

"Wow, a blonde and a brunette. How'd I get so lucky?" he asked. Jenny giggled as she looked at me. My eyes did a complete rotation in their sockets. A guy this eager to live with two girls was not an ideal roommate. This wasn't summer camp —it was supposed to be a professional environment for students.

"Hi, I'm Elise," I said with an outstretched hand.

He took my hand and shook it. "Leo."

Our eyes made contact, and I could tell from the look he was giving us he was interested in getting to know his new female roommates further. I wasn't looking to get involved with anyone while I was here studying. I was here to study forest conservation, and trees were the only *wood* I was interested in. Lucky for Leo, it seemed he might have a willing participant in Jenny, who was standing there like a nervous schoolgirl meeting a boy for the first time.

When I turned to look at her, she snapped out of her trance and smacked me playfully in the arm. "Gosh, I'm such a talker that I didn't even ask you your name. Elise. That is such a pretty name," she said. "How did you end up stuck in a cabin with us? You're pretty enough that you don't need to rough it out here."

I laughed uncomfortably. I couldn't tell if she was teasing me or was serious. Maybe she was nervous like I was. I wasn't used to the attention she was giving me.

Hoping to change the subject, I answered her question. "I'm from the East Coast. I've been studying forest conservation around the mountains for the last couple of years."

"I've never been to the mountains. There usually aren't the predators I'm interested in out there," Jenny said. "I'm here for the wolves. I study pack behavior and hierarchy."

"I'm a water guy myself. Winding streams, wet marshes... any damp environment, really."

Jenny's eyes widened as Leo finished his sentence. My head tilted to the side, trying to read the situation. I couldn't tell if he purposefully spoke in sexual metaphors. Maybe I was reading too deeply into the situation—I tended to do that.

I made a move to excuse myself and unpack. Jenny quickly grabbed my arm at the elbow and pulled me down the hall to my bedroom. I could hear Leo laughing to himself.

My room was at the back of the house. A full bed with a patterned quilt took up most of the space. There was one large window that looked out into the woods and a small closet with minimal hanging space. I made a mental note to grab my plants from the car. They would be happy on the sill of the window here. A sizable desk stood under the window, complete with a couple of drawers and a chair. I set my bags on my bed. Luckily I didn't have much to unpack.

Jenny bounced on my bed, making herself comfortable. "Was it just me, or did he come on...strong?" she asked.

"I think he came on super strong."

"He's cute." Jenny played with her curls, wrapping them around her fingers.

"He's all yours. I'm not here for any of that."

"Good. Because I might be interested in some of that."

Raising my eyebrows, I looked at her. "Well, he seemed very interested. Especially in wet and damp places."

Jenny groaned and rolled her eyes. "Not you too, with the sexual innuendos. I'm going to be in trouble this summer. I just know it."

Shaking my head with a smile on my face, I started unpacking my clothes, hanging what needed to be hung and folding the items that couldn't fit on a hanger.

"You sure have a lot of athletic clothes," my new roommate concluded as she watched me unpack.

"Yeah, I do a lot of running for exercise and hiking for research," I said.

"Makes sense. I have a lot of athleisure too."

I noted her words. Athleisure usually meant a two-hundred-dollar sweat suit, like the one she was currently wearing. My athletic clothes were not as nice.

"I brought a few jumpsuits as well. Never know when there will be an opportunity to go out." Jenny looked hopeful. "There's one jumpsuit in my closet that might be a little short, but you could make it work."

I couldn't imagine what I would need a jumpsuit for out here—they seemed like a bitch to pee in—but I thanked her anyway.

Just as I finished putting the last of my clothes away, Jenny and I turned our heads to the sound of glass shattering in the kitchen. Meeting each other's eyes, we rushed out of my room and down the short hall to find Leo with a tray of two shot glasses. One shot glass was shattered on the floor.

"Well, jeez, that's what I get for trying to kick off our research program with shots," Leo said. He looked defeated as he set the tray down and picked up the pieces of glass. Jenny and I laughed as I grabbed a rag and started to wipe up the floor.

The smell of strong liquor hit my nose as I cleaned. "Is this tequila?" I asked.

"Yep, I thought we needed some welcome drinks to start this semester. And you two look like tequila drinkers to me."

I couldn't deny that I enjoyed an occasional margarita. Leo took my rag and threw it into the sink as we watched Jenny pour a shot into a fresh glass.

She raised her glass. "Cheers to new friends and a new summer semester!"

We raised the glasses to our mouths as Leo said, "May the marshes be damp and rivers flow. Here's to the friends I'm about to get to know!"

Tequila sprayed all over the kitchen as Jenny started laughing. I couldn't help but join her. She had one of those contagious laughs that drew everyone in. Unlike Jenny's, my shot went down my throat. It burned and settled in my stomach, warming my body.

"We have to do another one! I didn't even get to drink mine!" Jenny said. She started pouring from the tequila bottle into our empty shot glasses. "No toasts this time! Just drink!"

Jenny, Leo, and I raised our glasses and then drank the second shot. This one went down easier as the warmth spread to my extremities.

It was fun talking with my new roommates. The tequila loosened our lips, and we got to know each other quickly. Leo was from Canada, as Jenny had thought, and was studying water ecosystems. It seemed like he had quite a few articles already published. He was starting a research project involving the freshwater amphibians that lived here. Although she never said it, I deduced from stories of her upbringing that Jenny had lived a very comfortable life. Her interest in wolves stemmed from her family's frequent ski trips to Canada when she'd been growing up.

Leo and Jenny grew even more comfortable with each other, and they found themselves cuddled up on the couch together at the end of the night. After one too many shots, I said good night to the lovebirds and found my way to my room. Closing the door, I collapsed on the bed and fell asleep on top of the covers, still fully dressed.

CHAPTER FOUR

The smell of bacon hit my nose as I rolled over onto my back. The taste of tequila was still on my tongue. Grumbling, I stumbled out of bed and made my way to the shared bathroom to brush my teeth. After cleaning every surface to get rid of the taste of liquor, I made my way into the kitchen to find Leo hard at work making breakfast.

"Wow, did you get lucky last night, or are we just lucky to have you?" I asked as I made my way to the cabinet. Grabbing a plate, I dished up the eggs and bacon that Leo had spent the morning cooking.

"Nothing happened!" Jenny chirped from the kitchen table, already enjoying her breakfast.

"Then I guess we're just lucky to have you." I thanked Leo as he got himself a plate. The food was delicious, and I gobbled it down, hoping it would help my stomach.

"We have to soak up the tequila somehow," Leo joked with a mouthful of food. "Professor Robinson is coming by the cabin later this morning to check in on us."

I groaned at the reminder of our lead professor's visit. Each of us had a professor that we were working under, but Professor Robinson was the closest to the cabin and had volunteered to supervise us and help us as needed with each of our projects. Based on the emails we had already exchanged, he sounded like a hard-ass that let nothing slide.

I needed to get my life together before the professor arrived. There were a couple of hours before he would be here, and I wanted to be a little more alert. Jenny offered to take care of cleanup this morning, so I made my way down the hall and found a sports bra and running shorts. After changing quickly, I tied my long brown hair into a bun.

My shoes had taken up most of the space when I'd packed. It might've seemed silly to have so many shoes, especially when they all looked the similar, but they weren't the same. There were shoes for walking, running, trail running, and speed work. With as much as I ran, the shoes were on constant rotation. The blue trail-running shoes were my choice today.

There were several miles of trails around the cabin that would be good for running. Worn down by the previous students, some trails were wide enough to fit an ATV. Walking back through the house and out the front door, I yelled to Leo and Jenny—who were busy at the sink washing dishes and bumping elbows—that I was going for a run. I got a distracted reply as the front door screen slammed and I walked onto the porch.

The dew that dusted the foliage was still present, making my shoes glisten as I walked down the drive. Birds called in the distance, having already been up long before me. I reached up and stretched my arms, jumping in place for a minute to warm up my body. I had researched the trail system around the cabin before arriving and easily found the trailhead about a hundred feet away and started jogging.

The woods were truly beautiful in this area. Wild and free

to grow as they please, plants wove through the tall trees that provided shade over the trail. Tiny wildflowers littered the sides of the path, their perfume hitting my nose as I breathed deeper.

After about a mile, my muscles loosened and my breathing became more regular. I had entered my favorite state of running, where I could finally turn off my mind and flow through the movements. My even footfalls became a metronome in my mind—*left, right; left, right*—and I entered the meditative trance that made running so addictive to me.

Left, right.

Left, right.

Left, right.

A breeze flowed over my face, cooling my forehead that had beads of perspiration forming on it.

Crack!

Just like that, I was pulled out of my trance. I glanced around my shoulder, finding nothing of suspicion. An acorn had fallen behind me, maybe.

Continuing, I came to a fork in the trail and followed the right path, making a mental note to explore the left path another time. The trail was a little rockier, and I had to watch my footsteps a little more carefully. A flash of gray entered my peripheral vision, and I swung my head to the right, but there was nothing there. How much tequila had I drunk last night? Shaking my head, I slowed my jog to a walk and began scanning the surrounding area, my breaths heavy.

There were wolves in these woods—Jenny was here to study them. I hadn't had a chance to ask her if she knew where any were located yet, and while I'd once read up on what to do if you encountered a wolf in the woods, of course right now I'd completely forgotten anything I'd learned. The rocks on the trail were getting larger and more difficult to walk on without accidentally rolling my ankle. My eyes went from scanning my surroundings to having to watch each step so I wouldn't fall and injure myself. Could wolves smell blood? I didn't want to fall and find out.

"Hey!"

At the sudden voice, I spun around quickly. My foot landed on the rounded rock in front of me and skidded off the side, causing me to lose my balance and fall. A small yelp left my lips as I landed on my butt.

"Hey, are you okay?" the voice, deep and male, asked.

I glanced up from my position on the ground, taking a mental account of all my body parts. Other than the bruise that was surely forming on my butt, I was fine. Luckily I hadn't rolled my ankle or cut up my hands in the fall. Out of the corner of my eye, I could see six feet of a man was coming my way.

"That was some fall," he said.

"I'm fine." I brushed off the dirt on my hands and attempted to stand, trying to find my footing among all the rocks.

Suddenly a hand reached out in front of me, and I gasped at how close he'd gotten. Just a second ago he'd seemed to be a good fifteen feet away.

I placed my hand on the stranger's; my hand was so small in his. Without effort, the man pulled me to my feet, and I found my footing, quickly letting go. Rubbing my own on my shorts loosened a thick scion with a couple sprouting green leaves onto the ground. It must have been ripped from its root-stock when I'd fallen on top of it.

"Damnit." I didn't like disturbing plants. I picked up the scion and looked at the stem. It seemed like a clean break. "Do you have a key or anything pointy?"

He dug into the pockets of his jeans and pulled out a single car key with a black head cover.

"I can't just leave it like this," I said, mostly to myself.

Taking the key, I searched for the rootstalk the green stem had broken off from. It was easy to find, the stalk sticking up from the ground right where I'd fallen. Crouching down near the rootstalk, I pushed the key's sharp tip straight into the cylinder of the stalk. This was a delicate procedure, especially since I was using a key instead of my usual tools. I pushed the key about a quarter inch into the stalk, widening the diameter. The stem easily slid into the hole, its diameter smaller than the rootstalk I'd just widened. I held it in place with my fingertips, searching for some long grass to tie it off with. I settled for some blue oatgrass that I recognized and was within reach. The oatgrass was long, and I was able wrap it around the stalk several times and tied it, assured that it would stay in place.

"You seem to know what you're doing," the man said, watching me.

I jumped back from my rescued plant; I had forgotten that he was here.

"Yeah, I've done it a few times before. It's usually successful." I sat back and admired my handywork before handing him his key.

"I wouldn't go much farther. The rocks get even bigger. I had to turn around myself," he said.

The man wasn't dressed for the woods. He wore light blue jeans that had maybe been nice at some point but were now ripped with several holes. His simple black T-shirt also had seen better days. There weren't any holes, but it was faded from consistent wear.

Closing my eyes and shaking my head, I tried to regain my composure. As I opened my eyes, I looked at the man's face. He was tan from all the time he must have spent outdoors. His dark hair was long enough that he had to use his hand to push it back over the top of his head to keep it from falling into his face.

His face lit up with a smirk—he'd caught me looking at him. "I'm headed back the way you came. Can I join you?"

I squeaked a "No" as I turned around and started walking.

The man easily caught up to me and kept pace alongside me. This was my worst nightmare as a runner—a man approaching me in the woods and now following me.

Keeping my eyes to the ground, I took in his shoes. His old sneakers didn't look like something I would choose to walk in the woods with, but nothing about the rest of his outfit did either. Right now, I was beating myself up for not telling Jenny and Leo exactly where I would be running. Maybe I should have brought something with me to defend myself or something to leave behind in the case this man wanted to murder me or eat me alive. In these woods, a girl like me could easily disappear.

Finding the nerve to lift my head, I looked over at him. He had already trained his bright blue eyes on my face. Unlike myself, he didn't need to watch his footing. He seemed to glide over the rocks gracefully.

"What are you doing out here?" I asked.

"I'm out for a run myself. I had to turn around back there. The trail got a little too...wild for me."

A run? Who ran in blue jeans? The man looked me over. Now regretting my scantily clad running attire, I put my hands protectively over my stomach. Like that would do anything in my defense.

"I could ask the same question of you. What's a pretty girl like you doing out here in the woods, dressed like that, all alone? There are all sorts of animals out here. Wouldn't want them to catch the scent of you."

"I was running," I blurted out, picking up my pace. "My friends back at the cabin are waiting for me. I need to get back."

My fast footsteps betrayed me as I tripped and lurched forward. With my arms crossed around my stomach, I yelped as I began to fall face-first into the rocky ground. Two firm hands grabbed my shoulders and steadied me back onto my feet. With him standing right behind me, I could smell earth and sweat. He didn't smell like a typical man would, but much to my dismay, I sort of enjoyed the earthy scent.

Breathing deeply, I let out an exhale as the man leaned over my shoulder and whispered into my ear, "Careful."

It took me a moment to shake myself out of his hands, putting a couple feet of distance between us. I turned around quickly, looking the stranger in his blue eyes.

"Thanks..." I struggled to maintain my composure. The man had saved me from a fall, but I still didn't feel comfortable with the way he was approaching me. His scent was throwing me off. Sure, he was attractive, but he obviously didn't know how to approach a single woman on a run in the woods.

"My name's Wilder. I live around here, but I've never seen you before."

Trying and failing to break eye contact, I tried to calculate a coherent answer. "I'm new, I guess. I'm here doing research for the university. There's a cabin not far from here where I live... which I need to be getting back to." I immediately regretted my answer—I'd just given this large man, Wilder, way too much information.

"Ah, I've heard about that cabin. I've never seen it, though."

"Great!" I squeaked awkwardly before turning around and saying, "I gotta go!" over my shoulder.

"I'm sure I'll see you around, Fumbles. Don't fall without me."

I could hear his chuckling as I jogged out of there, careful not to fall again. Glancing back over my shoulder, I saw that Wilder stood casually in the middle of the trail, watching me jog away. His hands were in the pockets of his blue jeans, and a smirk was on his lips. Apparently he enjoyed watching me run from him.

Once I hit the gravel trail that was more conducive to running, I broke out into a fast run, my legs turning over quickly, until I reached the clearing by our cabin. Hunched over, I brought my hands to my knees, trying to catch my breath. There were always stories about women getting approached on their runs by creepy men—you just never thought you'd be one of them.

Shaking off the adrenaline that flowed through my veins, I walked up to the cabin and opened the door. Leo and Jenny were nowhere to be found. I walked down the hall, hoping I wouldn't see anything scandalous in one of their rooms as I made my way to my own. Fortunately Jenny was alone, sitting on her bed with a book.

She set it down once she saw me walk by and followed me. "How was your run?" she asked.

"Not the best. The trail I ran on turned out to be rocky, and a creepy guy in the woods approached me." I kept the feeling of my attraction to Wilder to myself. I wasn't supposed to feel something like that for a random man who'd approached me in the woods. He'd saved me from a nasty fall that would have ended with me covered in cuts and bruises, but I couldn't let my guard down just because a man had used his reflexes and caught me. I wasn't a damsel in need of a prince to save me.

"What?" Jenny said. "I didn't think anyone lived close enough to our cabin that you would run into someone. What did he say? He didn't touch you, did he? Are you okay?"

"No, no," I said, realizing that she was starting to spiral. "He didn't do anything. He was just very flirty when he approached me. I don't like talking while I'm on a run, much less with a guy who comes up to me out of nowhere in the woods."

"Yeah, that's so weird. He didn't follow you back here, did he?" Jenny asked.

"No, I left him about a mile away and he didn't follow me. He said he didn't even know there was a cabin back here."

"Good. I'm glad you're all right. Maybe there's mace or something in the cabin you can bring with you next time."

"Yeah, I should look for something like that." My clothing was chilling my skin as the sweat that soaked the fabric cooled. "I'm going to take a quick shower before Professor Robinson gets here."

I needed to wash off the conflicting feelings from my body and my mind.

CHAPTER FIVE

AFTER MY SHOWER, I quickly got dressed in leggings and a T-shirt, then met Jenny and Leo at the kitchen table. Professor Robinson was just sitting down, handing out folders from his bag, when I slid into the last seat. He was an older professor, probably in his late sixties. His gray hair was short, military style, and he had groomed his mustache similarly. Opening the folder, I found a map of the area surrounding the cabin as well as some pamphlets from the university about codes of conduct and other human resources documents.

Clearing his throat, Professor Robinson began speaking. "I know you all have professors you'll be conducting your research under, and you'll be expected to check in with them weekly, but I'm here to supervise you physically."

Jenny and I made eye contact and smirked—we were so mature.

The professor's voice was stern and unwavering. It was obvious he took his job seriously. "You can go through all that human resource mumbo jumbo on your own time," he said. "Why I wanted to meet with you today is to lay down the ground rules and give you some information about the local region."

I felt like a freshman looking over a syllabus on my first day of class all over again.

"We've had some issues in the past with run-ins with the residents who live in this area. They don't like that the university is out here conducting research on the land." An irritated expression fell across Professor Robinson's face. "Apparently they see it as an intrusion of their personal space as well as an intrusion of the natural order." He paused, shaking his head before continuing. "Our differing philosophies aside, you are all here to work and begin your graduate studies. I would suggest staying clear of the locals."

My face heated, and my stomach dropped. One day in and I had already broken the rules.

"I've highlighted the homes that are within a twenty-mile radius of this cabin," Robinson said. "The closest one is five miles away. Anything within that distance seems to be fine. Once you are outside that perimeter, I want your guards up and for you to be aware of your surroundings."

Looking at the map, I noticed there were a handful of homes highlighted. Glancing at those, my eyes caught the black curved lines denoting trails. My fingers followed the lines, tracing all the different running paths I could soon explore.

"What happened with the locals and students that were here before us?" Jenny asked, looking concerned. She glanced at me before her gaze returned to Robinson, obviously disturbed for me and my recent run-in.

"Mostly verbal threats and reports back to the university of trespassing students," he said. "One incident occurred two years ago where a gun was pointed at a student. That resident has since moved away, but I would strongly suggest you steer clear of the homes that are highlighted. A lot of the people out here have limited contact with the outside world, and we don't know anything about them. Best to keep to yourselves and keep to your work."

Nodding, Jenny kicked me under the table, urging me with her eyes to tell the professor about my run-in earlier today. I subtly shook my head. I didn't want Robinson to target me as a problem before we'd even begun working.

Robinson gestured to our folders on the table. "Keep your maps and go through the rest of the paperwork. I'll be around next week to pick it up. I think you know how to act as mature adults, but you know how it is nowadays."

We all nodded. Paging through the paperwork, I saw a code of ethics, sexual-harassment policy, and the safety waivers ready for my signatures.

"I'm sure you know how to keep the cabin clean," he said, clearly not planning to wait for any questions we might have. "The university expects you to pick up after yourselves and maintain the cabin for future students to use. The outside of the cabin is also your responsibility. The last group here oversaw repainting the windows. Since it's summertime, you're responsible for cleaning up the landscaping around the cabin. I need weeds pulled and some general cleaning up around the perimeter of the cabin."

I tried not to let my frown show. Great—another thing to add to my to-do list.

Professor Robinson pushed out his chair and packed up his bag. "Oh, Elise, I have a letter for you. It came late this morning." He handed me the yellow envelope with *Elise Wilson* in large letters, and I immediately recognized my mother's handwriting. "Sorry about the sat phone. It broke last semester, and the university has been slow release the funds to replace it. Once I can get it ordered, I'll bring out the replacement."

All three of us looked at each other in surprise. We hadn't

even checked the satellite phone since we'd arrived, let alone realized it wasn't working. My mother was probably in a tizzy, unable to call the cabin and check on me.

"That was shorter than I thought it would be," Leo said. He looked at Jenny and me as we stood up to see the professor out the door. Robinson moved slowly across the cabin as if he was trying to remember if he had forgotten to tell us anything important.

He turned around to address us again. "I can't come out here any more than I need to. Do your work and act right, and you won't be seeing much of me."

Professor Robinson walked toward the door as we said our goodbyes. Leo opened the door and closed it behind the professor, exhaling loudly. Feeling the information overload, we all decided to go our separate ways to read through the materials he'd left with us.

Sitting on my bed, I opened the yellow envelope from my mom. She'd said she would write to me, but I hadn't thought it would be so soon. I looked at the postdate—two days ago, in Illinois. I shook my head as I unfolded it.

Elise,

I hope you're settling into your new life. I wanted this letter to get to you on your first days at the cabin so you would know we're thinking of you and miss you already! We are so proud of you! I'm sure your father and I are settling in nicely into our new home. I hope you're doing the same.

Don't worry about us at all! Focus on your studies! I'll write soon!

Love, Mom

I rolled my eyes as I finished reading and tucked the letter back into the envelope. My mother still caused me to roll my eyes, even from two hours away. How had she snuck the letter into a mailbox? Probably while I'd been on one of her imposed timed bathroom breaks at a truck stop. I was sure Professor Robinson would have a stack of letters by the next time he visited.

With the letter read, that left the folder of paperwork he'd left for us to review. But I wasn't in the mood to look over papers.

My backpack lay on the floor against my desk, empty from the unpacking I'd done earlier. Now seemed like a good time to start looking into what plants grew here. There was a list somewhere in the information I'd brought with me that detailed rare plants found specifically in this region, but again, I was avoiding the growing paperwork piles on my desk. There were a few I had committed to memory. It would be enough to get started.

I pulled out a fresh field journal from my desk, bringing my nose to the new pages. The smell of possibilities. I tucked the map Robinson had provided between the pages and dropped it into my backpack along with a few glass sample containers, a pair of clippers, and two pencils. I couldn't find my water bottle—I'd likely shoved it somewhere—but since I didn't plan to be gone for too long and I was itching to get out, I figured I would be okay to do without it for one day. With the backpack slung over one of my shoulders, I made my way through the cabin to the front door, passing Jenny's and Leo's rooms on the way out. Their doors were closed—they'd probably felt the same motivation to get going on their research as I did.

I purposely chose a different trail than the one I'd run down earlier, hoping not to run into any other locals today. The scent of pine filled my nose, the resin flowing fast this time of year. I let my fingers graze along the pokey pines of a nearby evergreen, admiring the new bud of needles forming along its tip.

This part of the country was so different from what I was used to. Back east, the woods were more manicured, still slowly recovering from the extensive lumbering and agriculture of the eighteenth and nineteenth centuries. Up north here, the forest had been less affected, left to grow wild and unruly—nature in its most natural form.

It didn't take long to find a plant that caught my eye, jogging my memory back to the list of the plants I was in search of. *Achillea alpina*, also known as Siberian yarrow, grew just off the trail to the right. Its white flowers and leaves surrounded by sharp teeth gave it away.

Coming off the path, and careful to not disturb the other foliage, I lowered myself to my knees and dug through my backpack for my journal and clippers. After observing the plant, I found the best spot to take a sample. It had to be small enough that it wouldn't hurt the plant in the long term yet big enough that it could be an adequate model to display pressed flat in my journal.

I unlatched the safety from my clippers and took a clean snip of the plant. "Steady," I said under my breath.

Picking up the sample, I admired the clusters of flowers on the stem. The leaves were hairy, with sharp teeth along the edge. It would look good pressed between the pages of my journal. I had never seen one in person before. It was like a text-book had become three-dimensional right before my eyes.

With the clipping safely put away in one of the sample containers, I got to work writing notes about where I had found the plant and what was growing around it. All these details were important, especially with rare species. It was helpful to know what the plant grew well around. Future conservationists could read my research and apply it to their own work, particularly in places where the plant was struggling to survive.

Finishing my notes, I zipped up my pack, ready to continue. The sun had crossed the sky and was on its descent into the horizon. There were probably four hours left of light. Enough time for a mile more of scavenging.

It was hard for me to keep my eyes on the ground where the plants I was looking for grew. Birds talked to one another high in the trees, flying from nest to branch and back again, protecting their newly born young. The canopy of trees overhead let light filter down through their leaves, creating shadows and flashes of light as the branches shifted in the breeze. It was enchanting, being caught in the kaleidoscope of light.

I closed my eyes for a moment, taking a deep breath of fresh air through my nose, letting it sit in my nose before blowing it out of my mouth. My happy place. Where I felt most myself, most in my element, with only the trees and the breeze.

Without my sight, I could feel the forest hum beneath my feet. I liked to pretend that it was humming to me, like a song, giving me the same energy lyrics and melody gave their listeners. This forest hummed in a different key than the forest back east. The sound ran flat, low in pitch, less spirited.

My eyes opened slowly, looking at the path ahead. Two tiny eastern hemlock seedlings grew from the ground, the sun shining down through the canopy, cooking the plant and its tender needles.

"Poor things." They didn't stand a chance out in the open with no protection. The light green needles were soft as I stroked the branches, careful not to break any of them off. I glanced around the surrounding forest for a log, a large one, that would shade the seedlings.

Decomposition was natural in a forest, and it only took a moment for me to find the right size of log. It had been the trunk of a large tree, probably fifty or more years old before it had fallen because of wind or illness. Now I would give it another life, one that would be just as important as its previous one. I used my body weight to roll the log toward the hemlocks, placing it in the right spot to give shade to the seedlings during the hottest part of the day. The log would become a nurse log to the seedlings, giving them not only shade but preventing the sun from absorbing too much moisture from the soil they grew in. As the log continued to decompose, it would provide nutrients to the soil and ultimately to the new hemlocks themselves. A fitting ending to a tree's life—helping another tree live.

I brushed my hands together, removing the bark and dirt from them. Two miles away from the cabin, it was time to turn back. With the yarrow in my backpack, I considered my first day successful. The sun was scorching. Beads of sweat along my forehead made me regret not taking the time to dig out my water bottle. Thirst motivated me to hike back to the cabin quickly, and I swore to myself I would find it before going out next.

I was the last to arrive back at the cabin. Leo sat on the couch in jeans and flannel button-up even though it was way too hot for that. Jenny popped out of her room when she heard the door open, sporting a form-fitting pink track suit, part of her athleisure collection. Everyone had finished up with research for the day, and judging from how damp and fatigued my roommates were looking as well, they were just as thirsty as I was.

CHAPTER SIX

<hr>

Leo mentioned a bar that was down the road about ten miles, so we headed that way, squeezed into the front seat of his old pickup truck. Jenny, in a mix of excitement and the seat's coiled springs, was practically bouncing in between us as we drove down the gravel road. None of us had bothered to change clothes, although I'd borrowed a pair of wedge sneakers from Jenny. She had insisted, showering me with compliments about how great my legs looked wearing them. I took her word for it.

A wooden sign that had seen its fair share of weather pointed us toward a small building that looked like a couple of trailer homes put together. There were a few trucks and cars parked in front of the building, and we pulled into an open spot between two older sedans. Jumping out of the car, I could read the sign on the door that said *No Bars* in hand-painted black letters.

"No Bars, like no cell service, get it?" Leo playfully pushed Jenny in the arm as he held open the door for us.

The bar was dark, with blinds covering the few windows along the wall. Neon beer signs lit up the space and cast a blue glow in the air. A stale smell hit my nose. I was sure there was poor air circulation in the bar. A long counter dominated the space, with a couple of tables littered about. The counter was surprisingly full of patrons, all male. They all turned around in unison when we walked through the door, as if surprised there were more customers.

Running down the line of faces, my eyes caught a familiar smirk that I had seen earlier today. *Oh boy...*

"Fumbles! You're here! Come join us and let me buy you a drink."

"Who's that?" Jenny leaned in, whispering.

"The weirdo from the woods today." I lowered my voice as well, keeping eye contact with Wilder.

He looked good casually sitting at the bar. Balancing on the barstool that seemed too small for his frame, he exuded confidence. Brushing his hair back and away from his forehead, he made a motion with his hands for me to come up to the bar and join him. His two friends who sat on either side of him smiled at Jenny and me with knowing eyes. I felt Leo step next to us in a defensive stance.

"Well, you didn't say he was cute. He doesn't look like such a weirdo to me. A free drink is a free drink, right?" Jenny swayed up to the bar and stood between Wilder and the friend to his right. "Are you buying us a drink, or what?"

"Only if Fumbles joins," Wilder continued, staring at me with his bright blue eyes that looked even more blue because of the neon lights in the bar.

"Come on, Elise! These guys seem friendly." Jenny looked over at Wilder's friend, who smiled at her predatorily. Leo walked over to the bar and pulled Jenny to the other side of Wilder's friend, out of the man sandwich she was standing in.

Left alone by myself at the entrance of the bar, I had no choice but to walk up to the counter. Wilder grabbed my waist and pulled me close. My lower back was in line with the barstool he was sitting on. "So, Elise, is it? I still kind of like Fumbles," he murmured into my ear from behind me. I could feel his breath against my cheek.

I balked at his overconfidence. "You can call me Elise. I don't make a habit of falling." I refused to let him rattle me like he had earlier today in the woods. We were in neutral territory now. I turned to face him, ready to challenge his banter.

Up close, Wilder was the epitome of his name—*wild*. His skin was tan from the sun, and small thin scars covered his forehead as if he had once run through a thick brush that had cut up his face. His eyes, of course, were blue, and his chin was clean-shaven and defined. White teeth made up a smile that told me everything—he was someone who frequently got what they wanted and was rarely disappointed.

"So, *Elise*, what would you like to drink? Whiskey? Beer?"

Looking along the counter, I saw that Jenny and Leo already had mixed drinks in their hands. Sighing, submitting to the fact that we were staying here, I ordered a beer. Quickly, a frothy beer appeared in front of me, and Wilder grunted "Scoot" to his friend to the left. The stool opened, and I climbed onto the seat next to him before taking a drink of the beer. It was cold and refreshing, something I'd needed after the intense warnings from Robinson.

Turning to face me, Wilder opened his legs, caging me in with his knees around my barstool. I looked down at his knees and followed his chest back up to his face. His eyes stared me down as he picked up his beer and took a sip.

I couldn't help but comment on his effort to trap me. "That's forward of you," I said, glancing down at his knees again. Wilder turned the swivel seat on my barstool so that my body was facing his, now my own knees pointed toward his seat. Closing his knees, they sandwiched my legs. I knew I couldn't turn my body away. I didn't want to move and seem scared. If I was being honest with myself, I wasn't even sure I wanted to move. There was something about the unwavering attention that kept me captivated.

"I'm just trying to get to know the pretty new girl. Never know when you're going to run off again."

Flushing, I blurted out, "You came up to me in the woods! I didn't know what you were going to do to me!" I looked around the bar for escape routes. Besides the room behind the bar, there were no other doors in the bar besides the entrance I had just walked through. I was fast—I could still make a run for it.

Wilder took in my words and put his face close to mine. I could smell the earthy scent of his skin and see a glimmer in his eyes. It was like he was daring me to run so he could chase me. "I don't do anything to a woman unless they ask for it," he said.

Snorting, I tried to turn my body away from him, forgetting my legs were trapped in his. My upper body tilted too far, and I almost fell off the stool.

Wilder caught me, his large hands on my shoulders, straightening me back in my seat. "See why I still prefer Fumbles?"

My stomach fluttered. What was it about him that made me feel so off-center? I tried to give him a glare as I grabbed my beer from the counter.

He just smirked and picked up his own drink. "Oh, I think you'll continue to fall tonight, Elise. I'll be calling you Fumbles by the end of the night."

I didn't have anything to say about that. His boldness was both repulsing and intriguing. I took a big gulp of my beer. I would need more drinks to deal with him. He seemed set on getting to know me. I had experience with guys like him, tunnel vision on me for the night until they got what they wanted. Of course, it wasn't something that happened unless I wanted it to.

I had a lot of practice turning down men during my undergraduate days.

Curly blonde hair entered my peripheral vision. Turning to my right, I looked down at Jenny, who smiled, glancing at me and Wilder, trying to read the situation. "Can you come to the bathroom with me?" she asked.

Thankful for the escape, I chugged the last of my beer and pushed Wilder's legs apart so I could slip off the barstool. As I landed on my feet, I realized I had put myself in an even more precarious position. Wilder's knees trapped my body, with my chest in line with the more intimate parts of the male anatomy. Rough fingers caught my chin and tilted it up so my eyes once again connected with the sky-blue ones.

"Hurry back, Fumbles. Don't go falling into the toilet. I would gladly help you up, but it might be embarrassing for you."

Hearing Wilder's comments, Jenny covered her mouth to hide her laugh. This guy was so cheesy. I pushed Wilder's knee, and he let the barstool turn his body so I could escape his hold.

Jenny linked her arm through mine and pulled me toward the back of the bar, where I assumed the restroom was. I glanced back at Wilder, who had turned back to the bar, clearly gloating with his friends.

We weaved through a few empty tables and walked around the one that held patrons. An eerie feeling came over me as I felt eyes staring at me. The table had four people sitting around it, each with a mixed drink in front of them.

They had stopped their conversation and stared at me as if they were trying to recognize me. Three large men sat facing one smaller woman. All the men looked similar with their dark hair and tanned skin. They all had tattoos on their necks and arms.

The woman, who had long strawberry blonde hair, leaned over and whispered to the largest man at the table. He kept his gold eyes on me, following me as I walked. What an odd eye color. His gold irises stuck out in stark contrast to his tanned complexion. A beard covered his chin and cheeks. The brown hair on his face looked just long enough for me to run my fingers through, and—

Where did that *thought come from?* I asked myself. What was it with these locals? Was there something in the water here? I turned my attention back to hiding away in the bathroom with my friend.

Jenny hauled open the restroom door and pulled me inside. "Tell me everything right now. Leo and I have been watching you and that...guy. He's huge! No wonder he scared you in the woods," she said. "If a guy like that came up to me when I was running alone, I probably would've peed my pants."

Cutting off her spoken trail of thoughts, I interrupted. "Doesn't it seem a little weird here?"

"What do you mean? It's a bar. In the middle of nowhere." Jenny checked her makeup in the mirror. I suddenly realized I hadn't put any on.

"I mean, don't the people seem just a little off to you? Everyone's staring."

She dismissed my worries with a flick of her hand. "I'm sure it's just the locals Robinson warned us about. They don't seem so bad. Free drinks and good company, right?" Her eyebrows rose suggestively.

"He's super intense. He obviously wants to take me home," I said.

Jenny immediately dismissed my estimate of Wilder's intentions. "Maybe he does? Maybe this is a one-night stand? Who cares? You should do what you want. Enjoy yourself before you lock yourself in your room to write your thesis."

Ready to get the attention off me, I turned to face her. "Is that what you're doing with Leo?"

"Leo and I are going to be *good* friends. If I'm going to be stuck in a cabin in the middle of the woods, I might as well have some fun with the guy I'm stuck with." Jenny fluffed her hair, posing in the sink mirror. "He's cute and smart. I need something to do during my time off. I'm not looking for anything serious—a fun summer fling. Maybe that's what you should have with Wilder too."

She turned to me abruptly, ending our conversation. "Good girl talk." Jenny grabbed my hand and led the way out of the bathroom, on the hunt for another drink.

Smiling at her words, I followed. My new friend was right —I needed to loosen up and have some fun before I got caught up in my work. For the last four years, I had been so focused on supporting myself and furthering my education that I'd lost sight of the part of life that was supposed to be fun for a girl in her twenties.

Maybe it was the first beer taking effect or Jenny's pep talk, but I felt pleasantly surprised to see another beer waiting for me on the counter in front of my empty barstool. Wilder stopped his conversation as I climbed into my seat. Smiling, he clinked his glass on mine and looked into my eyes.

"Glad you didn't fall in," he said.

I couldn't help but smile back.

CHAPTER SEVEN

THE POUNDING in my head woke me up. Sunlight felt piercing as I opened my eyes to find my face directly in front of a window with broken blinds. Groaning, I stretched my arms above my head and turned over to see Wilder sleeping quietly in the bed next to me. Now that it was light out, I could see what the room looked like. It was definitely a bedroom decorated by a guy—sparce furniture with a couple of random band posters on the wall.

I sighed. My body wasn't sore in places where I should have felt that delicious ache from a good night with a hot man. Last night Wilder had not lived up to his wild name. Disappointing, for sure.

BAM! BAM! BAM! The pounding returned, and it took me a couple of seconds to realize it wasn't in my head. Wilder roused and rolled out of bed. He pulled on his boxers before answering the door to his bedroom, mumbling something about roommates. I sat up and swung my legs over the side of the bed, my feet immediately hitting the floor. His bed was just a mattress. He didn't have a bedframe. Grabbing my sweatshirt and leggings, I tried to get dressed before Wilder opened the door. My shirt was barely on and my leggings pulled to my thighs when he swung the door open.

"*What?*"

"You were supposed to be at Camp forty-five fucking minutes ago!"

"I was a little busy." Wilder looked behind his shoulder at me. The large man in front of him took a glance at me and sighed loudly. I quickly pulled my leggings up to my waist, hoping he hadn't seen something he wasn't supposed to.

"What the fuck, Wilder. You knew you had to be at Camp this morning. It's mandatory. You don't have a choice. And now you drag a girl into this?" The man rubbed his hands over his face. "What were you thinking? Get dressed. I don't have time to drop her anywhere." He took a few steps backward. "Hope you have enough food for her in this shit hole for the next three days because that's where she's staying."

"Umm, I would like to go home," I said. Adjusting my leggings, I grabbed my purse and made my way to the doorway. What kind of mess had I gotten myself into? This was the trouble Robinson had warned us about yesterday. Never again. I was stuck here without a car or a phone, with Wilder as my only way home. Great.

Glancing at his watch, the man looked at me and then back at Wilder. "No time. Your boyfriend was supposed to be at Camp an hour ago now. As much as I would love to drive you home after your date night, I can't. I need to get this idiot to Camp right now."

Smacking Wilder on the arm, I made him look at me as he pulled on his clothing. "You're not leaving me here for three days. I don't know where the hell I am, and I don't have a car to get back to my house."

Wilder pushed his hair back from his face as if I was now a

problem that he didn't want to solve. I looked at the man for help, but he just shook his head.

"Trouble follows this kid wherever he goes."

I did a double take at his face. It was a little fuzzy, but I was almost certain this was the same guy from the bar last night that had been staring. He had the same golden eyes, the same beard —if not a little longer today, the same shaggy hair, and I flushed as I remembered the wayward thought I'd had about running my fingers through it.

The man's biceps bulged as he grabbed Wilder's arm and pulled him through the house to the front door. Looping my purse across my body, I followed them, dodging empty cans and food boxes that the man knocked over, dragging Wilder through the house. This had been such a mistake. What had I been thinking last night? Now I could be stuck here for days with a couple half-eaten leftover burgers for sustenance.

Wilder struggled to stay on his feet as he stumbled down the stairs of the house. I tried to be as careful as I could, stepping down the loose stair treads, trying not to fall too far behind. How I hadn't broken my neck last night was a miracle.

Parked at the end of the drive was a black SUV with tinted windows. The man opened the back door and all but threw Wilder into the back seat. He turned around and faced me. I tried to stand up tall and look commanding, but I was sure my wrinkled sweatshirt and uncombed hair made me look ridiculous.

"I'm not staying here," I said, trying to make my voice big, but I detected a shake in my vocal cords as I spoke.

"Sure, you are. There's nowhere else to go. Get back in the house."

The man climbed into the driver's side and slammed the door closed. The window slowly rolled down, revealing his face, staring at me, daring me to defy him. I looked around outside the cabin. My memory was fuzzy about the car ride home from the bar. It had been about a ten-minute car ride with no defining road markers. If I knew what direction the cabin was in, I could get home, maybe by lunchtime.

I looked up at the sky, shielding my eyes from the sun while still reading its position in the sky. It was probably early morning, the sun not yet risen to its highest point. If I assumed the sun was facing east, I would just need to head south the eleven miles back to the cabin. I could do it. I'd run far distances in the past. My toes disagreed, wiggling in Jenny's borrowed wedges. Shit. Maybe I could make them work.

I took one look back at the SUV carrying the serious man and my flop of a one-night stand, and I decided to run. Expletives rose from my wake as I heard a car door slam behind me. I tried for speed. My purse hit the side of my body in a rhythm that matched my footsteps. The muscles in my legs had woken up not ten minutes ago, and I profusely apologized to them as they strained to warm up to support my speed.

I tried to keep an eye on the placement of the sun, but there wasn't time between dodging rocks and navigating the uneven ground. I leaped, dodging a tree root that had briefly escaped the dirt before diving back down into the worms. Midair, an arm wrapped around my waist and pulled me out of the air. My back hit a warm wall of muscle before my feet found the dirt. I didn't make it very far.

"You're fast." I recognized the man's voice. He was breathing heavy. "Even in those ridiculous shoes." He swung my body so he had me in a suitcase carry at his side, his arm still holding me around my waist.

"Put me down!" I yelled and kicked, but he held me securely against him, not seeming to notice my struggle. I stopped struggling, trying to catch my breath. It was hard to breathe with the pressure of his arm against me.

It took several minutes to get me back to the car that he had left running. He set me down on my feet, loosening his grip on me, and I immediately took the opportunity to get away from him. A few feet away, I bent over, my hands on my knees, finally able to take a deep breath.

"Fuck." He pinched the bridge of his nose between his fingers as if I was yet another headache in this migraine of a day. "Get in the car. You're coming with."

"I'm not getting into the car with you," I said, my hands still on my knees.

"You have three choices," the man said. "One, you go back into the house and stay there for the weekend. Two, you keep running and I keep catching you. Or three, you get in the car."

I lifted my head to look at him. He looked larger standing next to the car than he had in the house.

"Maybe I'll go back in the house just until you leave. I think my odds of finding my way home are pretty good." The man looked at me, glancing down at my shoes and up my body. I felt the heat of his gaze even through my clothing. His eyes looked yellow from where I was standing, but maybe it was just the reflection of the sunlight.

"I think the odds of you running into something unsavory in these woods on your way is quite high." Okay, so he'd read my bluff. I didn't know where I was. But I thought running still might be the better choice...

Turning my head, I looked back at the house. Did it even have running water? I glanced down the trail the man had just brought me back from. Maybe if I tried again, I could lose him. Who was I kidding? I was fast, but he was much faster. And in these shoes?

The man was still standing there when I rotated back to the car. Damnit. The choice to get into a car with ultimately two strangers seemed like the only option. I took a step toward the man, who smirked at my choice, happy he had won.

I quickly climbed into the back seat next to Wilder. He wouldn't even look at me. The man closed the door and climbed into the driver's seat and started the car. This car was much nicer than the car Wilder had taken me home in. The cool leather seats grounded me as I let out a breath.

The man glanced at me in the rearview mirror before accelerating quickly down the road. He turned up the music as he drove well over the speed limit. Gravel flew up, creating a tan cloud around our car.

I looked at Wilder again. He looked straight ahead, obviously angry that someone had awakened him and forced him out of his house. Where was the guy that I'd been with last night who couldn't break eye contact with me? Now he wouldn't even glance my way.

"Where are we going, Wilder?" I kept my voice low enough that the driver couldn't hear. Wilder continued to stare forward as if I wasn't in the car. "Wilder!" I said, a little louder. This caught the driver's attention, and he glanced at us through the mirror. He shook his head as if he expected nothing less.

Wilder jerked his body toward mine, nothing but annoyance on his face. "You should've gone home last night."

"How? I don't have a car. You fell asleep right after..." My voice trailed off as the man's eyes glanced at me again in the rearview mirror. He'd obviously heard that. Wilder shook his head and turned to face forward.

"There will be people looking for me," I said, turning to the man in front. At least I hoped Jenny and Leo would be concerned if I didn't show up today.

"I'll have someone alleviate their concerns. Once we enter Camp, we won't be leaving until Sunday," the man said.

What had Jenny been thinking, pumping me up like that

last night? Her pep talk had been the worst advice ever. These were the locals we'd been told not to interact with, and now here I was in an unknown black car with an unknown driver headed to an unknown location. I was powerless as we barreled down the road at what anyone but a race-car driver would consider a frightening speed. All that time spent studying, not going out often with my friends had built up, and the one time I was a little wild, this happened.

Spending the summer in a research cabin that was cut off from the world with no service had seemed like a dream opportunity—a chance to immerse myself in the natural world and not have to worry about any other distractions. But right now, I desperately missed the security a phone gave me.

"My parents! My professor! They'll all be expecting to hear from me," I yelled, trying to entice the driver to stop, let me out, make him see that letting me go would be to his advantage.

"You live with roommates, right? Not your parents?" he asked, although he already knew the answer. I nodded. "And a professor? So you're a student, probably a good one?" I nodded again. "Then you weren't listening. It's the weekend. No professor is going to come check on you on the weekend. I'll take care of the roommates. Come Sunday, you'll be back home, safe back in your world. They won't even notice you're gone."

I looked away from Wilder and the rearview mirror, slumping over in my seat with my head in my hands. Last night had been such a mistake. I should have stayed in my lane and focused on doing what I'd come here to do. I was here to study and research the forest, not the local men. When they found my body buried in the woods in a couple of months, I was sure Professor Robinson would be nothing but disappointed.

"Wilder!" I whisper-yelled at him, trying to get his attention from my bent-over position so he could give me any clues about where I was going.

"Don't bother with him—you'll be nothing but disappointed," the driver said. There seemed to be a lot of disappointment going around. "I hope you have nowhere to be for the rest of the weekend. You're going to be stuck at Camp."

"What's Camp?" I asked. I was fine sleeping in a tent if my tent was far away from Wilder's.

"If you're expecting s'mores and campfire stories, don't."

"So, I'm your prisoner until Sunday?" This one-night stand had turned into an unwanted weekend affair.

"If I remember correctly, I gave you three choices. You chose the car. That hardly makes you a prisoner."

The car sped up even more. The man's white knuckles gripping the steering wheel were the only sign that he felt flustered. A sharp buzz sounded behind the car, and I whipped my head around to see what the noise was. Out the back window was nothing but the gravel road we had just driven over.

As I turned to face forward once again, we slowed down considerably to dodge the tents and people that had appeared in front of our car. My eyes must have bulged out of my head as I looked out the windshield.

"Welcome to Camp." The driver chuckled at my disbelief.

Wilder looked unimpressed next to me. He was acting like a teenage boy, unwillingly dragged along on a family road trip.

Large canvas tents lined the road we drove on. People were walking, laughing, and having conversations with one another outside the tents and along the road. Flags flew high above the crest of each tent's entrance. They were all different colors and had different symbols on them. We pulled next to the last tent on the road. The flag was black with a green cedar tree surrounded by a white moon like a halo.

Hopping out of the car, the driver opened my door and

made a hand motion for me to follow him. Wilder got out of his side of the car and followed us to the entrance of the tent. The man pulled back the flap of the tent and let me see inside before I entered. The tent was large and lit with natural light from the plastic covered windows on each of its sides. In the middle of the tent, there was a large table with five chairs on each side and a chair at the head and foot of the table. Several couches lined the sides of the tent. The mismatched fabric on them gave the impression that they had been bought from different garage sales.

A small group of people sat together on a couch near the back. Deep in conversation, they didn't seem to notice us entering. It wasn't until Wilder threw his body loudly onto the nearest couch that they turned around to look at us.

"You got him, Everett. Where the hell was he?" A man similar in size to the driver, apparently named Everett, stood up and walked over to where Wilder was lying on the couch.

Wilder looked undeterred by the large man coming at him. The man kicked the couch, rattling him. He sat up, glaring at everyone in the room like a boy receiving a lecture from his parents after they'd caught him sneaking out of the house.

"At his house, sleeping." Everett crossed his arms.

The large man walked over to where Everett and I were standing, keeping his eyes directly on me. "And who's this?"

He came up close to me, and I tried not to cower in front of his imposing size. Broad, muscular shoulders dominated his frame. He was wearing some sort of leather vest over his black T-shirt, accentuating his large pectoral muscles. Every one of these men was uncommonly large. I had to tilt my head back to see his face as he towered over me with a frown on his cleanly shaven chin. A thin white scar ran across his forehead. His hair was cut so short, you could see his scalp through the tiny brown hairs.

I clenched my hands together tightly to disguise that I was shaking.

"Don't scare the girl, Kostas," a feminine voice said from behind who I assumed was Kostas.

Everett sighed. "I found her with that idiot." He gestured with his head to Wilder. "The same girl we saw him with at the bar last night. I didn't have time to drop her anywhere with the wards closing."

"The side of the road would've sufficed," Kostas said.

"Like I said, there wasn't time. I was speeding to get here before the wards closed."

"We can't have a...girl here. This place is full of...us," Kostas said. His hands curled into tight fists.

"You're getting angry with the wrong person, Kostas." Everett kicked the couch Wilder had draped himself over. My *joy* of a date last night grunted before crossing his arms across his chest closing his eyes. "Wilder brought her home last night when he knew he had to be here early this morning. He should've taken her back last night like a decent philanderer." Everett kicked the couch again, and Wilder opened one eye before quickly closing it again.

"You should've left her where you found her. She doesn't belong here," Kostas said.

Everett grumbled, turning his glare onto me. I sucked in a quick breath and held it. "Believe me, I tried. She's a runner. Even in those shoes." Everyone turned to look at my feet.

A small woman with strawberry blonde hair pushed her way around Kostas's large frame. "Kostas! Everett! You're scaring the poor girl. Everett couldn't just leave her at that junkyard."

Moving around Kostas, the woman put her arm around my back and guided me away from the two menacing men. "Everett, let me take care of her this weekend. I'll handle the...

introductions." She gave me a closed-lip smile. Her expression was warm. "We could use some more feminine energy in the tent."

Everett nodded at her suggestion. "Fine. She's your problem for the weekend."

The woman brought me to one of the smaller couches and sat down next to me. Taking my hands in hers, she looked at my face, which I was sure looked terrified. "Hi, I'm Kleio. That brute that drove you here is Everett, and the other hulk is Kostas."

Gesturing to the table in the middle of the room, Kleio also introduced me to Jack and Gavrill. The two men got up from the table and walked over to where we were sitting. Although smaller than the other males in the room, Jack was covered in lean muscle. His blond hair stuck out in sharp contrast to his tan skin. Gavrill stood a little behind Jack. He had black hair and a closely trimmed beard. When he got close enough to the others, I could see why he had made Jack look small. I was glad I was sitting down, or I was sure my knees would have given out.

"Back up, you guys," Kleio urged. "You forget how big you are around humans."

My mind started racing. Humans? Weren't we all...humans here? These guys might've seemed more like Greek gods than humans, but they sure looked to be the same species as me.

With a huff, Jack planted a kiss on Kleio's lips and dipped his head to her shoulders to nuzzle her neck. I was sitting close enough, my hands still clasped in Kleio's, that I could hear a low growl coming from Jack as he pulled away. Then he walked to the table in the middle of the tent, Kleio's eyes following him with a hungry stare. Kostas and Gavrill also made their way to the table, shaking their heads in amusement at the couple.

Everett stayed behind for a moment, looking at me. His

yellow eyes connected with mine. I involuntarily squeezed Kleio's hands.

"Everett! Get back over here—we need to strategize," Kostas said.

He blinked quickly three or four times, shaking his head before turning around and heading to the table where Jack, Kostas, and Gavrill stood over large pieces of paper that looked like maps.

Kleio pulled her hands from mine, shaking me from my stupor, and I sent her an apologetic smile. Delicate strawberry blonde eyebrows arched over blue eyes. Her features were soft, and she had tiny orange freckles that dusted her nose. When she smiled back at me, her pink lips slowly opened to reveal white teeth framed by two large, pointed canines. Those were not human teeth.

Seeing that I'd noticed, she said, "You're safe here. No one's going to hurt you." Then she added, "Are you from around here?"

I quickly shook my head, my hands still covering my mouth.

"I didn't think so. Most girls around here know to stay away from that one." She nodded toward Wilder, who was still slouched on the couch but had shifted his head so he was staring at us. "But don't worry about that. We all make mistakes. What's your name?" Her hands reached up, and she slowly pulled my hands away from my face so I could answer her.

"Elise."

"Well, Elise, we're stuck here for the weekend. Might as well get to know one another," she said. "Let's go for a walk and let the insensitive men debate over their maps."

A scoff from Jack was the only acknowledgment we got as Kleio pulled me up from the couch and brought me through the tent flaps. We walked down the makeshift street lined with similar tents. People bustled around, chatting with one another. The overall mood was cheerful, and it seemed like everyone buzzed with a level of excitement. Kleio nodded, greeting people who gave us curious looks as we walked by.

"You didn't catch feelings for Wilder, did you?" she asked bluntly as we walked by two men playing some sort of lawn game with wooden blocks.

I didn't know how much I should divulge to Kleio. Wilder hadn't been pleasant to me this morning, but he was the only person I kind of knew here. I decided I should just be honest. "No, he was just a guy I met last night at the bar."

"Oh, good. I couldn't tell. You both seemed familiar at the bar last night." She raised her eyebrows at me.

I could feel the red embarrassment travel up my neck and onto my cheeks. "You were there?" Of course this would happen on the one night I let loose. I couldn't have an anonymous one-night stand. That would have been too easy.

Kleio laughed. "Oh, I was *right* there. I'm surprised your tongue didn't accidentally make its way down *my* throat."

I was sure I looked like a tomato as I groaned, covering my face with my hands. If a sinkhole could just open in the ground, I would gladly fall into it.

She grabbed my hands, pulling them away from my face for the second time today. "Don't feel embarrassed! We've all been there. Well, I haven't been there for a while, but I have definitely been there. I remember when Jack and I got together, there were more than a couple of nights that I humiliated myself at the bar. I don't think they ever fully fixed the sink in the girl's bathroom." She tilted her head, reminiscing. "It's possible that it became detached from the wall at some point." I almost laughed out loud.

"You and Jack?" I didn't know why I was suddenly interested in Kleio's love life, but her candor was amusing and I was desperate to talk about something besides my night with Wilder.

"Yeah, Jack and I are together. Don't go getting any ideas." She smirked at me in a teasing manner as we walked. Toward the end of the road of tents, there was an open field full of tall grasses and wildflowers, which rolled into dense woods that looked impossible to traverse.

"Where are we?" I didn't remember seeing this road or encampment on any of the maps Robinson had given us. If he knew that this many people were gathering this close to our cabin for some sort of event like this, I was sure he would have warned us.

Kleio stopped and turned toward me. "So, this is going to be hard to explain. You aren't from this area and aren't familiar with our customs." I looked at her with confusion on my face. "You're at Camp— Oh shit, move—quick!"

She grabbed my arm and pulled me forward as I felt the air whoosh behind me. I turned my head in time to see two enormous wolves run past us and into the field.

"We should probably stand somewhere else," Kleio said.

The two wolves chased each other in the fields, tackling and nipping at each other playfully. My feet cemented to the ground as I stood there watching them. I had never been that close to a wolf before. Their fur had brushed against my skin as they'd run by.

"Come over here." Kleio pulled me away from the road and sat down in the grass with her legs underneath her. I followed her, keeping my eyes on the wolves in the field. "Let's start simply. I'm actually a little nervous," she said with a laugh. "This is Camp. We are..." She took a minute to pick her words. "The technical term is *Lycans*. We can shift our forms if we want to—into a wolf. Most humans call us shifters."

I blinked at her. Wolf shifters? Like the wolves from myths?

"Am I doing okay so far? This is the first time I've personally given 'the talk' to a human before," she said, using air quotes.

I nodded at her. I didn't know how it could be going better or worse.

"Okay, good. I've heard it can be quite shocking for humans to learn about us." Kleio looked out into the field before continuing. "We've had humans in our pack before. Occasionally a shifter falls in love with one and brings them around." She tilted her head, looking up at the sky, then snapped her head back to look at me. "But you're not in love with Wilder."

"Definitely not," I said.

"Then it's just a happy mistake that you're here. Welcome to the world of Lycans." Kleio opened her arms in a sign of welcome, but I didn't know how to react. I must have been staring at her mouth with my own mouth gaping open in shock.

"I know you saw my fangs. Don't worry—we don't bite. Hard." Her lighthearted smile flashed her sharp canines, and she pushed me playfully on the arm. "Okay, that was a corny joke. We don't eat humans. We enjoy the same foods as you humans do."

I had so many questions. "Shouldn't you be, like, in hiding or something? How do people not know about this?"

Kleio laughed. "Hiding? I think I can pull off a pretty good human." Then she smiled at me with closed lips, hiding her teeth, but when I didn't say anything in response, she shrugged. "Everyone around here knows who we are, and we don't get many visitors. When we do, our good looks can distract even the most curious of humans. You were sure distracted enough last night."

I couldn't help myself from snorting. "Seriously?" Staring her down, I gave her the nastiest look I could muster.

"Fine, fine! I won't bring it up again. I just always like to tease the girls that get caught in Wilder's web."

Great—so I was one of many. "Finding girls at bars and taking them home is a common occurrence for him?" I asked.

"Only the girls who are desperate enough to follow him home." It was my turn to push Kleio in the arm. She held her hands up in surrender. "Okay, okay, I'm really done this time."

It hit me then that I had just slept with a shifter. Sex with Wilder hadn't seemed any different from any other encounter I'd had. Except for my lack of enjoyment. And I definitely didn't remember any fangs. But all the same, last night I'd shared a bed with a mythical creature. I could feel the blood drain from my face.

"I know this is probably a shock to you, but you're safe with us here," Kleio said. "We need to get through the next couple of days, and then you can go home and have the wonderful memory of living with wolves for the weekend."

She laughed as I looked at her unbelievingly. Kleio seemed so normal and so human. How could it be that Lycans were a real thing? Did this mean that vampires and witches and dragons and Bigfoot were also real? Were they all just living under our noses?

"I can see your mind spiraling," she said. "I promise we're very normal. We just have fangs and can turn into wolves... maybe that isn't the most normal, but other than those abilities we're just like you!"

I had to laugh out loud at that. There wasn't anything ordinary about these shifters. The two wolves that had almost run me over earlier were still bounding around in the grass, playing and chasing one another. Other than their size, they looked like regular wolves. There was something majestic about seeing wolves so close. Their fur looked shiny and soft, flowing through the breeze their bodies made while running.

"So, you can turn into one of those?" I gestured out to the field.

"My wolf isn't as big as theirs, but yes, I can." My eyes must have bugged out at her because she quickly added, "Don't worry—I'm not going to shift! I wouldn't scare you like that."

Shift, yet another word to add to my Lycan vocabulary. I nodded, trying to process everything.

Kleio's face shifted from teasing to something softer. "I know this is a lot to take in. Since you're going to be here a couple of nights, let me ask Everett where he wants you to sleep. You can have some time to yourself before we eat."

The tent town behind us was large and organized, but I couldn't imagine they lived here. I had seen no sleeping areas. We got up and walked back to the tent with the cedar-tree flag.

The map-studying session seemed to be over. Everett, Jack, Gavrill, and Kostas lounged on the couches, talking and joking with one another. They were clearly close friends. Wilder sat sulking in a chair at the table in the center of the room. I still didn't know why he was acting like that. The other people, or should I say shifters, in the group didn't pay any mind to him, as if this was normal behavior. They obviously weren't fans of him. His dejected face was such a contrast from last night that I almost felt sorry for him. Why had Everett retrieved Wilder this morning only for everyone to ignore him?

"Does she know?" Kostas asked as he saw us enter the tent. Everyone's conversation stopped, waiting.

"She knows enough for now," Kleio answered. "Where's she going to sleep, Everett? I'm sure she wants some time to herself to process everything. It's kind of been a whirlwind for her."

I appreciated her looking out for me. I really did need some time to get my bearings and consider everything I had just seen and heard.

"We only have enough tents set up for us right now," Kostas said.

"Oh, maybe you can bunk with us, Elise!" Kleio said. "That'd be fun, right, Jack?" She looked at Jack, who threw his hands up as if he was fine with the idea.

My eyes got big at the thought of having to share a tent with a couple, especially one that was as affectionate as Kleio and Jack. Gavrill seemed to sense my apprehension and quickly mentioned that there was an extra tent available but it needed to be set up. Everett nodded at Gavrill and looked to where Wilder was sitting.

"Go with Gavrill to grab the tent and set it up for Elise," he ordered. "That is the least you can do after dragging her into this mess." Everett's voice was authoritative and deep. Wilder didn't hesitate to stand up and follow Gavrill to retrieve the tent.

"Let's go sit in my tent until Wilder is done," Kleio said. She grabbed my hand and walked me to the back of the tent. There was another set of flaps, and she pulled me through them.

Behind the main tent was an entire city of smaller tents. Many of them placed in a circle around a firepit, like what I had seen camping with my family when I'd been younger. There were even more people around these tents, milling about and conversing. A couple hundred people relaxed, stoked the fires, and laughed with one another. It almost seemed like a family reunion.

Kleio led me to a tent that was farther away from the others and wasn't next to a campfire. I could only assume why her tent with Jack wasn't close to any of the others. It was small, but it had a bed and a chair in the corner.

"Sorry for the mess. We didn't clean up this morning," Kleio said. She quickly made the bed, finding the sheets on the ground and the blanket draped over the chair. My mind went wild imagining how the bed had gotten in such a state of disarray. I hesitated to sit on the bed, but it seemed clean enough.

She plopped next to me onto the bed. "I need to go see the guys, but you can stay in here and rest," she said. "You'll be fine. No one will bother you. Everyone stays away from our tent. Never know what you're going to find inside," she added, wiggling her eyebrows at me and laughing. It was nice to have someone provide some comedic relief in a situation that was anything but funny.

I nodded and thanked her for letting me borrow her tent for a bit. Being up late last night was catching up to me, and the ambient noise of people's muffled conversations made my eyes feel heavy.

Lying down, I made sure my shoes were off the bed. I wasn't comfortable enough to remove them, and I wanted the ability to run if I needed to. My eyes closed. I meant to just rest them, but I fell into a heavy sleep.

CHAPTER EIGHT

A LOUD HORN woke me up to a tent that was darker than when I had fallen asleep in the middle of the day. The canvas flaps rustled before a large hand reached inside to pull them open. I saw the top of his head, covered with tousled brown hair, before he lifted his face to meet mine, standing tall. What was he doing barging in here like this?

"I want to talk to you," Everett said. His beard was long enough for me to run my fingers through—and ugh, why was I thinking about my fingers in his beard?

He paused at the foot of the bed, looking over me. I looked down to where his eyes fell as his nostrils flared. My shirt had ridden up while I'd slept, my midriff completely exposed. Sitting up, I pulled the shirt back down, pretending I was unbothered by his stares.

He closed his eyes and shook his head quickly. "You're a guest here."

My mind snapped to attention. "*Guest?* Do shifters use that word interchangeably with the human word *prisoner?*"

"I see we have a linguist on our hands. Did your big words confuse Wilder last night?"

"What I did last night is none of your business."

"Very well, it isn't." Everett ran his hand through his hair, smoothing the tousled locks on the top of his head. "But now that you are here, everything about you is my business." I opened my mouth to mock the certainty of his words, but his voice stopped me. "Now that you're at Camp for the weekend."

"For now," I quipped.

A stern look came over Everett's face. He took a step toward the bed. I bit down on my tongue to stop the instinct that came over me to scoot back.

"Do you want to know what will happen if you try to leave Camp?" he asked in a low voice.

I sat there with my lips pressed shut. He was going to tell me the answer to his question whether I wanted to hear it or not.

"You will be...what's the human word for it? Ah, *electrocuted*," he said, and it took a lot of self-control not to roll my eyes. "There are wards surrounding Camp. Big walls of energy that keep everything and everyone inside. You humans can't see them from the outside. Like invisible walls. No one can leave until they're lifted. Not even me."

"I'm surprised. I thought you were a big shot around here, kidnapping girls and all." I smirked at him, ready for his rebuttal.

But I was surprised to see a hurt look flash across Everett's face, his eyes looking toward the ground and his eyebrows pinching together. He quickly recovered, but not before I'd noticed.

"You need to keep a low profile when you're here—humans aren't allowed at Camp. I don't want you attracting attention," he said. "Just keep to yourself, and no one will know the difference."

"Fine," I snapped. "I don't want to be here with you shifters anyway."

Everett took another step toward the bed, his shins hitting the end of the mattress. He lunged forward to grab my arm, but I pulled it away before he could reach me. His fingers made a fist, curling into his palm, as if he was fighting for control of his body.

"You will not insult us while you're here," he growled. "Do you want to eat this weekend? To sleep on a bed? Because I can change your accommodations real quick. Don't test me, Elise. Like you, I ace every single one."

With that, he turned around and stormed out of the tent. As I watched, Everett looked over his shoulder at me, those yellow eyes scorching. Then he was gone.

I sat up on the bed and wrapped my arms around my bent knees. I'd heard what he'd said, but the only thing I could focus on was how he'd said my name—that he'd remembered my name.

After some stretching, I got up and peeked my head out of the tent. The sun was close to setting, and the campfires glowed orange and red. I spotted Kleio walking briskly toward me.

"What was Everett doing in our tent?" she asked. "I just saw him come out."

"Giving me another 'talk,'" I said, making air quotes.

"Hmm. I thought he agreed that I'd oversee that."

"I prefer your talks to his."

With a chuckle, she said, "Of course you do. I'm not a grump. Maybe I should be the one in charge of giving all the new humans 'the talk.'"

She didn't ask anything further about Everett—maybe pleased that I obviously preferred her over everyone else at

Camp so far—and that was fine by me. She linked her arm through mine. "You need to come with us to the opening ceremony. We're all required to go, and there won't be anyone here to watch you."

Leaving me with no time for questions, Kleio started walking through the large field next to the tents and toward the forest. There was already a crowd of people standing in front of a wooden stage. I weaved through the crowd with Kleio until we found Gavrill. He was standing next to Jack and Kostas, waiting for us. They made space for us and closed us in, surrounding us like a triangle.

"Overprotective brutes," Kleio said under her breath. A high-pitched yelp came out of her mouth as Jack snickered, having pinched her playfully in the rear. As she turned to swat at him, an enormous white wolf on stage interrupted her by howling.

Everyone turned to face the stage, ending whatever conversations they'd been having. The large wolf sat on his haunches on the stage. Snout pointed toward the sky, he let out a loud howl that vibrated my eardrums. His head came back down, and his purple eyes looked back at the crowd.

The wolf shook his whole body, starting with his head. As his head shook, his jaw opened and continued to fall to the ground, unhinging from his skull. His snout and upper lips began retracting into his head, and his ears sunk into the top of his skull. Behind his head, his spine lifted toward the sky, elongating his body. His front paws retracted to the sides of his chest and lost the black claws and white fur that covered them. The back legs that had once been curved bone turned into straight human legs.

I stepped back in shock as white fur gave way to human flesh. There was no fur left on the man's body. No clothing either.

"Close your eyes if you're prissy," Gavrill mocked at me as I stared in shock at the naked man standing in front of the crowd, and I realized I had bumped into him.

The man didn't seem surprised or embarrassed, and neither did anyone around me. In human form, he was large, like all the men here. Muscled and covered with symbolic tattoos. His hair was graying, showing signs of age, and his face was tanned and beginning to wrinkle. I didn't look below his shoulders. Someone from the side of the stage handed him a pair of shorts, which he pulled on before he addressed the crowd.

"Welcome to the Deca Tournament! My favorite event of the decade!" he said. "For the last hundred years, we have come together as one Great Northern Pack to celebrate our strength and allegiance. This year, like every other year before, you will pick two of your strongest pack members to enter the hunt. At midnight tonight, in the forest behind me, we will release the one hundred rogues for the hundred-year celebration."

He gestured to several large cages tucked to the side of the stage that held wolves of all sizes and colors. Many of them had missing patches of fur, and some even had missing patches of flesh. They were snarling at the crowd and at each other, stalking around the cages.

I grabbed Kleio's arm, looking for an explanation.

"Those are rogues," she explained. "Lycans without a pack that have gone senseless. They hardly know what day it is."

She looked back at the speaker on the stage as he continued. "You'll abide by the Lycan Code during the hunt. Disobeying the code will not be tolerated."

Kostas faintly shook his head.

"As per usual, the pack that captures the most rogues at the end of the three-week event will be named Pack Preeminent and will have all the bragging rights for the next ten years," the man said. "Let's come together as the Great Northern Pack that we are tonight to feast and enjoy one another before the competition begins. Before I release you to your dinners, let's introduce the hunters entering this year's competition."

Slowly the speaker brought pairs of shifters to the stage, introducing them by pack name. There were teams of male shifters, teams of female shifters, and coed teams. The speaker introduced an especially rough-looking team of males from the Juniper Pack. The two men snarled at the crowd, showing off their bulging muscles.

"Oh, great—Kip and Elijah are here," Kleio whispered to herself. She caught me listening and divulged, "They're a bunch of assholes from the Juniper Pack. They love to beat up on weaker packs."

The man on the stage continued to call hunters from the different packs forward.

"Is this like the Olympic Games or something?" I asked. All the flags in front of the tents made sense.

Kleio smiled, amused. "Kind of like the Olympic Games, except there aren't any medals. And you have a high likelihood of dying."

"Why do you guys even do this? What's the prize?"

"We're here because the True Alpha"—she pointed to the older man on the stage—"commands it. Every ten years, he brings all the packs underneath him to join in a pissing contest for his own amusement. Survival is the only prize." Kleio then shushed me before I could ask anymore questions.

The True Alpha's voice continued to rumble from the stage. "From the Cedar Moon Pack, Everett Silas and Wilder Dendron."

Everett climbed gracefully onto the stage, followed by Wilder. They looked out into the audience, eyeing their competition. Everett's golden eyes scanned over the crowd until they found mine. He looked powerful from my vantage point below.

His brown hair was a little shorter than Wilder's but still gave him a cad look. His tan skin almost glowed under his white shirt. I could see the defined muscles in his chest and arms.

My breath caught. Everett must've been one of the strongest pack members if he was up on the stage. What confused me was why Wilder was up there with him. Kleio had said nothing to suggest that Wilder was a strong pack member.

The last two pairs were called to the stage. In the end, there were ten pairs lined up for everyone's viewing. Some looked confident and strong, while others looked nervous.

The True Alpha spoke again. "The wards are closed for the weekend. There will be no distractions. Enjoy your meal before the real feast is unleashed."

As if on cue, the rogues rattled their cages and snarled at the audience. Members of his own pack surrounded the True Alpha as he exited the stage and walked away. The pairs walked down the stage and found their way to their packs.

"Come on, Elise. Let's go eat before they leave for the hunt." Kleio led me back to the main tent that flew the Cedar Moon flag. Looking back down the road lined with more tents, I viewed more carefully the flags that flew above them. Each had a different type of tree on it, designating the name of the pack.

It was almost fully dark outside, and I could hear my stomach loudly rumble. I hadn't eaten yet today. Pulled into the tent, Kleio put me to work gathering plates and cutlery from the trunks that lined the back wall of the tent. We brought them to the table that had maps spread across it earlier in the day and set the table for seven.

"Why was Wilder up there?" I asked. "I get that Everett is strong, but it seems like Wilder hasn't been interested in being here this whole time."

Kleio sighed before she answered my question. "Wilder is the best tracker in the pack."

"Tracker?" I asked. "Like...looking for animal footprints and scat?"

"It's a little different for shifters," she explained. "For us, tracking is an ability kind of like a supertaster. Everyone can taste food, but only certain people are able to really taste every flavor at a heightened intensity. Wilder can smell every separate scent at a high intensity. It's rare enough that not every pack has one."

That was interesting. And for Wilder of all shifters to have that ability.

She went on, "Everett is the strongest shifter in our pack. Between Wilder and the alpha, they're good at finding and capturing the rogues in the forest. Everett had to drag Wilder in this morning because we need him if we're going to win again."

"Again? Alpha?" I felt entirely in the dark. It seemed like for someone who prided herself on knowing a lot about plants and forestation, I knew nothing of what really lived in these woods.

"Everett's the alpha of the Cedar Moon Pack. That's the pack we"—she motioned around the tent—"belong to. He's our leader. Ten years ago, during the last Deca Tournament, Everett and Wilder won. It was by the skin of their teeth, but they won. The True Alpha hasn't messed with us for the past ten years, probably because he knows how strong we are. Everett will keep it that way." Kleio continued carefully setting the table while she spoke. "If you couldn't tell by his pompous attitude, the True Alpha is an actual piece of work. He can make pack life very difficult if he wants to. For the past several decades, he has kidnapped members of the losing packs and forced them to join his pack—all female shifters." Kleio's nose wrinkled in disgust. "Everett would never let that happen to his pack."

As if my stomach knew what was coming, it rumbled as Wilder and Gavrill carried in plates of grilled meats they had been cooking over the fire. Kostas followed with grilled corn and squash. Everything smelled delicious. We all sat around the table and ate family style, passing plates and food. Now that I knew that Everett was the leader of the pack, it surprised me that everything was so informal, though he did sit at the head of the table. The rest of the meal he spent laughing and talking with his pack mates. He seemed at ease and happy here with all his people.

I felt a warmth in my body that I hadn't felt before. It wasn't just the good food I was eating; it was the warmth of comradery and acceptance. Even Wilder seemed more at ease. He spent much of his time talking with Gavrill and shoveling down food.

When the meal was over, I helped Kostas clear the plates while Everett and Wilder disappeared to their tents to prepare for the hunt. Kleio and Jack were happily tucked away on a couch together. Gavrill stood in the middle of the tent, unsure of what to do. He looked at Kleio and Jack, and then at Kostas and me, and then he rubbed his face and mumbled something about going over the plan with Everett one more time.

Kostas laughed to himself. "Gavrill has never been one to help with the dishes."

We settled into a rhythm cleaning the plates. He washed the dishes in a bucket of water that he had brought in, and I dried them with a towel I'd found in one of the large trunks of supplies. I was careful to put each dried plate back where Kleio and I had found them earlier. Even if I didn't want to be here, they were feeding me, and—for the most part—being nice to me, and I wanted to keep it that way.

When the dishes were done, I was about to sit on one of the empty couches when Wilder and Everett walked through the back flaps of the tent, dressed for the hunt. My mouth opened, but I quickly snapped it shut, not wanting to let anyone know what I was thinking. Wilder probably looked fine, but my eyes fell to Everett. He looked the part of alpha. Forget Wilder—if he had approached me in the woods, I probably would have peed my shorts like Jenny had claimed.

He'd covered himself in black. The black pants he wore hugged his thighs tight up to his waist. My tongue pushed against the back of my teeth, trying to banish the inappropriate images in my head of what lay underneath.

No, he kidnapped me and is holding me hostage here, I reminded myself. *I shouldn't be having these thoughts at all.*

I tried to swallow as my eyes traced his body up his abdomen and up his chest. The shirt he wore was thick but still athletic enough that he could move freely. He wore black gloves, made of leather, that had to have been custom made to fit his large hands.

I stood up as Kleio and Jack made their way to the hunters. Kleio whispered something to Everett that I couldn't hear. He nodded in agreement, briefly glancing my way. Jack shook his hand and wished him luck.

I didn't know what I should be doing. *Do I sit and keep to myself? Or should I go up and say goodbye?* It seemed like I should do something. Before I could figure out what to do, I found myself walking over to Everett and Wilder.

"Good luck," I mumbled. "I hope you catch a lot of rogues."

Everett smirked as he reached out his hand to shake mine. His hand and fingers completely encapsulated mine. Our eyes met, and shivers traveled down to my tailbone. Every time I looked into his eyes, my mind went to mush. He blinked, breaking the trance his eyes had put on me. Abruptly, our hands separated, and I took the hand he shook and brought it close to my chest. I turned to wish Wilder well, but he was already on his way out of the tent with Gavrill's arm slung around his shoulders.

I mentally berated myself. That had made me look like an idiot. I shouldn't have done that.

Kostas came up from behind Everett and slapped him on the back. "It's almost time, alpha."

As Everett walked with Kostas out of the tent, I waited for him to look back at me, but he never did.

"I'm not going to be able to sleep tonight," Kleio said, slowly pacing the tent.

"Sounds good to me." Jack was sitting on the couch, watching her with an eager look on his face.

"I'm not going to be able to do *that* either, Jack." She rolled her eyes. "I'm just too nervous. Why can't Gavrill go on the hunt? He's almost as strong as Everett, and then we wouldn't be putting our alpha at risk."

"Everett would never let him go with Wilder," he said. "Gavrill would worry about keeping his brother safe instead of focusing his attention on the rogues. Dangerous for everyone."

"Wait, Gavrill is Wilder's brother?" I asked.

"Yep, you've already met your boyfriend's family," Jack said.

I narrowed my eyes at him. "Not my boyfriend."

"Jack!" Kleio swatted at his arm. "I promised her we were done with the teasing."

A chorus of howls from outside filled the tent. She stopped her pacing and cuddled up next to Jack. "Wake me up on Monday morning."

We sat in silence for several minutes until the howling

stopped and Kostas flipped back the flap of the tent. He walked inside and sat down on one of the empty couches. "Well, they're off. Kip and Elijah bullied their way to the front, of course, but Everett and Wilder have a leg up on them tracking wise. I'm sure everything will be fine."

"They'd better be," Kleio said. She ran her fingers through her hair, twirling a section between her fingers. "This is the most stressful month of the decade. I can never sleep with all the backstabbing and riffraff that goes on during Deca."

Kostas rubbed his hands together as he spoke. "Rules never get followed during Deca. No one is watching, and accidents always seem to happen. But I have faith in Everett. He's the strongest shifter here. Let's just hope he comes home tonight with a decent number of rogues. It would take the pressure off."

"I know. It still worries me," Kleio said. She looked over at me. "Elise, you must be tired. Let's go find the tent Wilder so kindly set up for you."

I was thankful the pack had an extra tent for me. While I appreciated the thought, there was no way I was going to share a tent with Kleio and Jack. Had she expected me to share the bed with them? On top of the simple awkwardness, I would also have a much harder time sneaking out if there were others in the tent with me.

What I had told Everett meant nothing to me. His talk of wards didn't scare me either. They were probably some scary story shifter parents told their kids at bedtime that he thought would get the "dumb human" too. Magical electrocuting invisible walls? Mm-hmm, okay, right.

Shaking my head, I refocused myself. I needed to get back to the cabin. I couldn't stay here with a bunch of shifters.

Thankfully Wilder had set up my tent far enough away from the others that escape seemed actually possible. Everyone had been so nice to me, except for Wilder. I kind of felt bad leaving everyone without a thank-you or goodbye. Especially Kleio, who I had taken a liking to. She was fun and open and confident in her choices. Something I wished I could be.

I sat on my cot, waiting for the sounds of the camp to die down and for everyone to retreat to their tent for the night. Once the crickets became louder than the voices, I grabbed my purse, putting it securely across my body. I kicked off Jenny's wedge sneakers. They'd done me dirty earlier today when I'd run from Everett.

Delicately, I pulled the flap of the tent back so I could peek out. There was no movement. I slithered my body out and crouched with my back to the side of the canvas tent. A few campfires still glowed with red embers.

Between the red glow and the bright stars in the sky, I had enough visibility to make my way through Camp. I dodged the ropes and stakes that held the tents down, breathing easier. This escape was looking promising. If I could make my way behind the main tents and follow them, I would be parallel to the main road. From there, I could follow the road out of Camp and hopefully I would find a landmark that was familiar.

My footsteps picked up in pace as I made my way from behind the last tent in the row at the start of Camp. Looking behind my shoulder, I saw nothing. Silently congratulating myself, I took off into a full run. The gravel road appeared to have endured frequent driving, breaking down the gravel rocks into fine pebbles and dust. It was perfect for running. My muscles were warming, and my breathing leveled out as I set a pace that was comfortable but kept me moving.

I wondered if Jenny was worried about me. How could Everett have gotten a message to her that I was okay when he had been at this "Camp" the whole day? What kind of excuse had he given her as to my whereabouts?

My purse shifted down my body as I ran, and I looked

down to rearrange it to the other side. I didn't have time to lift my gaze before I was flying backward, having hit something solid in the middle of the road. My head flew back, leading my body to the ground. A loud thud echoed in my ears as my skull hit the gravel, my body following it like a rag doll.

CHAPTER NINE

Floating in a sea of darkness, I couldn't move or see anything. Like waves in the ocean, my hearing came in and out. One minute I could hear what was going on around me, and the next only the blood whooshing through my head synchronized with my heartbeat.

"What have you done, Lyka?" a deep voice asked.

Strangely, I felt like I was floating in the water, rocking back and forth. I was lying braced on something firm, wind rushing past me. Moving?

Another voice joined. The rocking never stopped. "What the hell is going on?"

"She ran into the wards."

"Where was she going?"

"I don't know. I need to get her back and get her head looked at."

"Give her to me—I can bring her to the tent."

Something shifted, tightened around me. "Don't touch her."

———

Opening my eyes was painful. My head felt like I had been on a rickety roller coaster one too many times, my brain jostled. I rolled my head to the side to look at my surroundings. I was in the pack's main tent, on one of the floral couches. Someone had draped a tan fleece blanket over me. I tried to sit up, but the pulsing in my head immediately humbled me, so I lay back down.

"You're awake!" Kleio's voice rang out. "You had us all scared, Elise. How are you feeling?" She came over to the couch and sat down next to my knees.

"Not great. My head hurts," I managed to mumble. "What happened? I was running, and then I hit something."

"You ran into the wards. I wasn't kidding when I told you that you were stuck here for the weekend. Nothing gets in and nothing gets out until Sunday afternoon."

Groaning, I tried again to sit up. Wards? Was that what I had laughed off as a bedtime fable? I hadn't run into a solid wall, that was for sure. But I had definitely hit something. My pounding head was evidence of that.

"Thank goodness Everett found you," Kleio said.

Everett had found me? I hardly remembered anything from when I'd hit the ground to now.

Confused, I tried to gain some clarity. "I didn't see any walls."

"Of course not, silly. You can't see the wards," she said. "Most humans can sense them. They give them the feeling of unease, and they usually turn around. You must have been running so fast that your body didn't have enough time to sense them. Coming at them with some speed can really do a number."

My hand felt my head. There were some paper towels on

the back of my scalp. Hissing at the stinging contact, I pulled my hand away.

"The escapee awakes!"

I turned my head to see Gavrill entering the tent, having to duck down to fit through the entrance. "Boss says one of us has to keep an eye on you the rest of the weekend. Doesn't want the human to get hurt again. Too much of a liability with all the pheromones around here."

"You should've seen it, Elise." Kleio giggled as she reminisced. "There was blood from your head on the ground—okay, that part wasn't funny—but the other shifters came out in droves. Everyone was wondering what had hit the wards and who the pretty human was lying on the ground. Gavrill, Kostas, and Everett had to get all tough and growly to get them to back off."

Suddenly Kostas sat up on the couch next to me. "Glad you found it so entertaining." He had been lying down, and I hadn't even noticed him there. "Everett and Wilder are out hunting for the day. You'd better hope they come back with more rogues than yesterday. Their hunt got cut short." The look he gave me told me he thought that was my fault.

I groaned, trying to sit up. The sun coming through the windows on the sides of the tent was evidence that I had been unconscious the entire night. The back of my head throbbed. My mind went into problem-solving mode, taking stock of what I had with me to help my recovery. When I'd gone to the bar Thursday night, I hadn't planned on being in the middle of a shifter tournament by Saturday. I didn't have any first aid supplies with me.

I could feel Kostas taking stock of me as I finally managed to sit up and tried lifting myself into a standing position. "Take it easy there," he said. "Everett isn't close enough to rescue you this time if you take another fall."

"I didn't ask anyone to help me." I glared as I spoke.

"You should be glad he was there. Those other wolves would have torn you apart just based on instinct. Head wounds bleed a ton." Kostas got up from his couch and went to grab a bottle of water from the cooler against the tent wall. "Where were you going anyway?"

Everyone paused what they were doing to look at me, curious as to my answer.

"I was trying to get back to my cabin. I have roommates who must be wondering where I am."

Gavrill shook his head at me. "Everett took care of it. As far as they know, you're spending the weekend with Wilder. He had one of Wilder's roommates go over there and let them know."

"Oh, great." I face-palmed with my hand. "Not only do they think I'm shacking up with Wilder all weekend, but you also sent shifters to my cabin."

"The shacking up you brought on yourself, but I didn't send a shifter near your friends. Wilder's roommates are human, locals who are aware of...us."

I scowled at Kostas and Gavrill. They looked at me like I was a burden. I didn't want to be here. I hadn't asked for Everett to come and save me. I was sure I would have been fine. Lying there, bleeding out on the gravel, surrounded by wolf shifters... My head pulsed at that moment. I needed to find something to treat my head wound.

"Do you guys have a first aid kit?" I asked. They all looked at me with blank faces. "You know, something with bandages, antibiotic ointment?"

"Well, no," Kleio answered. "We don't really need one. Most of our wounds heal quickly." She chewed on the side of her cheek for a second thinking. "Jack's performing his required healer shift at the chief tent, but I don't think we should bring you up there." She turned to the men in the tent. "Gavrill, Kostas, go see what you can find for Elise. She needs something to treat her human injuries."

They both grumbled while they walked over to the coolers along the side of the tent, flipping them open and slamming them closed.

Standing up, it took a minute for me to gain my balance. I was wobbling enough that Kleio came over to grab my arm. I appreciated the gesture—and that she hadn't lectured me about trying to run away last night.

"We'll get you fixed up," Kleio said. She looked behind my head and sucked in a sharp breath. I winced, not even wanting to know what it must've looked like. She patted my arm. "The boys will find something."

"This is all we've got," Gavrill said. He was carrying a roll of paper towels and some masking tape.

"I got some ice. That's good for head wounds, right?" Kostas emerged behind Gavrill, holding a few cubes of ice in each hand. They had already started melting against his skin, the water running between his fingers and dripping onto the ground. Great. That was super sanitary to press against an open wound.

I took the paper towels and tape in one hand, and Kostas rolled the ice cubes into my other. They continued to melt.

Kleio sighed and took the paper towels and tape from my hand and set them on the table. "I'm sorry we don't have anything for you to use. I don't—"

I cut her off. "Can we go for a walk? Close to the forest?" I knew enough about the vegetation here that I could find something to help me. There was a wide array of plants native to the area that had medicinal properties. I just needed to get close enough to find them.

"Of course. Just hold on to me. I don't want you falling

again." She guided me out the back of the tent. I threw the melted ice into the grass.

We walked across the field toward the forest in silence. Glancing down, I saw some yarrow growing near our path and slowly bent down to gather some. I could prepare a paste with the yarrow, put some against my head wound, cover it with paper towel, and wrap it up with the tape. It seemed like a bad idea to be stuck here with wolves and an open cut.

Kleio gave me a strange look as I shoved some of the plant into my pocket, but she didn't say anything, and so we kept walking.

When we made it to the edge of the forest, I took a deep breath. It looked so peaceful. The green foliage and bird sounds were inviting.

A snarl interrupted the nature's sounds. I turned my head toward the noise and heard more snarling and the rattling of metal. Just past the edge of the forest, the ten metal cages that had held the rogues during the opening ceremony sat in a row. There were more rogues in the cages than there had been yesterday evening. Each cage had a banner in front of it representing the name of the ten packs that were competing. Some cages had two or three rogues in them, whereas some were empty.

I scanned down the line of cages until I found the Cedar Moon banner. The cage behind it had three rogues in it. Up close, the rogues were extremely unpleasant. In their wolf forms, they paced and snarled at anything that came close to the metal bars surrounding them. They also picked fights with each other inside the cages. The fur on their bodies looked matted and greasy. Many of the rogues had entire chunks of flesh missing or pieces of muscle that hung off their bodies, only hanging on by a single tendon. The sight was enough to make me nauseous.

Grunting and yelling commands at each other, two men caught my attention a couple of cages down from the Cedar Moon's cage. The two naked men were struggling to subdue a rogue they had caught. The rogue wolf was in terrible shape. It was missing an eye and had a large gash on one of its hind legs. That didn't stop its aggression, fighting for its life against the two big, strong men in their human forms. They both worked together to contain the rogue and shoved it into the cage, then quickly closed the door as the rogue recovered and launched itself at the metal gate.

The two men bent down with their hands on their knees, trying to catch their breaths. It had clearly taken all their energy to get the rogue locked in. They looked at each other as they stood up and stalked back into the forest, ready to find their next catch.

"So, Everett and Wilder are out there doing...that?" I looked to Kleio for conformation, and she nodded.

I didn't get the point of this competition. Why release the rogues, who were wild and dangerous, only to catch them again? I asked her about this.

"I wish I had the answer, Elise. It's a hundred-year-old tradition that the True Alpha upholds," she said. "The pack laws require us to join. If we didn't partake, he would come after our pack. It's important that we win to protect the pack and show our strength."

Still, I had a hard time not feeling sympathy for the rogues. It appeared they had no thoughts or control over their emotions or bodies. It was pure survival for them, clawing and biting their way to live.

Kleio went on, "There have been more rogues showing up in the different pack lands for the past several years. We don't know why they're...like that. Some think it's because they don't have a pack. It can drive a Lycan insane if they don't belong to a pack, but others think that the land is changing and causing a disruption in the natural order, physically changing the makeup of Lycans, causing them to decompose as they mature."

I took in Kleio's words and stewed over them. It looked like the rogues were being taken advantage of because of their reduced mental and physical functions. They were being used as pawns in the True Alpha's games.

I turned away from the cages, shaking my head, and looked into the forest. There was a sense of peace that beckoned me. One more day and I could head into the foliage and get back to my research. I couldn't wait to get lost in the trees and find some solitude. If this weekend had shown me anything, it was that I needed to stay on the path I had laid out for myself before I'd arrived in Minnesota. The one time I'd tried to not care and do something without really thinking it through had led me to a weekend stuck in a shifter tournament. I wasn't making that mistake again.

Having seen enough, we turned around and walked toward the city of tents. Kleio invited me to come play a lawn game with her pack to pass the time, but I decided I wanted to rest in my tent.

Stopping in the pack's tent, I took the roll of paper towels and the masking tape from the table. I grabbed a bottle of water from the coolers and walked to my tent. I fingered the leaves and flowers in my pocket as I bent down to enter my room. Using a small amount of water and a couple of rocks I found on the ground, I made a paste with the yarrow leaves. Then I carefully peeled the paper towels off the back of my head. Dried brown blood covered the white paper. It didn't seem super serious, but I would need to keep it clean.

I blindly smoothed some of the yarrow paste over the cut and covered it with a clean rectangle of paper towel. I pulled strips of masking tape from the roll and taped it to my head the best I could. I would probably be losing some hair when I removed it. I lay on my side, listening to the muffled conversations going on around the tent. The warmth of the tent in the afternoon sun and the ambient noises lulled me into unconsciousness.

CHAPTER TEN

"Elise?" My eyes popped open to find Kleio's head poking through the tent flaps. "I just came to check on you. Gavrill decided he doesn't want to play our game anymore, and we need another player."

I rubbed my eyes and sat up. The pain in my head had subsided to a dull ache instead of a pulsing pain. "How long have I been in here?" I took a drink of my water, trying to wake up.

"About an hour? You humans sure take a lot of naps."

Wiping the sleep from my eyes, I stood up.

"So, the game," she said. "Will you join us?"

It was Saturday. Another day away from the cabin and my research, but at least I was still in the same woods, albeit an area I hadn't expected to study. It didn't feel right to be playing games when I could use the time to explore.

"I am going to have to pass on the game—sorry." The excitement left Kleio's face, and I felt an unexpected pang, like I was letting down a friend. "I'm going to go explore for a bit. Maybe you could come with me? It would help if I had someone familiar with the forest."

"Where are you going? Remember the wards, Elise."

Yes, the constant dull ache in my head was my constant reminder of the wards.

"I'm going to stay within the wards. I just want to look around, maybe take some plant samples if I find anything interesting."

Even in the enormous field surrounding the tent city, there could be something exciting. The possibility of finding ornamental grasses that hadn't been documented within the last century made my body tingle. And if I could get into the dense forest, even just a few feet, who knew what I could find? The prospects were endless in this forest.

"You like plants?" Kleio looked at me, surprised.

"Yeah, that's why I'm here. I'm on the hunt for rare plants in this region."

"So, it's like a scavenger hunt?" Her eyes lit up and the twinkle returned.

"Yeah, kind of." Essentially, that was what I was doing—scavenging for rare species.

"This is even better than the game! Let's go!"

"Wait, do you have any paper or pencil?" I didn't have my journal, but it would be nice to have something to write on in case I found anything of interest.

She thought for a few seconds. "I'll take one of their stupid maps. They have so many they don't even use. You can write on the back of it."

Kleio pranced away to the main tent on a mission to find me some paper. I laid my purse across my body. It wasn't my backpack that I took on research hikes, but it gave me a sense of constancy to have something with me.

Camp was almost empty when I stepped out of my tent. A

few fires smoldered, sending light colored smoke into the air. The shifters who sat around the fire closest to my tent turned to look at me. I tried not to make eye contact, remembering Everett's warning. *Act normal.* I felt their gaze leave me, and I let out a sigh of relief.

Kleio's strawberry blonde hair drifted behind her as she made her way back to me, paper in hand...and Gavrill's massive body steps behind her.

"I was told we require a babysitter." She handed me the map and a black felt-tip pen. I took the map and folded it twice into a square and stuck it into my purse with the pen.

"I'm just following the boss's orders," Gavrill said. He had a backpack on and looked ready to hike.

"He doesn't trust me with you," Kleio whispered into my ear in a teasing tone.

"I don't trust that you won't get carried away and find your-selves so deep in the forest that you can't find your way back by sundown."

"I'm a horrible tracker," she whispered to me again. "Oh, well. We'll just ignore him."

"I heard that," Gavrill said.

Kleio was true to her word and ignored him. "Lead the way, plant lady!"

I looked around, deciding where we should go. The field was enticing, with all the fluttering grasses, but if I had the chance to go into the forest, especially with those familiar with the land, I couldn't pass up the opportunity. I led the way around a few scattered tents and through the field, letting my fingers brush on the tips of the grasses. I glanced around my shoulder, always finding Kleio and Gavrill close behind. They weren't taking in the environment like I was. It was like when someone lived in a warm climate their whole lives, so they took the sunshine for granted. The slight breeze on my cheeks, the soft earth beneath my feet...it was a whole-body experience for me.

When we came to the edge of the forest where the rogue cages stood, I kept my eyes away from their decaying bodies. It wasn't that their bodies were unpleasant, or the smell; it was that they were stuck, living beings being used as pawns in someone's game. That made my stomach churn.

I ducked my head under a low-hanging branch as I entered the forest. The sounds of the tree branches rustling together and the birds chirping to one another masked the snarling sounds of the rogues. Our six feet made satisfying crunching sounds with each step—the dried leaves being mulched by our feet. We walked for what seemed like a while, but time never passed the same in the forest. For me, it always slowed.

The sound of trickling water running over rocks in my ear was the first sign that there was water ahead. It got louder as we walked, my hearing proving correct. A storybook stream lay ahead of us, about three feet wide. Its cerulean-blue waters flowed over smooth rocks that looked like gems beneath the water. Along the banks of the stream, broad green leaves caught my eye. I walked over to the sapling, no taller than my waist.

"It can't be," I murmured.

The plant rolodex in my head flipped through cards, finding the one I was looking for. *Morus rubra.* There was no way. I took a leaf between my fingers, rubbing the top of it with my thumb—it felt like sandpaper, my index finger tickled by the tiny hairs underneath the leaf.

"So, what exactly are you looking for?" Kleio asked. "It all just looks green to me."

I tried not to flail with excitement too much at the question. Turning to her, I said, "I'm looking for anything unusual, something that stands out against all the 'green,' as you said. It does all look green—unless you look closely."

I bent my knees along the side of the stream, crouching down. Kleio followed suit, with Gavrill standing with his arms crossed behind us. I took a small leaf, one close to the ground, and snapped its petiole. Milky-white sap covered my fingers.

"It's a red mulberry," I told Kleio.

"Is that good?" she asked.

I laughed, the corners of my lips pulled toward the sky. Good? This was amazing. "It's remarkable. No one has seen a red mulberry in this region for at least a hundred years," I said. Kleio looked taken back, surprised. This was exactly what I needed for my research. I could see myself presenting my thesis, surprising my professors with my find. I slipped the leaf into my purse.

The tree was small, still a sapling—and still fragile. Its location so close to the stream worried me. "I don't think it's going to survive, though," I said, frowning.

"What? Why not?" She grabbed my arm, demanding an answer.

"It's growing too close to the stream; its roots could easily get overwhelmed if the water levels rise from a rainstorm."

"Well, we need to save it! What do you need me to do?"

Kleio's enthusiasm motivated me. I looked around the forest floor, going through my options. It was tempting to take the mulberry tree, find a pot, and bring it back to the cabin with me, but that wouldn't be ethical. The tree needed to stay where it grew—in its natural habitat.

"We could try to transplant it," I said. "Move it away from the stream."

"Let's do it! Tell me what to do." Kleio rubbed her fingers along the leaf as I had, petting it, clearly emotionally attached to the tree now.

"Well, usually I have a trowel to dig." I looked at her, my hands void of tools.

"I've got you covered," Kleio said, opening her hand, letting black claws emerge from her fingernail beds.

I stepped back, although it shouldn't have surprised me. Of course Lycans had claws—they could turn into wolves.

Kleio looked eager to put her claws to work. I directed her to dig up the tree along the edge of the canopy of leaves it had grown. Any closer and she would damage the already-fragile root system. She made quick work of digging, reaching deep into the earth to get all the roots that had grown beneath. I admired her tenacious spirit.

Once the tree was free from the earth, I picked a spot several feet away from the stream and directed her to dig another hole to put the tree in. It was a nice spot for a sapling to continue to grow; it would get morning sun and afternoon shade. There was enough space for it to stretch its branches horizontally and up to the sky, reaching for the sun.

Together, we lifted the tree from its original hole and put it in its new home. We filled in the hole, covering the roots and patting it down the soil so the tree would stand sturdy should a gust of wind blow by.

I looked at the transplanted tree proudly. I had done my part as a conservationist, making sure the tree had its best chance of survival. "There—let's hope it continues to grow, produces mulberries for the birds, and lives here in this forest for a hundred years."

"Is there anything else we can do? I feel bad leaving it here to fend for itself." Kleio continued to pat down the soil around the tree.

"We need to give it a big drink of water so its roots reach out into the new dirt. If I had fertilizer, that would also provide extra nutrients to the tree, but I don't..." I looked around, thinking. A solution popped into my mind, but they would never go for it.

"What is it? You have that thinking face again, Elise." Kleio narrowed her eyes at me.

"There is something we can do, but I don't think you guys will go for it." I looked at her and then back at Gavrill, who had been standing by us the entire time we had been working, quiet with his arms crossed.

"Lay it on me." Kleio stood up, brushing the dirt from her hands. Her claws retracted beneath her skin.

"Well, I've read about fertilizing a plant with...blood." Neither of them said anything, and I couldn't gauge their reactions. "Blood has potassium in it, among other nutrients that are good for root development."

Kleio looked at me and smiled. "I know whose blood would work great!" She turned to Gavrill; a startled look covered his face.

"Nope, not happening," he said, shaking his head at her.

"Come on, Gavrill. You've been standing there his whole time while Elise and I have been hard at work saving a life. It's the least you could do."

Kleio walked over to him, making big doe eyes at him. He stood there, avoiding eye contact with her on purpose.

"Elise and I are covered in dirt. It would be just a little bit of blood, right?" She turned to me for reassurance.

"Yeah, just a little bit," I said.

"See, Gavrill, just a little blood and you can save a life today!"

Gavrill looked at me before he made the mistake of finally looking Kleio in the eye. I could see his willpower breaking as his face went slack. Kleio was hard to say no to.

"Fine—only a little blood," Gavrill said.

"Yay!" Kleio clapped her hands together before looking to me for direction.

"We need to dilute the blood with water," I said.

Gavrill took off his backpack and reached inside, pulling out a bottle of water. He handed it to me, and I opened the cap. He brought his left index finger to his mouth, pushing the pad into one of his sharp canines. Blood immediately pooled around the wound when he removed it from his mouth. I held out the bottle as he squeezed his finger. The blood dripped, then expanded as soon as it hit the water, creating billowing red clouds that disappeared, turning the water an opaque red color.

"That's enough," I said. I closed the cap and shook the bottle, mixing the homemade fertilizer. Gavrill brought his finger to his mouth, sucking on it to end the bleeding.

I extended the shaken bottle to Kleio. "You do the honors." She brought it close to the trunk of the tree, sprinkling the mixture gently over the dirt.

"Wow, that felt good. Let's save another tree!" she exclaimed.

I laughed at her enthusiasm. It was always a good thing to have another plant person in the world.

"We'd best head back—it's getting late," said our babysitter.

Kleio and I looked down at our hands and arms, both blackened with the rich soil of the forest. She winked at me before leaping onto Gavrill, hugging him with her dirty arms. "Oh, Gavrill, thank you for saving the tree with your blood!"

"Ugh, Kleio get off me." Gavrill pushed her off him. He did his best to brush the dirt off his own arms and shirt, but he was unsuccessful.

"Maybe next time we go scavenging, you'll think twice before chaperoning us. You've been a grump all weekend." Kleio playfully stuck her tongue out at him.

Gavrill didn't respond to the juvenile behavior. He turned around and led the way out of the forest and back to Camp. Kleio linked her arm in the crook of my elbow, and we walked arm in arm out of the forest.

"Just in time," Kostas said as he greeted us inside the main tent, where he had been hard at work making dinner—more meat and vegetables. This seemed to be the shifters' diet. I wasn't complaining as I sat down and loaded my plate with medium-rare steak and green beans.

The tent flaps flew open, blowing in a breeze that smelled like sweat and blood. We all looked up from the table to see Everett and Wilder enter the tent. They both looked exhausted. Dark bags rimmed under their eyes, and their brown hair was wild and unkept.

"How'd it go today?" Gavrill asked Everett as he made a plate of food for him.

"We caught ten more. Up to thirteen." Everett dropped into his chair and didn't pause before he started shoveling food into his mouth. I doubted he had eaten yet today.

Wilder sat next to him with a plate of food that Gavrill had also dished up. I found myself staring at Everett, mesmerized by how fast he was eating. Did he chew his food? He caught me staring, and I quickly found a bean on my plate that was very interesting.

"That's good," Gavrill said. "We're on track. Are any of the other teams giving you trouble?" He had a concerned look on his face. I remembered Kostas shaking his head knowingly when the True Alpha had spoken about following the tournament rules.

"Nothing we can't handle. I'm sure it'll get worse over the next two weekends as teams get more desperate." Everett finished his food and began scooping seconds onto his plate.

"Well, we had an interesting day." We all looked at Kleio as she spoke, and my face turned red as she beamed at me. "Elise saved a rare tree today." Everyone but Gavrill stared at her with a blank look. "She used Gavrill's blood to fertilize it."

Kleio smiled before she popped a piece of steak into her

mouth and chewed. Then everyone turned to look at Gavrill. He continued to eat his food, unbothered by the sudden attention.

Everett stopped eating as he turned to where I was sitting. "I thought I told you to keep a low profile."

Kleio quickly stepped in, saying, "It was just us, Everett. No one saw. We were deep in the woods. Gavrill didn't even cry when his finger was pricked."

Gavrill stabbed the food on his plate violently, grumbling something unintelligible. Everett shook his head and continued to eat.

"Well, I thought it was fun." She smiled at me.

The meal was finished in silence. Jack and I picked up the dishes and stacked them next to the bucket of water we used for washing. I could feel a prickling sensation on the back of my neck as I placed the last dirty plate on top of the stack.

Rubbing my neck, I turned around to see Everett and Gavrill talking quietly to one another on a purple floral couch. Gavrill glanced at me quickly before looking away. Something told me I was the topic of their conversation.

Kostas broke my line of sight as he stepped in front of me. I sighed. "I wash, you dry?"

Halfway through the dishes, Kostas bowed his head as a gesture of goodbye to Everett and Wilder as they exited the back of the tent. I looked up to see Everett staring at me, but he turned away, leaving me to stare at the flap of the tent he left fluttering in his wake.

"Are they headed back out to hunt?" I asked.

Kostas turned to me and nodded. I couldn't believe they had energy to keep going.

"They'll be out there all night and most of the day tomorrow," he answered. One more sleep and one more day until I could go back to my cabin and restart.

Everyone retired early to their tents. Jack chased Kleio to their tent, and I could hear her giggles across the campsite.

Maybe someday, after I had completed my schooling and gotten a job that could support myself and help my parents, I would allow myself to find someone. Kleio and Jack seemed so happy together. Their love was contagious and made me want some for myself.

Lying on my side in the bed, I promised myself I would get there one day. I just needed to follow the path and not stray like I had this weekend.

No more distractions.

CHAPTER ELEVEN

On Sunday morning, I woke up surprisingly refreshed from last night's sleep. Maybe it was the fresh air or maybe it was my head injury, but I had slept soundly. Not being woken up by pounding doors or with a headache made it easier to roll out of bed reenergized.

I reached my arms above my head, stretching and groaning loudly as my muscles released. I could smell myself. Not taking a shower for the last two days had taken its toll. I no longer smelled of the cucumber soap I used during my showers. First thing I would do when I got back was jump into the shower and get all the sweat and grime off my skin.

Unwrapping the bandage around my head, I cringed as I felt some follicles pull from my scalp with the tape. The wound was almost healed. It barely hurt when I felt it carefully with my fingers. There was no need for more paper-towel bandages.

Next, I rubbed some of the bottled water under my arms. It wasn't the best, but it would work for now. I made a mental note to put a small stick of deodorant in my purse moving forward.

Thinking of my purse, I reached in and pulled out the red-mulberry leaf I had stowed there yesterday. When I got back to the cabin, I would press it into my journal. The sap was still sticky on the end of the stem. I made a mental note to harvest that before I pressed the leaf. It was interesting that it had sprouted near a stream. Maybe it was an undocumented species of red mulberry? One that tolerated waterlogged soil? My body tingled with the possibilities.

Tossing my bag over my shoulder, I exited my tent and made my way to the large one. I could smell bacon even before I lifted the flap to enter. Gavrill was finishing dishing up breakfast when I sat down at the table. I thanked him as he set a plate of eggs and bacon in front of me.

"Today's the day," he said, sitting next to me with his own plate of food. "Everett will drop you off at your cabin once the wards lift at noon."

A sense of relief came over me at his words. Everyone here had said I would be returned home, but having an assured time brought me comfort. My cabin couldn't be too far away from here. I should be home by one o'clock. Enough time to shower and get my life together before Monday.

A worry crossed my mind. Having only learned about the wards two days ago, I didn't know enough about them. If they were going to lift the wards and hadn't caught all the rogues, would they just run free? I would not be running alone in the woods if that was the case.

When I asked Gavrill, he didn't make me feel like I was asking a stupid question when he answered. "The True Alpha's pack is large, with a bunch of trackers and hunters. They go out and clear the forest of the rogues before the wards get lifted. They throw all the loose ones into a cage until next weekend."

I was relieved I wouldn't run into any of the rogue wolves. Gavrill's answer solidified the ridiculousness of the tournament. If the True Alpha's pack could just catch all the rogues quickly, it really was just for his own sick amusement.

Kleio and Jack came to join us at the breakfast table. We all chatted until it was almost noon. Kostas showed up at the tent with his backpack already packed, and eventually Wilder and Everett entered the tent as well.

"I have everything packed up," Kostas told them.

"Great. Let's get out of here," Everett said. He and Wilder looked like they could use twenty-four hours of sleep and some hot showers.

Kleio gave my arm a squeeze, mouthing goodbye before Jack whisked her away into a car. Everett opened the passenger side of the black SUV he had driven me here in, leaving the door open for me before he walked around the back of the car to the driver's side. I tried not to take offense that no one had said goodbye to me. It was for the best. I was an unwanted weekend guest who they wouldn't be seeing again. No reason for goodbyes.

The car ride with Everett was silent, but my head was filled with noise. He kept his right arm draped over the center console, close enough that if he were my boyfriend, I would be able to reach over and grab his hand. My hands twitched. I clasped them together tightly in my lap, hiding the involuntary movements. Without turning my head, I glanced over at Everett. His jaw was clenched tight, his head slightly askew toward me, his nostrils flaring in and out with every breath. It almost looked like he was in pain.

"This is as far as I can take you." Everett stopped the car on the road in front of the driveway to the cabin.

It seemed a little silly that he couldn't drive me the last one hundred yards to the front of the cabin, but I'd gotten through the weekend relatively unscathed. I wasn't about to complain.

I hopped out of the car without saying goodbye. I didn't

know what to say. *Thank you for kidnapping me this weekend? Thank you for not killing me with your giant fangs and claws?* Everett didn't say anything either, but I could feel his gaze on my back as I walked down the driveway to the cabin. It took all my willpower not to turn around and look into his golden eyes one last time.

As soon as I entered the cabin, Jenny shot up from where she was sitting on the couch.

"Elise, you have to tell me everything." She didn't seem alarmed that I had been gone all weekend. Apparently Wilder's friend had eased any concerns she might've had. "I thought you'd spend the night, but the entire weekend? He must've really been something." I grimaced at her evaluation of my weekend. "When his roommates came by on Friday and told me that you were staying the weekend, I was shocked. Who turns a one-night stand into a weekend event?"

Again, I had no idea what I could even say. *Well, you see, I got swept up in this Lycan hunting tournament and spent the weekend with wolf shifters.* The shifters didn't seem overly concerned about keeping their presence in this area a secret, but I didn't know how much I should tell Jenny and Leo. It felt like something I should keep to myself, so I decided to play into Jenny's assumptions. "Yeah, it was a fun weekend."

Jenny looked pleased with herself. I felt a twinge of guilt come over me. She clearly thought I had fallen for Wilder, that we'd had a great time together all weekend. In truth, I felt nothing for him. It had been a one-night mistake. I would have to make it clear to her I wasn't interested in him. A different time. When I'd had time to process the last weekend. I needed to stay far away from the shifters and focus on my research. For now, I let her believe what she wanted to.

"I told you! I knew you needed a little fun."

I was already walking back to my room, ready to shower off the weekend. "Yeah, fun."

CHAPTER TWELVE

By Wednesday, I had fallen into a groove. My head was completely healed, and the plants I had rescued from my car were thriving in the window of my room. The clear pots I grew them in looked great against the sun shining through my window. I could see all the white roots weaving through the dirt, and it was easy to tell when they needed to be watered. I had even pressed the red mulberry leaf into my journal, jotting down what I had recalled from the woods that day.

Each day, I'd get up early to go for a run, exploring new trails and paths that had been laid out on the map Robinson had given us. After my run, I'd gather my research supplies in my backpack and set off into the forest, careful to stay within a five-mile radius of the cabin. Eventually I would have to go beyond those boundaries, but I felt more comfortable staying within them for now.

The forest was just as peaceful as I'd thought it would be. The large trees created a canopy over the trails. I felt like I was in a warm green bubble, complete with birdsong and a gentle breeze. This was my happy place. I scavenged for different plants to add to my stash and made notes about the different species that grew here. My notebook was growing thicker with the fresh leaves and stems I had pressed on its pages.

Today I went a little farther down the trail where I had first met Wilder. I'd had had no other wolf sightings this week, and I was beginning to wonder if last weekend had been a hallucination.

I wasn't jogging this time, so I could climb the rocks at a slower pace. After climbing over them for a time, the pile of rocks abruptly ended. It was like there had been a single avalanche of rocks over the trail. It seemed unnatural and purposeful. The gravel trail continued as usual after the pile of rocks ended. I brushed off my hands, removing the dirt and dust that had accumulated while I climbed the rocks.

Continuing down the trail, I noticed discrepancies in the forest floor. Some areas were lush and green, while others had turned a purple-brown color. Looking down the trail, this pattern continued as far as I could see.

Crouching down next to one patch of brown, I unpacked some containers from my backpack along with a pair of gloves. It seemed like the plant was decomposing, but it didn't look like any decomposition that I had ever seen before. The plants in the brown area had withered, devoid of moisture.

I reached with a gloved hand to gather a sample to bring back with me. The stem I grabbed shattered under my fingers, turning to dust. The crinkled leaves on the next plant did the same thing. I had trouble grabbing any of the brown plants before they disintegrated between my fingers. Using both hands, I grabbed a plant between my palms and carried it over to one of my glass containers I used to store specimens.

Carefully, I pulled my hands apart, letting the plant dust fall into the container. I covered the sample with a lid and looked through the glass. How could a plant disintegrate into dust? I couldn't remember reading anything like this from my textbooks or in my previous research. What made it so odd was that there were perfectly healthy plants growing green next to all the brown ones. Taking out another container, I gathered some of the soil the brown plant had grown in. I wrote some notes in my notebook, then headed back to the cabin.

Professor Robinson would be back to check on us tomorrow. After I labeled the sample containers, I planned to send them back with him to the lab so they could run some tests to tell me what I was looking at.

For a moment I sat there, taking in the stillness around me. It was peaceful but, for the first time, also a little lonely. I missed Kleio and even Gavrill. They had been my pseudo research assistants, helping me navigate the woods. Kleio had been so enthusiastic about the whole experience. Had she told Everett more about our day exploring? Part of me hoped that she had. He'd seemed annoyed with me for going out scavenging, so hopefully she'd explained the innocence of the day.

Why did I care what he thought? I would never see him again. But the way he had flared his nostrils at me, almost like he was smelling me? That had been weird, right? Or had I just imagined that? Everything last weekend seemed more like a foggy dream, fading from my memory every day.

I spent Thursday working on the landscaping around the cabin. A plant with purple flowers covered the entire perimeter of the cabin. The flowers were pretty enough, but I didn't think the plant was native to the area.

Remembering all the books in the cabin, I headed inside to see what I could find about it. I didn't want to get in trouble for pulling out the wrong thing. My fingers brushed along the line of book spines until I found one titled *Native Plants of the North*.

I thumbed through the pages until I saw a picture of a

flower that looked like the ones outside. *Aconitum—also known as aconite, monkshood, or wolfsbane—is indigenous to the North.* I read from the page. They were native but extremely overgrown around the cabin. My eyes caught on the name *wolfsbane*, and I wondered if it was a coincidence.

I closed the book and headed back outside to pull the overgrowth. The plant was easy enough to remove from the ground, and in a couple of hours, I had cleared most of the wolfsbane. I carried the piles I'd made of it over to the edge of the forest, where the vegetation became thicker, and tossed them into the forest.

Leo came up the trail, having completed his work for the day. He had waders on that were still dripping with pond water. "Can I help with that?"

I nodded, motioning to the pile of wolfsbane still needing to be brought to the woods.

He grabbed a pile of the plants and helped me carry the rest. "Thanks for cleaning up. I've been so busy with my research."

"It's not a problem. How's everything going?" I asked.

"Good—everything's good. I met one of the landowners. He has some good insights. There's a lot going on in these woods."

I couldn't agree more. Had he found rot in the land too? I was about to ask, when Robinson's car pulled up our driveway.

The professor entered the cabin, his white scrub-brush mustache leading the way. He never looked particularly happy, but today he had an air of annoyance about him. He set his bag on the table as we all pulled out the chairs and sat.

"I see you made some progress with the outside of the cabin," Robinson said. "It looks nice." He puckered his face like the last phrase was hard for him to say. The outside of the cabin did look a lot cleaner and more groomed. I was proud of the work I'd done out there.

"I hate to bring this up"—Robinson's slight upturn of his lips suggested the opposite—"but you all missed your check-in calls with your professors last week."

I froze in my seat. Shit. I had forgotten to update my professor. Friday was my scheduled check-in day, but I'd been with the shifters on Friday. I looked over at Leo and Jenny, who looked equally as stunned.

"I'm sorry, Professor Robinson. It won't happen again," I said. Leo and Jenny mumbled apologies.

"Now, I understand the sat phone isn't working," Robinson said. A smirk grew on his lips, his eyes bouncing between each of our faces. He enjoyed making us panic. I exhaled, the tension releasing from my body. Right, the phone wasn't working. It wasn't our fault. "I'm still waiting on the new phone to get delivered. Hopefully by next week we can get it up and running." Jenny and Leo also looked relieved. "Next week, I expect check-in calls from you all." I nodded. "I know it doesn't seem important, but your professors need weekly updates to track your progress and know that you're doing what you came here to do—what the university is paying you to do." He pointed that last sentence at me. My scholarships.

Robinson finished talking and gathered his belongings. He took my samples, promising a one-week turnaround time for the results. To my relief, Robinson had brought no letters from my mother. I hoped next week I wouldn't get a backlog of letters she had sent.

Jenny, Leo, and I sat on the couch after he left. This was the first time all week we had hung out together. I was sure Jenny and Leo had made time for each other during the evening hours, but we all had been busy getting set up and getting our research going.

"That was rough," I said to them both.

"No Bars has drink specials on Thursdays." Leo wiggled his eyebrows suggestively.

"We met Wilder there last week. Maybe Elise wants another *wild* weekend."

I rolled my eyes at Jenny's comment. "I won't be having another wild weekend. Wilder was a one-weekend stand. That's it," I said.

She eyed me suspiciously, making it obvious she didn't believe me. Getting away from the cabin and having a drink did sound wonderful. I had been out on the trails or locked in my room, typing on my computer for the last four days. A change of scenery would be nice. There had to be other bars around that Wilder and the wolves regularly haunted. The chances of running into them again were probably low.

"I'll go for a drink." Leo clapped his hands together at my answer and said he would drive us in twenty minutes after he took a shower.

"One drink," I insisted. "Just to help me relax. I need to get back to it tomorrow."

Jenny grabbed my hand and dragged me to her room. "You have to let me dress you, Elise! You've been wearing nothing but hiking gear all week. It'll feel good to dress in something nice."

The "hiking gear" she was referring to was my regular everyday clothing. Athletic clothing that I could easily move around in and didn't break the bank. Her fancy athleisure wasn't in my price range. She seemed so excited to play dress-up that I went along with her and sat on her bed while she looked through her closet.

"Here! This will be perfect." Jenny pulled out a pink spandex jumpsuit with thin straps. It had shorts that went well above the "finger test" from high school. "Put it on!"

She turned around and continued rummaging through her closet to find something for herself. The jumpsuit was not what I would have picked, but what did I care? I was going to a bar in the middle of nowhere, trying to impress no one. If it made Jenny happy, then what did it matter?

I took off my leggings and tank top. The sports bra I was wearing wouldn't work with the suit, so I took that off too. I slipped into the suit and pulled it up my body, slipping the thin straps over my shoulders. I could tell without looking in the mirror that the jumpsuit was shorter on me than it would be on Jenny. My legs were longer than hers, and her clothes just fit me differently.

Jenny turned around with a matching pink tennis skirt and tank top in her hands. "You little harlot! You look fantastic. Everyone is going to eat you up!"

She didn't know, but that was exactly what I was afraid of.

CHAPTER THIRTEEN

WATCHING MY STEPS, I walked into No Bars behind Jenny and Leo. The shoes Jenny had loaned me were not what I was used to. The tan wedges made me even taller. Jenny had styled my hair in loose waves that reached midway down my back. I was already cursing every hair that got caught in my lip gloss she'd insisted I wear.

We siddled up to the counter and ordered our drinks. Looking around the room, I saw two tables pushed together, surrounded by the very people I was trying to avoid. *Is there only one bar around here?* I thought. Gavrill and Kostas sat talking with Everett, while Kleio and Jack looked to be teasing Wilder. I tried to sink behind Jenny's curly hair, but I was too late.

"Elise! Oh my god! I'm so glad you're here!" Kleio's voice carried across the room. "Come over here and sit with us!"

Jenny turned to me, curious. "How are you meeting all these people? You seem to know everyone around here."

I looked around frantically, trying to come up with an

answer for Jenny that didn't involve the word *shifter*. "They're Evere—I mean, Wilder's friends. I met them last weekend."

Leo gestured to the table. "You'd better go over there and say hi. The blonde one is almost falling out of her chair."

Kleio was bouncing in her seat, looking at me expectantly. I grabbed my drink and walked over to the table. Leo turned to Jenny and began flirting with her, making her laugh. He seemed happy to have her to himself.

As I approached the table, Wilder got up and walked over to the bar, rushing past me with no acknowledgment. What a nice guy I'd picked last weekend.

Kleio rolled her eyes at him and patted the seat next to her. I sat down, suddenly noticing who was seated at the other side of me. I felt his body tense as he looked over and met my eyes. The golden swirls around his pupils were hard to look away from.

"Hi, Elise." Everett's stare was possessive, as if he dared me to look anywhere else but into his eyes. I accepted his dare and held contact. The feeling didn't make me nervous as it had with Wilder last week. This was more commanding, but he emanated so much assurance in his actions that I felt safe.

"Hi, Everett." My voice came out so quiet that it was almost a whisper. He looked much more rested than when I'd left him on Sunday. The dark circles under his eyes had disappeared, his hair tamed.

Sitting in the chair next to Everett was as close as I had ever been to him. The skin on my shoulders hummed where I had brushed against his black T-shirt as I sat down.

I glanced down at his arm and couldn't stop myself from looking over the full sleeve of tattoos. The designs all flowed together seamlessly, weaving through one another. My fingers reached out to trace the lines that reminded me of the map of trails I had left in my room.

Before I could touch his skin, Everett pulled his arm away. I felt my face heat as my eyes snapped up to his. He smirked at me as if knowing what I had just tried to do, and I couldn't believe that I had just done that. It was like I had involuntarily moved and had no control over my body. I curled my fingers into my palm to control myself.

Kleio touched my left arm, breaking the hold Everett had on me. "How have you been? You look so cute tonight! How's your head doing? I've been thinking about you all week."

"My head's fine. It's pretty much healed," I said.

"Already healed? Wow, you must know what you're doing with all those plants you gather," she said. I was kind of surprised that Kleio had remembered me picking the yarrow. "We'll have to go on a scavenger hunt again soon."

I nodded in agreement. Feeling a mental pull to my right, I turned to see Everett listening to our conversation. Kleio turned to yell something to Gavrill, who was laughing with Kostas across the table. Everett looked down at my jumpsuit that barely covered half of my thighs. I immediately felt exposed in front of him.

"I like your outfit." His low voice rumbled through me.

"Thank you. It's my roommate Jenny's jumpsuit. This isn't what I normally look like." God, I was babbling. What was it about Everett that made me feel like this?

"I know what you look like. You always look beautiful." Everett's words sent those tingles down my spine that reached all the way to my tailbone.

I took a moment to compose myself. "I should go check on my friends." I got up to leave, but a firm hand on my thigh pushed me back into my seat.

"They look like they're just fine," Everett said.

When I turned to see Jenny and Leo, I saw that they were doing fine, probably more than fine. Jenny had her tongue halfway down Leo's throat, and he looked like he was enjoying every minute of it. A few barstools away from them was Wilder, chatting with a couple of blonde girls that had their breasts pushed up to their chins.

I sighed, turning back around. It seemed I wouldn't escape that mistake until I finished my research. Everett removed his hand from my thigh, and I immediately missed the warmth and touch of his fingers.

He noticed my gaze toward his packmate. "Wilder's always been like that. He's a flirt and immensely insecure. Don't feel bad that you fell for his charm. He's perfected his flirting game to make up for what he's lacking."

Everett opened his mouth, tapping on his large canine teeth. I gasped at the sight of the large white fangs. Last weekend I had seen Kleio's, but these were much larger. I didn't fear his teeth as much as I was curious about them. What would it be like to kiss him with those teeth? I could see him using them to nip at my lips and tongue. What would they feel like dragging across my body? A dull scratch against my skin followed by a warm tongue...

I shook my head to get those thoughts out of my brain. Where were they coming from? I needed to stop drinking. The one drink I'd had was already messing with my mind. I pushed my glass to the middle of the table.

"Wilder never got his fangs. It's rare, but it happens. I think he tries to make up for the lack of them in other ways," Everett said.

He looked over to the bar where Wilder had an arm around a girl's waist. I didn't feel jealous—everything Wilder had showed me after our night together solidified that he was nothing more than a one-night fling.

I found it interesting that Wilder had never gotten his fangs. Did it make him less appealing to other wolves, so he had to seek human companionship? Or maybe, like Everett had said, it was a major insecurity, causing Wilder to isolate himself from the rest of the pack. Either way, I wasn't interested in anything Wilder could offer, fangs or no fangs.

Everett and I joined back in on the conversation at the table. Jack was in the middle of animatedly telling the story of the last time Kostas had gotten drunk at this bar.

"He disappeared from the table. He was gone for five minutes. Longer than it takes a guy to piss," Jack said. His eyes were lit up. Kleio was smiling, her fangs on full display.

Something warm sank onto my bare thigh, slowly getting heavier by the second. I glanced beneath the table, seeing a tan hand on my leg. I followed the tattooed arm it was attached to to the man sitting next to me. Everett continued following the story, acting as if this was normal behavior. His hand was on my thigh. Again. I didn't move. A tingling sensation traveled down my leg—it seemed to come from his hand.

"I went to see what was going on, and I found him at the end of the hallway," Jack was saying. "He never made it into the bathroom."

My mouth fell open as I looked at Everett for any sign he knew where his hand was at this current moment, but he revealed nothing. If anything, maybe his lips upturned slightly. His thumb began making rubbing small circles along my inner thigh. Goose bumps peppered my skin, and he must've felt it. He increased the pressure of his thumb against my skin. His hand felt so warm against my skin that it was suddenly so cold. I shivered at his touch. My hearing went fuzzy for a moment. The only thing I could feel was Everett's hand against my thigh. Stroking my skin slowly, as if he was relaxed in this situation. Like this was a casual touch between two lovers.

His calloused thumb drug across my skin, the rough texture stimulating. My mind went places it shouldn't—his rough skin against my soft core... I was not relaxed. My muscles were tense and my core tightened. Everett was dangerously closed to *that* area. He could slip his hands beneath the shorts of the jumpsuit and... No one at the table would know.

Jack's voice came roaring back into my ears. At first quiet, then loud. "He was stuck at the mirror at the end of the hall-way, continually running into it and apologizing to his reflection."

Everyone at the table laughed. Everett's fingers squeezed my legs quickly before releasing my thigh and returning to the tabletop to grab his drink.

My reaction was delayed, as if my body couldn't send neurons fast enough to the part of my brain that controlled my reaction to stimulus. I looked around the table to see if anyone had seen what had just happened, but it seemed that no one had. Everyone continued laughing, unbothered. I laughed a little too loudly, trying to blend in, keeping my eyes trained on Everett. What had just happened? Last weekend I had been an unwanted guest at his shifter tournament, and now I was "beautiful" and worthy of a thigh squeeze?

I shivered, taking my eyes off him, trying to follow the conversation at the table. I had goose bumps again, this time because I had lost his touch.

"Hey, Elise. It's late. We should head back." Jenny inter-rupted the trance I was in. She stood behind my chair nervously, glancing at the shifters who sat around the table.

"Give me a minute—I'll meet you out there," I said. I didn't want to leave, but Leo and Jenny were my ride home. She nodded and turned around to leave.

When I shifted back to the table, Everett looked at me and cocked his head to the side.

"Do you always do what people tell you to do?" he asked.

"No...I don't," I answered. Jenny and Leo were my ride—I

wasn't about to let them leave without me for the second Thursday in a row. We all saw how that had turned out for me the first time.

"I think you get easily persuaded to do a lot of things."

My jaw dropped. Who did Everett think he was? We had barely had a full conversation. "I do not."

"Who picked that outfit for you? I know you didn't pick it for yourself. If you would have chosen an outfit, it would be some of those tight leggings and a baggy T-shirt."

I frowned, but he wasn't wrong.

"Who left you to hook up with Wilder last weekend? I'm gonna bet that it wasn't entirely your idea."

Everett had some nerve. I had said less than twenty words to him the entire time I'd known him, and he now was stepping over the line. His touch might've been confusing to me, but this entire conversation was getting too personal. What did he know about my decision-making? Why did he even care?

I glared at him, and he gave me a confident smirk.

"Kleio." I said her name louder than I intended. She imme-diately turned to look at me. I stood up, pushing my chair out from behind me with the back of my knees. "I've got to go."

"Oh, okay," Kleio said. She looked between Everett and me, somehow sensing the tension. She gave me a quick hug. "It was so nice to see you, Elise. I'll see you soon."

I didn't think that would happen, but I nodded. "I'll see you all...later," I said to the table, avoiding eye contact with Everett. If he was going to comment on my decision making, I could easily show him I could decide not to acknowledge him.

I left the table and made my way to the door. Not once looking behind me, I walked through the exit and took a moment to calm my racing heart. Everett. Something about him just pushed my buttons.

"*I think you get easily persuaded...*" I mimicked his dumb

deep voice as I searched through my purse to make sure I had all my things. "Who does that guy think he is?"

Scanning the parking lot, I saw the bed of Leo's truck sticking out from behind the side of the building, and I turned to walk that way.

As my body turned, I ran into what felt like a brick wall. A brick wall that was all muscle. I backed up a step and felt large hands grab the sides of my upper arms. That warm, tingly sensation shot through my arms and out of my fingertips. There was only one person I had met who could elicit such a feeling.

I let out a small yelp as Everett pushed me back against the building with his body. My nose was stuck between his pectoral muscles as we both breathed heavily against one another. He smelled like outside. Not the dirty, sweaty outside smell, but the smell of fresh air after it had rained. Like a spring day after all the snow had melted and warmer days were on the horizon.

His inhales expanded his body, pushing his chest into me, pushing my back harder into the wall behind me. My hands at my sides felt the rough texture of the brick. I couldn't move my arms with Everett pinned on top of me. He moved his upper body away from my head and grabbed my chin with his thumb and first finger.

Tilting my head to his, I looked into his golden eyes that I always seemed to get lost in. Right now, they looked desperate. They scanned my face frantically, attempting to read my feelings. His index finger hooked under my chin as his thumb grazed my bottom lip, slowly rubbing along its edges.

I hadn't come here for another hookup, but at that moment, I wanted Everett to kiss me. Between my rapid breathing, being pinned to the wall, and the prickling feeling I was getting between my legs, I craved it. He might have just been an asshole to me, but since when did I do what my mind wanted?

I closed my top lip over Everett's thumb, and a feral look flashed through his eyes. He took my permission and ran with it, slamming his lips into mine.

The kiss wasn't gentle. It was hungry and searching. The shock of him coming at me with such force opened my mouth, and he took full advantage, running his tongue along my own. He tasted like a mixture of whiskey and mint, a strange combination that made me weak in the knees. His hand found the back of my head and his fingers weaved through my hair, protecting the back of my head from the wall behind me. I broke my hands free from the pressure of his hips and pulled them up to his chest.

Grabbing onto his shirt, I pulled his body closer to me, needing to feel more of his frame on mine. A growl from deep in his chest vibrated my hands. It made me even more frantic, and I tilted my head to the side to give him more access. I could feel the pulse between my legs spread up into the bottom of my stomach. I needed more pressure, more friction, more anything with Everett.

My lips felt naked as he pulled away abruptly. I let out a small whine of discomfort. Everett tucked his head into the space between my neck and shoulder. His body still pressed me against the wall as I clung to his shirt. I could feel his short, rapid breaths against my neck as he tried to catch his breath. He seemed just as needy and desperate as I felt.

He opened his mouth against my neck. Instead of the soft lips I was expecting, I felt the prick of his fangs touching the tender skin of my shoulder. The sensation was wildly carnal and made me gasp. My eyes flew open, and my breathing became even more rapid. He closed his mouth and nuzzled the side of my neck. I felt his large hands grab hold of my wrists, which had been trapped between our bodies. The grip was firm but not uncomfortable.

Everett's low voice vibrated through my hands that were against his chest. "I knew it," he growled.

He pushed off me and stalked away from where I was standing. I was suddenly cold without his body heat. Trying to catch my breath, my mind reeled from what had just happened. I leaned back to steady myself.

What had he known? Had he kissed me as some sort of test? Was this a joke that one of his buddies had put him up to? There was no way he hadn't felt what I had. That hadn't been an ordinary drunken kiss from a cute guy at the bar. That had been...animalistic. Like we'd both craved each other's touch and needed it to survive. The fangs that had once scared me were now intriguing. I felt my body pulse as I remembered the sensation of his teeth dragging along my neck. It had felt better than I'd imagined.

My fingers gently rubbed along the side of my neck where his fangs had touched. I wondered if there would be a mark there tomorrow. I made my way from my neck to touch my lips. They were puffy from the rough kiss. Looking around, I was thankful that I was alone and there was no one around to watch me recover from that.

Eventually I pulled myself together, getting into Leo's truck and sliding next to Jenny on the bench seat. Luckily they seemed too occupied with each other to notice how flustered I was. We made it back to the cabin, and I said good night to them before I brushed my teeth and got into my pajamas. My head hit the pillow; I was glad I had made it to my own bed this Thursday.

CHAPTER FOURTEEN

A RUSTLING NOISE outside my window woke me up from the deep sleep I was in. I glanced at the clock next to my bed. It was three in the morning. What could have made that sound? There weren't any trees close enough to the cabin to be rubbing against the outdoor walls of my room.

I pulled the covers up to my chin, curling myself into a ball. The sound met my ears again. This time it was closer. Listening carefully, I tried to hear over the loud heartbeats coming from my chest. It sounded almost like an animal sniffing around, foraging for something. The sniffs were loud enough that the animal was probably bigger than a possum. Maybe it was an overgrown raccoon looking for garbage. I would have to make sure our garbage containers had the strap adhered in the morning.

Rolling over, I tried to ignore the animal noises outside my window. A low growl met my ears and made my whole body stiffen up. After a couple minutes my heart rate lowered, as I hadn't heard any more strange noises. The animal must have moved on.

I closed my eyes, trying to get myself back to sleep. The single drink I'd had tonight was no longer in my system, and it had left my mind racing about the kiss. It had been a good kiss. Better than good. It was probably the best kiss I'd had in my entire life. The memory of his overwhelming frame pushing against me and the light scratch of his fangs sent tingles from my stomach to between my legs.

I crossed my legs under the covers, trying to contain the feeling. He was an alpha. A leader in the pack and one of the strongest Lycans. The boldness he'd had to take what he'd wanted really outshined any of the physical aspects of the kiss. There was a part of me that enjoyed being the one he'd wanted, and being submissive to his wants was something that felt refreshing to me. Having to take care of myself and my parents for the last several years, it felt good to let go.

Rolling over in bed, I squeezed my legs together even tighter. Maybe I had been letting other people decide for me lately. I just hadn't had the mental capacity to decide for myself after the last whirlwind of a month. Helping my parents, graduating college, and moving to a new part of the country had taken a lot out of me. Everett's power was intriguing.

I rolled over again, changing positions once more. The cool pillow beneath my head changed my perspective like the flip of a coin. This was another mistake that could derail the plans I had for myself. Everett wasn't just a cute guy from the bar—he was a Lycan. A mythical creature. The second shifter I had hooked up with in the last week.

Ugh, this was not what I had planned. Not only was Everett distracting me mentally, he was also distracting me physically as I lay in bed with so much pent-up sexual tension. I needed to get some rest before this weekend. My research was behind from having spent the last weekend at Camp. I would need to work through the weekend to catch up.

Whisper-listing all the plants I had cataloged in my note-book, I tried to distract myself from the hormones running through my body. I made it about halfway through before my eyes got heavy and I fell into a restless sleep.

———

Later that morning, I woke up determined to get some research done. It was Friday, and that meant it was the second weekend of the tournament. The wards would be going up around noon. If I kept close to the cabin, within a couple miles, I could avoid them. I hoped.

The clock next to my bed said ten o'clock. Shit. I never slept in that late. This was Everett's fault—if I hadn't been up late trying to calm myself down from the kiss, I'd already be out in the forest. The last thing I wanted was to be trapped inside them again. This weekend I needed to get work done.

After packing my backpack with more collection containers and an extra stick of deodorant—just in case—I ran through the cabin and found Jenny typing on the couch.

"Why did you let me sleep so late?" I asked.

"Who wakes up early after drinking?"

There was no time for a big breakfast, although my stomach growled. I grabbed an apple off the basket on the counter.

Jenny closed the screen of her laptop and tilted her head to the side. "Sorry. I should have knocked on your door earlier."

I filled up my water bottle at the sink. It was probably already hot outside. "It's fine. I just wanted to get an earlier start."

"I'm just glad you made it back from the bar this week!" she teased. "If I don't see you the rest of the weekend, I'll just assume you're crashing with one of the many attractive guys you keep running into."

"Ha ha. Very funny, Jenny. I'm about to head out and explore one of the trails on Robinson's map," I said.

"Let me know if you see any big wolf tracks. I keep finding wolf footprints, and I follow them, only for them to suddenly disappear. It's the weirdest thing," Jenny said. "I started wearing my necklace again." Jenny pulled a small silver whistle out of her shirt. It hung around her neck from a dainty silver chain. "The sound is high pitched enough that it stuns them, giving you enough time to get a head start."

If only I could tell Jenny why they were vanishing. Or should I say shifting.

Not wanting her to see how conflicted I surely looked, I headed out the front door before she could say more.

"Oh! Elise! The new satellite phone got dropped off this morning. I'll install it so we can make our calls this afternoon." I gave her a thumbs-up on the way out.

After finding the head of the new trail I planned to explore on the map, I let myself become lost to the serenity of the woods around me and the sound of my footsteps crunching the gravel.

The sun was high in the sky when I finally stopped for a water break. Glancing around, I saw more of the brown patches about ten yards off the trail. Putting my water bottle away, I stepped carefully until I was next to the brown, withered foliage. It looked like the plants I had seen before, but this was a new area. I took out my clean containers and gloves and started gathering the plant material. A buzzing sound entered my ears, then disappeared. I absently waved my hand around my head in case anything was flying past me.

Quickly, I finished gathering the specimens and zipped everything in my backpack. Time to go back.

Back on the trail, I started heading back the way I'd come. It was around lunchtime, and my stomach was rumbling.

I made it ten steps before something zapped me. Static electricity in the woods? Had I gotten stung by something? Odd. I turned slightly and took a few more steps. Zapped again. I held out my hand cautiously, reaching in front of me. My hand shook. There it was again, the zap. I pulled my arm back against my body. *No.*

I bent my knees and launched myself forward, shoulder first. My body bounced off an invisible wall, and I stumbled, trying to catch myself before I fell. The wards weren't that strong, were they? Maybe I could power through it. I went slowly this time walking forward, driving my feet into the soil as leverage. I braced myself and pushed my shoulder against it. My muscles strained as I pushed. I vibrated with the electrical current of the wall flowing through my body.

It wasn't budging. The invisible wall pushed me back for a second time. I tripped over my feet before righting myself. The ward was stronger than I'd thought. I reached out with my hand, my fingertips searching for the barricade. I found the invisible wall, and tiny electrical shocks danced along my fingertips. It felt eerily like the last weekend when I had been knocked unconscious.

Maybe I was on the outside of the wards. It was a giant invisible wall, right? I was probably on the outside, I tried to convince myself. I hadn't traveled too far from the cabin. My fingers grazed the ward as I walked quickly along the wall. I continued feeling small zaps skipping along my fingers as I traced it. At some point, if I was on the outside of the wall, I would stop feeling the buzz and know I'd made it past the ward. The ward had to end. I wasn't trapped inside. I was on the outside. I had to be.

My fingers continued to feel the zaps as I walked along the invisible partition. Drips of perspiration fell down my back, tracing my spine. I couldn't be... This wasn't happening. I wasn't trapped inside, was I? For the second weekend? I shouldn't have slept in. Should've paid more attention to my surroundings. The wards wouldn't open again until Sunday night. I couldn't be stuck in the forest all weekend. I didn't have any food or supplies with me.

A stick snapped behind me, and I turned to find nothing. I continued along until I heard another snap, this one closer to me. Twisting around, I came face to face with a brown wolf with his lips curled, showing his sharp white teeth. Instinctually backing up, I hit the ward with the side of my body and lost my balance. I fell onto my side, halfway on top of my backpack. Swiftly, I got up onto my hands and knees looking up at the wolf, who was in the middle of shifting.

He slowly morphed into a towering man with sandy-brown hair. The process of shifting still wasn't pleasant to watch. All the stretching, bone elongating, and nakedness both shocked and disgusted me after he'd finished. The shifters seem to have no qualms about nudity.

"Hey, Kip! Get over here. I got a live one." The man paraded over to me unclothed, his appendage swinging back and forth. My brain tried to focus on what was happening around me as my eyes took in what was in front of me. Where had I heard the name Kip before?

Another man made his way out of the woods, equally tall and equally naked. "Good find, Elijah. Not a rogue, but a plaything. She'll make the weekend much more enjoyable."

Kip and Elijah. Kip and Elijah...

My brain flew through the names and faces I'd seen at last weekend's opening ceremony, and suddenly I recalled where I knew these two men from. They were the hunters from the Juniper Pack that Kleio had told me about. She had said nothing good about them.

Still crouched down, I scanned my surroundings for a stick

or something I could use in defense. I saw a decent-sized stick a few feet away, and I scurried over to grab it. Standing up in a defensive position with my new weapon in front of me, I stood ready to protect myself from these assholes.

"Stay away from me!" I yelled. They didn't even flinch.

"Look at the human with a stick. She's a feisty one," Elijah said. "We like a little fight in our girls, don't we?"

They stalked around me.

"That we do," Kip said. "I'll let you have the first go with her since you got the last rogue. Don't tire her out too much, though. I want some of that fight left in her."

With the ward to my back, I had nowhere to go. I swung my stick at them like an amateur fencer, trying to get them to back off. My actions seemed to only excite them. They laughed at me as if this was a fun game. Their naked bodies were showing how excited they were as they got closer and closer to me, licking their lips hungrily.

"Get back!" I yelled again as loud as I could.

I lunged forward, trying to jab my stick into Kips torso, but he was too quick. He yanked it out of my hands with little effort. Taking the stick with both hands, he snapped it over his knee like a twig. Throwing the broken pieces behind him, he nodded to Elijah.

I turned my head just in time to see him charge at me, grabbing my right forearm. He swung my body around, holding my back to his chest. Grabbing my other wrist, he pinned my arms behind me, holding both wrists with one of his massive hands. I could feel the dull zaps and pulses of the ward as he held my body against it. The front of my body was being repelled off the ward, pushing me into Elijah's back. My backpack kept my back from contacting his chest, but I could still feel the hard bulge of his erection against my backside. I gagged as he bent over and started trailing his tongue along my ear. I tried to squirm away, but any movement either zapped the front of my body or pushed me against Elijah's naked body.

"You taste sweet. Kip, come have a taste."

My eyes squeezed shut as I felt Kip approaching. I waited for his tongue to run over my skin, but it never happened. A loud growl vibrated my body, and my eyes shot open in surprise. A huge black wolf leaped toward us, landing on the ground with four giant paws. The ground trembled with the impact.

No sooner had the wolf landed than Kip's leg was in its jaws. A loud crunch of cracking bones made me grimace. He cried out in agony as the wolf kept his broken leg in his mouth and began shaking him violently back and forth. In his human form, Kip was no match for this massive wolf.

"Oh, shit," I heard Elijah say under his breath as he continued to hold me against him.

As Kip's cries became louder, Elijah began looking around for an escape route. He backed away from the ward, still holding me against him. I wanted nothing to do with this crazed wolf man and his intentions for me. As he continued to retreat, I took a risk and slammed my foot down on top of his bare one. He yelped in surprise, loosening his hold on my wrists.

Spinning my body around, I broke his hold and quickly lifted my right leg to meet his naked cock. I easily made contact with my shin, and he doubled over in pain. Rolling to the ground, he cursed me out as I backed away slowly. Looking behind me, I saw the giant black wolf in a wrestling match with a smaller red wolf, which had a broken leg hanging from its torso.

The red wolf, Kip, seemed to be growing tired, probably from the blood loss and injury to his leg. He snapped at the black wolf a couple more times before he backed away and retreated into the woods, dragging his leg.

Behind me, bones were cracking, and I turned to watch Elijah transition to a silver wolf. He snarled at the black wolf, who was pacing behind me. I turned slowly to face the black wolf, whose white teeth were still showing as he snarled.

I backed away, raising my arms in surrender. This wolf might have saved me from Kip and Elijah, but I didn't know what its intentions were for me now.

Then a gray wolf leaped from behind me, placing himself between us. My hands stayed up as the gray wolf quickly shifted back into his human form. With elongating of bones and retracting claws, I watched the gray wolf turn into Wilder. Or at least a scruffy, bearded version of him.

"They're gone, man. She's fine," Wilder said. He approached the black wolf, who was still pacing near me. He fell down to his knees and tilted his head to the side, exposing his neck.

Before I could question what Wilder was doing, I spotted a large cut along one of the wolf's front legs that oozed blood.

"You gotta shift, man. You're hurt," Wilder tried to reason.

The wolf's gold eyes stared me down, and I all but fell into the swirls of gold. Everett.

"Tell him you're fine. He needs to hear it from you." Wilder's voice was growing more frantic as he looked at me and backed up, trying to stay between me and the black wolf. I didn't know who this Wilder was, so concerned about not only Everett but apparently me as well.

"I'm fine," I said. I lowered my hands as I walked closer.

Everett tried to lie down on the ground slowly but collapsed as he got close to the dirt. A small whimper left his mouth as he shifted. Claws and paws retracted as his spine lengthened. His snout sunk into his skull as his face took shape. He had a brown, scruffy beard covering his face, and his brown hair stood disheveled on his head.

I ran to his side as he lay on his back with his eyes closed. Wilder was there, leaning over Everett, trying to take stock of his injuries. I knelt on the other side and took his arm into my lap. It was a deep enough cut that I could see white bone underneath all the blood. Blood soon soaked my leggings as it poured out of his arm.

"What do we do?" Wilder asked, looking up at me. "This is deep. I don't have any first aid supplies with me."

I searched around the forest, taking stock of what was around, and grabbed some large-leaved aster from the plants growing low on the ground. They were a plentiful forest "carpet" this time of year, and I layered them over the wound.

"Hold them tight against his arm," I said. I moved my hands as Wilder took their place, putting pressure on the gash. "Let me go see what else I can find."

My eyes to the ground, I walked several yards away in search of yarrow. The forest around here seemed to have plenty, and it had done wonders healing my head wound last weekend. The white flowers of the yarrow caught my eye, and I rushed over and began gathering the leaves.

I brought the plant over to where Wilder was kneeling next to Everett, keeping pressure on his arm. I found two medium-sized stones and put the leaves on one stone. Using the bottle from my backpack, I poured some water over the leaves and got to work grinding it into a paste. My arm was sore, and my palm had a fresh blister on it when I finished, but the paste was decent. I scooped the medicine into a fresh green leaf and carried it over to where Everett was lying.

Wilder looked at me with distrust. "Are you sure that's going to work?"

"I don't think you can carry him yourself, can you?" I asked. "I know I won't be of any help." Everett was huge. It would probably take a couple of men to lift him if he was dead weight.

"What is that, even? How do you know it isn't poisonous?" Wilder asked.

"I've made this for myself many times. It's safe. This is our best chance to stop the bleeding before he loses too much blood," I said.

Wilder tried to argue again, but Everett's deep voice cut him off. "Let her use it."

Sighing, Wilder followed his alpha's commands and moved out of my way. Standing above me, he looked down while I lifted the bloodied leaves and began packing the yarrow paste into the wound. It was deep. If I had a needle and thread, I would have sewn it shut, but that wasn't an option out here.

Everett grunted and grimaced as I applied the paste. The bleeding slowed and eventually stopped by the time I had finished. Finding some more large-leaved aster by me, I placed them over the cut. A couple feet away, I found some long grass to use as string. I tied the leaves to his arm, taking care to not wrap the grass too tightly.

When I was done, I looked to see Everett's eyes on my face. "How does it feel?" I asked.

"Much better." Some color had returned to his skin.

I found my water bottle next to the rocks I'd used to grind the leaves and held it to his lips as he took several sips.

"We need to get out of here. If any of the others know you're down, we'll become a target," Wilder said. He was standing and looking around, scanning the woods.

Everett used his good arm to push himself into a seated position. Despite his ragged breathing, he managed to start moving again.

I picked up my things and brushed my hands against my thighs, hesitating. I knew there was no getting past the wards, but I wasn't sure I wanted to go with them either.

Everett looked at me with resolve. "You're coming with me," he said.

Wilder groaned and argued. "We can't bring a human back with us again. She's too much of a liability."

"You don't get to make the decisions, Wilder, I do," Everett said with a labored voice. "She's coming back with us. She's touched the ward too many times. They already know she's here."

I opened my mouth to argue. "I can't spend another weekend at Camp! I have a life to get back to. I have work to do!"

Everett cocked his head at me, staring with an intensity that made my body stiffen. "I would apologize to you for this inconvenience, but I will never apologize for keeping you safe."

His words sent shivers down my spine. What did he care if I was safe? Maybe he felt he owed me something since I had taken care of his arm. Everett was sending so many mixed signals I didn't know which way was up. He flirted with me, provoked me, kissed me, and then walked away. Now he demanded that I follow him back to Camp. What was with this guy?

Howling filled the surrounding air. I had no choice but to look toward Wilder and Everett for guidance. The wards had apparently alerted everyone that I was here, and with Everett injured, I doubted he could fight at full strength. Standing slowly, he lifted himself one vertebra at a time. I'd forgotten how tall he was when he'd been lying down. I couldn't help looking past his stomach at his incredibly large...

"Like what you see?" Everett asked. He had his trademark smirk plastered on his face. I knew he was part animal, but jeez—the size took me by surprise.

I quickly looked away, feeling my face turn red.

"You can't be bashful around me, Elise," he said. "I'm sure it's nothing you haven't seen before."

I looked back at him with an angry look in my eye. How many times did he think I'd looked at a naked male body?

"Or maybe it's nothing like you've ever seen before?"

Was he flirting with me again? Two could play at that game.

"Oh, it's something I have seen before," I snapped. "Seems like something average. Nothing special. Don't worry—it'll soon get lost in the slideshow of male dicks in my head."

Everett raised his eyebrows at me. I didn't think he'd been expecting a rebuttal like that. It felt good to have the upper hand. "So, she has her own thoughts. I was wondering when you would start to speaking up for yourself. You are a lively little one, aren't you, Lyka."

Wilder interrupted our banter. "This is all so cute, but you're barely standing up straight, Everett. We need to get out of here."

Everett let out a wheeze as he pulled his eyes away from mine. Losing his gaze made it feel like the tight thread between us had snapped, leaving me with the ricochet.

Another howl, this time closer, met my ears, and I was ready to follow Wilder and Everett to safety. Wilder led the way, and Everett motioned me to follow before he took up the back of our line. Sandwiched between the two shifters, we traveled along as fast as we could without losing Everett. I could hear his ragged breaths behind me as we stumbled along.

CHAPTER FIFTEEN

THE FOREST soon cleared away and opened to the field where I had watched the two wolves play last weekend. A familiar city of tents loomed ahead of us, small orange campfires sprinkled throughout. Wilder and I turned around when we heard a loud thump behind us.

"Oh, shit," Wilder said.

Everett's body was collapsed on the ground, and he was unconscious again, having used all his strength to make it through the forest.

Wilder muscled Everett over onto his back. "You grab Kostas and Gavrill. We're gonna have to carry him the rest of the way."

I took off, trying to remember which tent was Cedar Moon Pack's. As I got closer, I spied Kleio absently poking the fire with a stick, looking bored. She glanced up as she heard footsteps approaching, and a surprised look crossed her face. "Elise? How did you get here? Why are you here?"

Between breaths, I told her to grab the guys because Everett was hurt. I stayed by the fire as she ran into the tent and was quickly followed back out by the hulking frames of Kostas and Gavrill. Following my pointing finger, they ran out to the field to gather up their alpha.

I'd been right—it took three men to carry Everett's dead weight back to the tent. Gavrill and Kostas each took a shoulder, and Wilder carried his legs. I followed them into the tent and watched as they laid him down on the couch, setting my backpack off to the side.

Kleio entered the tent, pulling Jack behind her. He carried a canvas bag that he set down on the floor next to Everett. Everyone got out of his way as he began his assessment.

"Who did this?" Jack looked at Wilder and me, pointing to the leaf-and-grass bandage I had concocted in the woods.

"Me." I barely squeaked out the words. I couldn't tell if Jack was pleased or appalled by my fieldwork.

"Genius." I breathed a sigh of relief. "Yarrow, right?" I nodded. "Probably saved his life."

Everyone looked at me while I pretended to be interested in my shoes. Jack took out supplies from his bag and cleaned up the skin around the gash. He replaced my leaf bandages with real ones and set to work cleaning the other minor cuts that littered Everett's skin.

Noticing my interest, he turned around to look at me. "They don't just keep me around because I'm pretty." His eyes crinkled as he smiled at me. "He'll be fine. He lost a lot of blood and needs some rest."

After he finished, Jack stood up and linked his arm around Kleio's shoulders. Gavrill walked over and handed me a quilt, motioning for me to cover Everett with it. I almost laughed out loud because I had forgotten that he was still naked. The quilt was probably for my benefit.

I unfolded the quilt and draped it over Everett's body, careful not to take another peek below his waist. As I tucked it under his shoulders, a warm hand grabbed my forearm and pulled. I ended up face-to-face with Everett.

"Thank you, Elise." His murmured words were soft and kind. They seemed genuine.

I could feel warmth spread from my forearm to my chest, where my heart was pumping rapidly. His eyes met mine, and the thread pulling us together was once again taut. I had never met someone who'd had such a hold on me. I was both annoyed and attracted to him at the same time.

His hand encapsulated my arm. I had thought Thursday night at the bar had just been a fluke, but I felt the same electricity pulsing through me. Tingling pinpricks made their way across my chest and into the bottom of my stomach. Everett's nostrils expanded as if he could smell my feelings.

I broke the thread of connection this time, looking at the audience that surrounded us. Everyone was suddenly busy doing nothing. I felt my face heat, knowing that everyone had just witnessed that moment between us.

Kleio broke the tension. "Elise, help me set the table?" I was all too eager to escape the situation, and I pushed away from Everett to help her. Glancing back, I saw his eyes closing, giving in to the rest his body needed.

Kleio was easy to talk to, and we fell easily into conversation. I could smell Gavrill's cooking waft through the tent, and I realized I hadn't eaten since the apple I'd had for breakfast. I snuck glances at Everett and felt comforted by the fact he was sleeping peacefully on the couch. He needed to rest since he still had two days of hunting ahead of him.

Dinner was pleasant, and once again I enjoyed everyone's company. I reached for seconds of the grilled chicken and almost moaned out loud at how delicious it was. Gavrill knew his way around the grill.

"You act like you won't get another meal for days!" Jack teased as he pulled Kleio in for a kiss on the cheek.

"I haven't eaten since breakfast. This chicken is delicious," I said, my mouth full of food.

Jack laughed. "Well, slow down. You're stuck with us for the weekend for a second time. You know you won't go hungry."

He was right. Since I had arrived at the cabin, the wolves had frequently been the only ones to feed me actual meals. As we ate our dinner, I settled into my seat to listen to Gavrill and Kostas debate with one another. It was comical to see the two hard-headed men get so worked up over trivial things.

Kleio and I were laughing and enjoying the show, and I realized I was comfortable here. Everyone was so inclusive and inviting. There weren't any expectations of me here. I could just be...me. Not someone who needed to complete her thesis with efficiency or take all the responsibility of caring for her parents or accommodate to everyone around her. I could slow down and remove myself from real life while I was at Camp. I'd come to the woods to escape and found a different freedom I'd never expected.

The tent flaps whipped open, and a huge male entered the tent. I immediately recognized him from last weekend as the True Alpha. Time seemed to stop, only beginning again when Kleio dropped her fork. The clanging of the metal hitting the porcelain dish shook everyone out of their stupor. Slowly, everyone stood from their chairs and bent down on one knee in submission. They all tilted their heads, showing the sides of their necks as Wilder had done to Everett earlier in the woods. I wasn't sure what to do, so I just followed what everyone else was doing and got down on one knee myself.

Gavrill was the first to speak. He walked over to the entrance of the tent where the True Alpha was standing. "To what do we owe the pleasure of your company?" Gavrill spoke so formally, it made me even more uneasy.

"I received news that my son was injured. I came to see about his condition." The True Alpha's words vibrated down my spine. *Son?* Everett was the True Alpha's son? "But now I see there are more pressing matters in the Cedar Moon tent."

His eyes shifted to me, where I was still kneeling. "Stand, human."

I stood up slowly as the True Alpha walked over to me. He leaned his head close to my chest and took a long inhale through his nose, smelling me. I tried my best to stand my ground, but I was trembling.

The True Alpha straightened. "Interesting."

Everyone in the tent, still kneeling, seemed to exhale as he turned away from me and went to inspect his son. Everett was still sleeping peacefully on the couch, unaware of his father's presence. Gavrill followed him over to Everett's body and explained what had happened in the woods.

The True Alpha seemed satisfied with Everett's care and pulled Gavrill toward the entrance of the tent, speaking in harsh whispers that I couldn't hear. They both looked at me before the True Alpha ducked under the tent flaps and disappeared into the night.

Everyone else slowly got up from their knees, groaning, and returned to their chairs, dinner forgotten. Gavrill sat down as well, looking pensive.

"What did he say over there?" Kleio asked anxiously.

"He wants a meeting with Elise," Gavrill said. My heart skipped a beat in my chest.

"Everett is gonna be pissed. There's no way we can let the True Alpha speak alone with Elise. He's so unpredictable," Kleio said. She took my hand in hers and squeezed it reassuringly.

Jack tried to ease my anxiety. "Everett won't let that happen. I'm sure the True Alpha is just curious why his son's pack has a human."

I gave him a thankful look. The pack had enough going on at the tournament without me attracting the True Alpha's attention. It wasn't like I wanted to be here, but nevertheless, it seemed I was becoming a dangerous distraction.

"I wonder what he smelled on her. Have you gotten anything interesting, Gavrill?" Kostas asked. He walked over to the back of my chair and motioned, asking me if he could take a whiff.

I obliged. "Go right ahead. I'm full of dirt, sweat, and blood. I'm sure I smell wonderful."

Kostas took a deep smell, careful not to get too close to me. "I smell human, earth, and Everett's blood." He looked satisfied with my smell, but I wasn't sure if that was a good thing.

Gavrill took a turn and nodded. "Same here. I don't catch anything out of the ordinary."

I felt like a scented candle, and not a good one.

Jack came forward to take a whiff. "But remember, the True Alpha is a tracker. He probably smells something we can't."

I backed away. "Okay, enough smelling me. Why didn't anyone tell me that Everett is the True Alpha's son?" I would've thought that at least Kleio would've told me. Maybe we weren't as close as I'd thought we were. I glanced between the three shifters, willing someone to tell me what was going on. "Is it some kind of secret?"

"I think you should go to your tent for the rest of the night." Kleio rubbed my arm, guiding me ever so slightly to the back flaps of the tent and picking up my backpack along the way.

Now they were putting me to bed like a child? I deserved some information. The True Alpha had noticed me, had smelled me. Maybe they couldn't tell me everything, but I needed to know what any of it had to do with me.

"Tell me what is going on, Kleio," I pleaded, feeling desperate.

"Let us handle it. You have nothing to worry about," she said. "Everett won't let anything happen to you."

I turned to look at him, still unconscious on the couch. What did he have to do with any of this? What were they hiding?

Kleio didn't let me say anything else before she pushed me out into the dark night, walking me back to my tent, which I was surprised to see was still set up. Campfires glowed orange, lighting our way. The air was brisk, having lost the warmth of the sun.

Frustrated, I dumped my backpack and paced inside my tent. Lack of information always made me uneasy. As a researcher, missing just one piece of data could change the entire result of your research.

With my mind made up, I slipped outside and snuck back to the main tent, careful that they wouldn't hear my footsteps approaching. Next to the back flaps, I crouched down, trying to look casual to those around their campfires enjoying the evening. Muffled voices from the tent became clearer as I focused.

"Everett won't be happy when he wakes up." It was a low male voice, probably Gavrill or Kostas.

"Was it too much that I sent her to her tent for the night?" Kleio's voice was easier to detect.

"No, Elise doesn't need to know about Everett's relationship with his father." That was Gavrill or Kostas. I couldn't tell the difference.

"What relationship, Kostas? We left his father's pack when

we were eighteen. He only sees his father every ten years at the Deca Tournament." That was Gavrill.

"But now that the True Alpha has taken an interest in Elise, we're going to have to deal with him. Everett won't want her anywhere near his father, and his father won't forget requesting the meeting with her," Kostas said.

"It was odd that he came to check on Everett. He never does that," Kleio said. I could tell they were walking around the tent as they talked.

"Everett is his only heir," Gavrill said. "Of course he came to check on him. His pack depends on Everett's leadership should he die."

"He'll never die." Kleio sighed, abruptly cutting off her breath as she sat down. "He's one of those Lycans that live forever, tormenting everyone because he's bored from living so long."

"Let's wait until Everett wakes up to see how he wants to deal with his father," Kostas said.

Mumbles of agreement filled the tent. I heard footsteps come dangerously close to where I was crouched down by the tent. I stood, rushing back to my tent, hoping no one noticed I had been listening.

Ducking under the flaps of my tent, I let out a breath. It was just how I left it last weekend, and I was grateful for the bed. Moving my backpack to the end of the bed, I climbed onto the mattress and under the sheets. I couldn't imagine what the True Alpha wanted with me. I was just some human stuck in his tournament wards. But from what I had heard, it seemed like there was a lot of bad blood between Everett and his father. Being stuck between two alpha Lycans was not where I wanted to be.

CHAPTER SIXTEEN

Camp was already chattering when I woke. I could hear people up and moving around. Rubbing the sleep from my eyes, I stood up and stretched my body. My wrists were a little sore from where Elijah had held them, but other than that, I felt good and rested. I dug through my backpack, thankful for the deodorant I had put in there "just in case."

Stepping outside, I made my way to the main tent, hoping Kostas was cooking something for breakfast. My stomach ached when I walked in and found muffins and eggs on the table. Beyond the table, the couch Everett had slept on was empty.

"It's a miracle," Jack said, seeming to have noticed where I was looking. "His arm looks way better than I thought it would. He woke up early this morning and was ready to hunt. You must really know your stuff."

I sat down and dished up my plate with food. I'd expected that Everett's arm would be better than last night, but I hadn't thought it would have healed enough for him to hunt today. Maybe Lycans healed faster than humans.

I relayed my thoughts to Jack.

"We do," he said, "but not to the capacity that Everett healed. I thought he would be out of the hunt for the weekend." Jack patted my back in appreciation as he dished up his own plate.

That was surprising to me. Yarrow had healing properties, but it wasn't anything magical.

After breakfast, Kleio approached me giddily, bouncing up and down. "We have most of the day to ourselves. Let's go on a scavenger hunt again—this time without the babysitter." Her eyes were alight with anticipation.

I nodded, ready to be back in the woods. Maybe we would get lucky again like last weekend.

We stopped at my tent to grab my backpack, my supplies ready to go from when I'd packed them on Friday. I slung my pack over my shoulder and followed Kleio across the field.

Snarls and growls broke up the quiet as we neared the edge of the forest. The cages holding the rogues were more crowded than last weekend. I could tell the difference between the rogues that had been in the cage since last weekend and the ones that had been freshly caught. The ones who'd been here longer were thinner and more aggressive. They looked dirtier and more ragged.

Looking up to the banners above the cages, I smiled, seeing that the Cedar Moon Pack was in the lead with fifteen rogues. The rest of the cages had fewer captives, although Kip and Elijah's cage with the Juniper Pack banner above it had about ten rogues. It was surprising they could continue to hunt after Everett had injured Kip so badly.

Quickly, the smile left my face as I felt overcome with bittersweet feelings. Yes, the Cedar Moon Pack was winning, but what were they winning at? Catching the obviously sick rogue wolves? It didn't seem fair that they should have to be locked up for a month in misery. And while my situation was certainly different than theirs, I knew a thing or two about being trapped here. Was there something that could be done to help the rogues who had been captured?

Before I could think more on it, Kleio pulled me past the cages and into the forest, the cool air from the shade of the trees blowing over us. I was coming to enjoy the quiet moments with Kleio. She was always insightful and willing to answer my questions. The yarrow was plentiful out here, and occasionally I would lean over and pick some, placing it gently in my pocket. Never knew when you'd need some around these shifters. The path in the woods widened, allowing Kleio and me to walk side by side.

"So, I saw you and Everett on the couch last night." She wiggled her eyebrows at me suggestively.

Not her too, I thought. At least she wasn't as overbearing as Jenny. She seemed to be genuinely interested in whatever was going on between Everett and me and not about to tell me how to navigate the situation.

A tree to my left caught my eye. It was growing almost sideways, parallel to the ground. I rubbed a leaf between my fingers. Nothing rare, just an oak tree growing oddly.

"I don't know what it is." I decided to be honest. "One minute he's all authoritative and bossy, and the next minute he's being sweet."

We continued walking on the trail. I scanned the forest in a back and forth motion, not willing to miss anything of interest.

"Male Lycans are known for being dominant and protective," Kleio said. "Jack used to drive me crazy with his domineering attitude. I put him in check real quick. It has gotten better, but you need to understand that they can't fight their instincts."

"Instincts to do what?"

"Protect, silly."

"If it's every Lycan's instinct to protect, then Kip and Elijah never would have attacked me," I said.

"Well, it's not about protecting everyone. It's their instinct to protect those who are...important to them." Kleio said, looking at me like I should know what she was talking about.

"How am I important to Everett? He's hardly talked to me, kissed me once, and spent the rest of the time ignoring me."

Kleio's eyes grew wide. "He kissed you?" I nodded, and she started smiling. "How was it? I mean, what did it feel like?"

I looked down, trying to put into words what the kiss had felt like. "It was a good kiss? I don't know what you want me to tell you, Kleio."

"Think about how it felt. What did you feel?"

I had felt a lot of things with that kiss. It was as if the world had gone fuzzy around us and all my senses had focused on Everett.

I tried to put what I had felt into words. "It was consuming. I felt like there was something between us that kept pulling us closer together." She nodded knowingly. "What, Kleio? What are you not telling me?"

She stopped walking and turned to me, grabbing my arm, making sure I had her full attention. "You're important to Everett. I think he likes you, Elise. He wouldn't have risked losing the hunt by coming to save you yesterday if he didn't care."

"Is that what you feel with Jack? The overwhelming feeling?"

She smiled at me, reminiscing. "Totally. I felt it from the first time we touched."

I broke eye contact with Kleio and looked around the forest where we were standing. It was calming, as it always was, its sounds soothing. Something inside of me felt unsettled hearing Kleio's words. I wasn't imagining what I was feeling—Kleio had the same feelings with Jack. But that made me even more uneasy. They were deeply infatuated with each other. I couldn't imagine getting to a place like that with Everett. It wasn't the reason I'd come to Minnesota.

"There it is!" Kleio broke away and jogged to the red mulberry we had transplanted last weekend. I followed her, eager to see how the tree was faring. Transplanting could be hard on trees, especially one so young.

She crouched down next to the sapling, admiring its leaves. "Looks good, right?"

I bent down next to her, letting my knees squish into the soil. I rubbed a leaf between my fingers and ran my hand along the trunk, giving it a slight wiggle to see if the roots had grown and stabilized the tree. Everything checked out.

"It looks great!" I said. "I would call this a successful transplant."

Kleio stood up, stepping back, admiring the tree. "It really feels good to save a tree, even just a small one."

"Every tree is important to the forest. Everything around us is in a symbiotic relationship, relying on each other to survive."

She looked at me funny, cocking her head to the side. "That's kind of like our pack house. We eat together, work together, and live together—everyone working toward a mutual interest."

"Yeah, kind of like a...pack house?" It was my turn to give Kleio a funny look.

"I forgot you know nothing of shifter culture." She could sense my puzzlement. "We live in a pack house, which is basically a large house with a bunch of smaller apartments for the families that are a part of the pack. Living together as a family is very important to us. Some members have their own places close by, but most of the pack lives in the main house. It's like living with all your extended family."

My face must have contorted into a disgusted look at the thought of living with my entire family.

Kleio laughed. "It's great. People who support you constantly surround you. Plus we throw some exceptional parties. You should come to the party we're having next weekend to celebrate the end of the Deca Tournament!"

Being at another event surrounded by shifters was not something I wanted to do, but I was polite and told Kleio I would think about it.

With the mulberry doing well, we spent the afternoon walking the woods, me naming plants for Kleio between bites of the sandwiches she had packed. She spent a lot of time trying to get information about Everett from me. I kept my lips closed. Her tracking skills weren't as bad she claimed them to be, and we made it back to Camp just in time for the evening meal.

Dinner was delicious, as always, and I retired early to my tent as the sun was setting. Tomorrow I could get back to the cabin. I knew Jenny would assume I'd spent the weekend with Wilder...which felt strange to play along with now. But what else could I tell her? That I'd been with...Everett? It wasn't like I could tell her the truth. For the past week and a half, I had basically done more of Jenny's research about wolves than I had done of my own.

In my head, I tossed around the idea of telling her about the shifters. I didn't know her that well; I had only just met her. While it would be nice to have a sounding board who wasn't a shifter, she seemed only interested in telling me what to do instead of listening and giving advice, and I didn't know yet if I could trust her with a secret like this.

I got ready for bed, still wearing my leggings and shirt from Friday. I made a mental note to pack a change of clothes along with my deodorant since I continued to end up in this situation.

Since it was a weekend-long event, no one showered or bathed. It was truly camping, with no running water or electricity. Luckily I had practiced in taking care of my needs in the woods, or being without a toilet would be mortifying. I scrubbed my teeth with my finger and a bottle of water, doing the best I could to keep clean. This level of hygiene was not what I was used to.

I lay in my bed for a while, the glow of the moon gradually lighting my tent. The cloudless night gave the moon nothing to hide behind, and it shone brightly in the sky. Even with my eyes closed, I could see the glow beneath my eyelids. I sat up in bed, rubbing my face. When I couldn't sleep, my mind raced. Mostly with thoughts about my research. It was hard to escape camping in a tent in the woods, the sounds and smells of nature constantly surrounding me.

If I couldn't sleep, I might as well put my wakeful mind to work. I still needed to sketch the red mulberry and take some notes about its surroundings. Now was as good of time as any.

It was remarkable how bright the moon was tonight. The moon was like a flashlight in the sky, lighting the earth. I crossed my fingers that I'd remember the way to the red mulberry. Twice now, I had been to the tree and the stream it grew next to. The topography class I had taken in undergrad taught me that water flowed at low points in the forest. If I was walking on a slight decline, I would be going in the right direction. Hopefully I was as good of a tracker as the shifters.

CHAPTER SEVENTEEN

The canopy of leaves above me only slightly dimmed the light of the moon. I could still easily navigate the forest floor, dodging the errant tree root. After second-guessing my sense of direction a few times, I heard the babbling of the stream and smiled as I saw the mulberry, its leaves fluttering in the breeze. Far enough from other trees, the mulberry stood alone under the moonlight, like a spotlight shone on it.

Sitting cross-legged next to the sapling, I unzipped my backpack and removed my journal and pencil. There was enough light from the sky that I could see the tree clearly and got to work sketching and taking notes about the foliage surrounding it. The sounds of my drawing mixed with the sounds of the forest, the rustling of the leaves in tune with the scratch of my pencil against the paper of my journal. A warm gust of air juxtaposed the coolness of the forest, lifting the hairs on the back of my neck. My pencil paused, mid mark.

"You shouldn't be out here alone." Everett's voice filled my ears.

I stood, turning to face him. How had he known I was out here? Had he come looking for me in my tent, only to find it empty?

He stood beneath the light of the moon. It highlighted his dark features, casting shadows beneath his eyes and accentuating the bulges of the muscles in his arms. I swallowed, my throat visibly bobbing. My mind flew back to Thursday night and the feeling of his fangs dragging over my neck.

"Do you need something?"

"I just wanted to check on you," he said.

"Check on me? I'm not the one who was unconscious yesterday. How is your arm?"

Without thinking, I stepped in front of him and grabbed his arm to examine the injury. Tiny zaps danced over my fingertips as I touched his skin. Maybe I wasn't imagining them because Everett recoiled slightly at my touch.

His wound was healing beautifully. Only a small line of open flesh remained, surrounded by new pink skin. "Amazing," I murmured.

"I heard you had a run-in with my father," Everett said.

Someone from the tent last night must have told him. Did he think I'd been weak for not being able to speak or even move in front of his father? I shuddered, remembering his presence, and looked away.

Everett reached his arms out and rubbed my arms up and down in a soothing motion. His hard, calloused hands felt rough against my smooth skin. "I don't want you to even think of my father," he said. "He's nothing but a sad man who uses his power to intimidate those with less. Let me handle him."

I let out a breath, releasing some of the tension that I had been holding since last night.

"I brought something for you." Everett pulled a small, clear bag of brown dust from his pocket.

I reached out for it, and holding it up at eye level, I immediately had an idea what it was. I knelt down and dug through my backpack, finding the jar of similar brown dust I had collected Friday before I'd gotten stuck within the wards. Holding the two side by side, there was no debating that they were the same plant.

"How did you know I was collecting samples of this? Where did you find this?" My curiosities overrode the tension for a moment.

He squatted down next to me. "I saw the jars of the plant in your bag when you were digging for water in the forest yesterday. It looked the same as the plants I've been seeing dying all over my territory."

"*Your* territory?"

"Yes, my territory. This is all my pack's territory. We're hosting the Deca Tournament this year."

"See, I thought this was a national forest—you know, owned by the government." I had never heard of land owned by the Cedar Moon Pack, let alone any other shifter.

"We let them use the land, as long as they take care of it." Everett seemed to have an answer for everything.

I held up the jar and bag. "Looks like someone isn't taking care of it."

"For the last two years, the brown rot has spread," he explained. "My father didn't believe the extent of the problem until he came here for the tournament and saw it himself. He claims that there's an imbalance. Too much death and not enough life present in my forest. I don't know what's causing it." A look of desperation came across his face as he spoke. "The land is slowly dying. *My* land is slowly dying. The *pack's* land is slowly dying. And I can't figure out why."

Everett didn't have an answer for this one. Even I didn't know what the cause was, and I was supposed to be an expert on these things. Professor Robinson had my samples, but I wouldn't get those results until the next time he visited.

"I'm looking into it," I said. Everett nodded, accepting my answer. "Can I keep this?" I held up the plastic bag as he nodded again. I tucked away the samples in my backpack. Standing back up, I found he was only one step away from me, his foot on top of the red-mulberry tree.

"Everett!" I screamed, pushing his chest with both of my hands. His body didn't move. "Get off my tree!"

Everett looked down at where his boot was pressing down on the sapling's trunk. "Shit!" He lifted his foot off the tree and took several steps back. "I didn't mean to step on it. I wasn't paying—"

"All this talk about saving your land, and you go around squishing baby trees under your foot."

I went into damage control, assessing the situation. The tree hadn't snapped under the pressure of Everett's boot because its root system was undeveloped. But the roots of the tree stuck out from the dirt, exposed to the elements as the tree lay on horizontally on the ground, and the bark was missing where Everett's boot had pressed. My fingers ran along a three-inch oval of raw tree. Less than twenty-five percent missing. This was good. Anything over that would be a death sentence. The tree still needed help, though. My hand dug deep into the earth, re-digging the hole that Kleio had previously made with her claws.

Warm hands wrapped around my wrist. "I can help," Everett said, his golden eyes looking into mine.

Maybe it was because it was late and I was tired, but I lost it. "I think you've done enough. Do you know how long it took me to save this tree the first time? Gavrill gave his blood to the tree, for god's sake."

I scooped more ferociously, flinging dirt behind me like a

dog digging a hole for its bone. Once the hole was deep enough, I tipped the tree back vertically, settling the roots back in the soil. The tree tipped, still unstable as I brushed dirt from in the hole. "Damnit!" I held the tree upright with one hand and used the other to drag the surrounding dirt toward the trunk.

Everett's large hands, like bulldozers, pushed piles of dirt into the hole, filling it quickly. I kneeled there, holding the tree up while he worked.

"Let me help you." His voice was calm, opposite of how I was feeling.

"It lost a lot of bark underneath your shoe."

"What can we do?"

"Well, *I* can do a technique called bridge grafting to help regrow the bark," I said. "It might not be enough to save it, but it's worth a shot."

Examining the mulberry, I picked a branch from its foliage that looked healthy and had a thick diameter. I snapped the branch off, laying it gently on the ground by my feet. The bridge grafting technique was difficult and not always successful. I had only done it one other time to a maple tree, and it had failed. The technique was just as it sounded—creating a bridge with a branch of the same tree from the top to the bottom of the area of the tree that was exposed. The hope was that the tree would use the branch to grow bark along the "bridge" covering the exposed part of the tree.

I needed to create two notches in the healthy bark for both sides of the bridge to sit. The backpack I had with me didn't have any of the tools I needed for this complicated procedure. My eyes scanned the surrounding woods, looking for something strong and pointy enough to make the notch.

"Let me help you." Those four words again came from Everett's lips.

I looked down at the poor sapling and at my hands, covered

in dirt, then at Everett's eyes. He seemed sincere, like he actually wanted to help me.

"Can you use your..." I made a claw motion with my hand.

"Claws? Sure I can." Everett flexed his hand, a long, sharp black claw extending from each of his five fingers.

"You just need one." I held up my finger. Everett did the same, all the claws retracting except the one on his right index finger.

I showed him where to carve the two notches and warned him not to go too deep into the sapwood. He stood right next to me, our bodies almost touching. He hadn't cleaned up since coming back from hunting, but he still smelled the same—fresh and clean, like the first day of spring. I breathed in his scent, letting it settle in my lungs.

Everett was careful with his carving. If I was less annoyed with him, I might have told him he had a future in conservation. Instead I just extended the branch to Everett, explaining that he needed to cut a wedge into each end. I held the branch while he wrapped his non-clawed hand around my wrist, keeping me steady. My arm stopped trembling as he did so. Had I been shaking?

His sharp claw made quick work of the cuts, diagonally cutting each end. I took a breath in as I watched him let go of my wrist, my skin now cold. He stared down at me intensely. My breath caught in my throat as he traced the top of my cheekbone, following it all the way to my mouth. His fingers lingered on my bottom lip, slowly outlining it. I couldn't look away from his swirling eyes, and I felt the thread again, pulling me in.

I tugged against the thread, unwilling to let it reel me in. "Now we need to insert it into the notches you made," I said.

I turned away from Everett, leaving his hand floating in the air where my face had been. My backpack had many odds and ends in it that I randomly needed in the field, and I knew I had push pins in there somewhere.

Finding them quickly, I crouched down next to the mulberry. This tree had been through a lot in the past few days. I inserted the wedged ends of the branch into the notches Everett had created. It fit perfectly, bending the branch into a slight bow shape, like an actual bridge. I pinned each end of the branch into the tree to keep it in place. Hopefully in a few weeks, there would be new bark growth and the tree would survive.

As I backed away from the tree, I turned around to find Everett right behind me. Instinctively, I put my hands on his chest, separating our bodies. I could see the tiny white lines that crossed his neck like tally marks. His neck was scarred like the tree we'd just saved.

"Thank you for saving the tree." Everett didn't have to speak loudly. Our bodies were so close.

"Well, that's my job." I tried to act unaffected by his kind words, but it was becoming hard, my body responding to his. I didn't want to pull away.

"I can tell you really care for the forest like I do."

"Of course I do—that's why I'm here," I said, replying automatically, my gaze finding where his tattoos peeked out of the top of his crew neck T-shirt. They looked tribal style with thick swirls and loops.

"I think you're here for more than that."

I watched his neck as he spoke, his skin vibrating with the deep tone of his voice. My hand reached out to trace what I could of the tattoos along his neck. I had wanted to touch them since Thursday night at the bar.

As soon as my fingers contacted his skin, everything around

us became fuzzy. My ears could no longer hear anything except our joint breathing and the increasing heartbeat in my chest. I moved slowly along the dark tattoo, casually dipping my fingers under his shirt before I found a new swirl to follow. He was warm and his skin was soft. I was close enough to his heart that I could feel the strong beat.

Everett's finger caught under my chin, bringing my face up to meet his. His dark pupils dilated in stark contrast to the gold irises that surrounded them. The thread pulled tighter, and I leaned into him, my hand now resting flat against his firm chest.

He groaned before he crashed his lips into mine. I opened my mouth immediately, ready for his tongue. His hand found his way behind my head to brace my neck for his rough kiss. I draped my arms around the back of his neck, pulling our bodies closer together. His kisses were like a drug. They had me needy and unable to quit. It was amazing how well our bodies meshed now that they were fully touching. Our size difference made no difference in our ability to fit together. My hips fit snuggly between his thighs, and my breasts found comfort right under his pectoral muscles.

I was in a daze as Everett and I exchanged unrestrained kisses. Nothing mattered to me except getting closer, pulling the thread tighter until it wrapped around both of our bodies. Instinctually, my body ground against his, needing friction. Purrs of delight left my lips as I felt the hard arousal through his pants rubbing against my stomach.

Everett let out a growl as he broke the kiss and put some space between our bodies. I whimpered, trying to pull my body close to his again. He grabbed onto my hip bones with both hands and firmly kept the distance between us, separating the parts of our bodies that needed the contact the most.

Our foreheads were still touching. Nose-to-nose, we breathed each other's air, unable to get enough.

"Did you feel that?" Everett's voice was strained. His eyes searched mine for confirmation.

I wasn't sure what he was asking. I had felt many things. I was still feeling them.

"Feel what?" I asked.

"The pull between us."

I leaned back slightly, and Everett pulled me back until our bodies were touching. He leaned down, meeting my eyes, searching. Neither of us could deny there was something between us. It was raw and electric.

"To me, it's like we're being pulled closer and closer together with an invisible thread," I said. That was the only way I could describe the attraction between us.

Everett let out a sigh of relief, and his face relaxed. "I feel that too."

Keeping one hand on my hip, his other hand cradled the back of my skull as he put his face between my neck and shoulder. I leaned my head to the side to give him better access. His warm face fit perfectly in the sunken spot along my collarbone. As he nuzzled my skin, I heard his lips part as he planted soft kisses along my shoulder and neck. Rough, his beard scratched my sensitive skin.

I wrapped my arms around his back, unable to touch fingertips because of his size. My body betrayed me when he opened his mouth and let his fangs drag along my neck. The moan I let out was louder than it needed to be. I was sure the entire Camp could hear it, even as we were out here in the woods. At the moment, I didn't care. Heat traveled from the skin where his fangs touched down to the pit of my stomach and pooled between my legs. I tensed with the pulsing need that rushed through me.

"Lyka," Everett whispered against my skin as he sniffed his nose along my neck. My sudden realization that I hadn't showered in a couple days caused me to push away from Everett. Self-conscious, I looked down at my feet.

"What's wrong?" he asked, lifting my chin again to meet my eyes.

"I just realized I probably smell horrible," I said.

Everett's eyes crinkled, and a smirk crossed his lips. He pulled me close once again, stuck his nose to my neck, and inhaled deeply. His voice vibrated against me. "I smell nothing but your desire for me. It's quite potent. I'm sure the shifters back at Camp can smell it too," he said.

Pushing away from him, my eyes grew wide and I was sure my face turned the darkest shade of red. I could feel wetness pooling between my legs. Wishing I had packed an extra pair of leggings, I looked straight at him. "You can't."

"I most certainly can." His eyes closed slightly as he leaned in. I could feel his warm breath against my ear. "And it smells delicious."

I squeezed my legs together to stop the pulsing between them, which only made it worse. My knees buckled, and Everett caught me around the waist, pulling me close for another kiss. I let out more embarrassing sounds that he muffled with his mouth.

We were hungry for each other. His hands never strayed beyond the back of my head or my waist, and that made me feel even more deprived. I needed him to touch me. Moving my legs apart, I straddled one of his thighs. My hands wrapped around his torso and pulled him closer to me. I was like a wild animal, grinding against his quad muscle, trying to relieve the tension.

Everett groaned against my neck. His fangs dragged across my skin. My body tensed at the feeling. I froze, my breath hitching in my chest. He froze as well. The lack of movement between us broke the spell.

I pushed him away. No, I couldn't be doing this with him. I couldn't get more entangled with him more than I already was. It would only cause problems for me in the long run.

What was wrong with me? I felt both frustrated and sexually charged at the same time. It was quite the combination.

He glanced longingly up and down my body. "What are you doing to me?" he asked, rubbing his chin.

"Too much. I'm doing too much." I tried to control my heart rate. "I can't be doing this with you," I said.

He took a step close to me and slowly took a deep inhale, running his nose from my shoulder and up my neck. I stood there, trying not to let a moan escape me. Everett backed up and shook his head with his eyes closed. He turned, putting his hands behind his head and looking up at the sky. "You're right. Everyone can hear and smell you out here. I don't like to share."

It was like a cold bucket of water had dumped over my head. The fuzzy surroundings became clear again, and I looked around the forest, surprised to be there. What was Everett doing to me?

I took a step back and covered my face with my hands. This was so embarrassing. I was in the middle of the forest surrounded by Lycans who could apparently smell me. This wasn't like me. I prided myself on being controlled, especially with my emotions.

"Should we head back?" Everett held out his hand like he expected me to hold it.

I planted my fists along my sides and marched past him, heading in the direction I hoped would lead me back to Camp. I heard Everett's footsteps behind me.

"Wrong way, Lyka," he said.

I stopped marching, not willing to look behind me. His voice sounded smug. I couldn't give him the satisfaction of knowing how deeply red my face was. I waited until I heard him walking away the opposite direction to turn and follow him.

Everett turned around to glance my way. I gave him the meanest look I could muster, which wasn't all that mean. He smirked and continued to lead me back to Camp.

CHAPTER EIGHTEEN

Camp was already bustling when I woke up to the sun illuminating the tent. I did my best to clean myself up before making my way to the main tent with my backpack hanging over one of my shoulders. It was Sunday, and soon I could get out of here and back to the cabin. Space was what I needed—space from Everett. He made my resolve fade and body disobedient. A good night's sleep had cleared my head. I would not get caught up with another shifter. The last one I had hooked up with had put me in this mess, and I didn't want to fall any further into this Lycan world I had found myself in. Stopping things with Everett last night had been the right thing to do. I had work to do.

Breakfast was simple and quick as everyone in the Cedar Moon Pack focused on packing up supplies and their personal items to head home after the weekend. Everyone was in good spirits. I could only assume it was because the tournament was going well.

Right before noon, Everett and Wilder stalked into the tent, looking dirty and disheveled from hunting all night.

"Everything ready to go?" Everett looked to Gavrill for confirmation, who nodded, motioning for everyone to head to the cars.

When we got there, everyone started throwing their bags into one of the black SUVs, but Everett took my backpack from me and put it in the back seat of the second SUV.

"You're riding with me," he said as he opened the passenger door for me.

I looked to Kleio for guidance, but all she did was shrug.

"He's the boss." She smiled with no sympathy as she climbed into the first car with Jack, Kostas, Wilder, and Gavrill.

I looked at Everett holding open the door for me. I was tired of arguing—I just wanted to go home. Climbing into the car, I buckled my seat belt. Everett, looking satisfied, got into the driver's seat, and we started the drive down the long gravel road.

"I hope you remember where I live because I have no idea where we are." My usual keen sense of direction was completely turned around every time I spent the weekend at Camp.

"I remember. The cabin is much more accessible, better now that the wolfsbane is gone." Everett glanced at me before he looked back at the road. How did he know that I had removed the wolfsbane from the cabin?

I scooted in my seat as far away from Everett as I could. He chuckled softly to himself. What a creep. Was he stalking me?

After a silent drive, we rounded a corner, and Everett pulled up the gravel driveway in front of the cabin. I climbed out of the car before he could put the SUV in park. I opened the back door to retrieve my backpack.

"You're welcome."

I lifted my eyes to see Everett turned around and staring at me from the driver's seat. "For what? I've been stuck at Camp for the second weekend in a row and attacked by deranged shifters. There's not a lot to be thankful for."

Everett smiled. "For the ride. Both in the car and on my leg last night."

Too much. That was too much. I let out a sound that resembled Everett's own growl as I flung my backpack over my shoulder and slammed the door closed. I stomped up to the front door of the cabin without looking behind me. The audacity of that man.

"I'll be seeing you soon." I froze mid-step as his voice met my ears. I took a breath and kept walking, keeping myself from turning around to look at him again.

Once I was inside the cabin with the door closed behind me, Everett backed down the driveway. I leaned my head against the door and closed my eyes, taking a deep breath.

"You're back, you minx! I knew you would disappear all weekend with those hot guys again. You need to introduce me. Sharing is caring!" Jenny was already on me before I could take a another step inside.

"I need a shower." I headed to my room to put my backpack down, hearing Jenny's footsteps following behind me.

"Yeah, you do. Did you just spend all weekend in the woods rolling around on the ground with those men?" Jenny said. "Ugh. What I wouldn't give for a weekend with one of those guys. I need some of your tricks. Maybe I can borrow some of your leggings and shirts? That seems to work for you."

I laughed with her. "That's pretty much what I did." If only she knew the truth. "But aren't you into Leo?" A couple of days ago, she'd seemed very much smitten with Leo.

"He's been gone most of the weekend. I guess he found a stream or something he likes?" Jenny said with a bit of a pout. "I don't know—he's been gone a lot and I'm lonely!"

"It's only been a few days since you had your tongue down his throat!"

"Well, I get lonely quickly." She laughed. "You should take a shower already, and then we can make popcorn and hang out so I won't be so lonely."

I agreed, and she left me to bathe in peace.

I allowed myself a long shower, probably using up all the stored rainwater. The water flowed over my body, washing away everything that had accumulated on me this past weekend. It wasn't just dirt I had collected but a whole new part of the world that I'd never known existed. A mythical place where humans shifted into wolves, something I'd believed only existed within the confines of a fairytale. It all should have scared me, but it didn't. The researcher in me thrived in the unknown, the mystery, the search for answers. Their world fascinated me, and I had a feeling I had only skimmed the surface.

Now that I had found the Lycans, I wasn't so sure I wanted them to be hidden from me. There was too much in it that intrigued me. Yes, Everett was a big part of it. He had sunken into my pores. My fingers brushed across my lips, still feeling the touch of his.

But the rot—it was affecting the forest in a way that I hadn't known was possible, easily killing the plants native to the area.

Killing wasn't the right word. It was vaporizing them, turning them into a fine dust. It was affecting the shifters too, turning the lush green forests of their home into brown wastelands. Although Everett didn't have answers about the rot, it was nice to have someone who was just as invested in the forest as I was. We would figure it out.

We. I talked about him in my head like we were already partners, not only in investigating the rot but in other ways. It had been so natural, letting him help me last night with the mulberry. The way he'd cared for the plant and then cared for me.

I wanted more. Maybe after I figured out the mystery of the rot, I would let myself explore Everett. I couldn't let him become more of a distraction from my research than he already was.

When the shower became more of a dribble than a stream, I turned off the faucet. Hopefully it rained soon to replenish our supply if Jenny and Leo needed to clean up.

Leo must've been busy working if Jenny hadn't seen him recently. His research brought him close to the ground like mine did, all the water ecosystems under our feet. Had he noticed the rot? I'd be surprised if he hadn't.

Cozy and clean, I met Jenny in the living room. "Is Leo coming back tonight?" I wondered where he was. The cabin was getting dark. Soon we would have to turn on the lanterns.

"He's been getting back super late," she said. "I've been hearing him come in well after midnight."

That was weird to me. I couldn't imagine Leo getting any work done in the dark. Especially in the water. What was he doing? I knew he'd been meeting with one of the land owners out here, so maybe those talks were keeping him out so late. I knew I'd be talking someone's ear off if they had any experience with my area of study.

After popcorn and chitchat, Jenny released a yawn and announced that she was going to bed. I followed shortly after her, excited to sleep in a proper bed in a house with solid walls.

CHAPTER NINETEEN

On Monday morning, I felt refreshed from a full night's sleep. I woke up early, put on my running clothes, and threw my hair up into a bun. Heading out on the trail, I fell into the comfortable meditative trance that I needed to reset myself from the past weekend. It had been too intense with Everett. I had never felt like that with a man before. He was addicting and made me forget what I was here to accomplish. I'd earned a scholarship to do research here, and that was what I was going to do. People like me didn't get many chances like this, and I had worked hard to earn the opportunity.

After three miles, my head was reset, and I felt ready to tackle some more thesis writing. I hoped Professor Robinson would bring back some results for me on Thursday, but I had other things to keep me busy and on track with my work.

I walked down to my room, passing Jenny's and Leo's rooms along the way. Leo's door was slightly ajar, and I saw him sleeping in his bed soundly. He must have gotten in late last night. Jenny was up working at her desk in her pink heart pajamas. I hurried past her door so I wouldn't get caught in a conversation.

The day flew by, and I only noticed it was the evening when my room darkened, signaling the sun beginning to set. I stretched my arms above my head to relieve the tension in my muscles from sitting in a chair for so long. It was well past dinnertime. I was terrible at remembering to eat when I was working, and I had skipped lunch. Leo and Jenny's rooms were both empty, and I was happy to have the evening to myself.

Looking at the floppy turkey sandwich I made myself for dinner, I missed the shifter's cooking. I certainly didn't go hungry when I was with them. Funny how my thoughts continued to come back to the shifters.

Even though I had sat at my desk for most of the day, I could still sense that my body was tired. Probably still recovering from the weekend. Pleased to find there was still rainwater, I took a quick shower before bed. After not having access to a shower the past two weekends, it was a luxury to smell decent before climbing under the sheets. Changing into comfortable pajamas, I got into bed for another night of sleep.

I heard the front door of the cabin open, and heavy footsteps alerted me it was Leo. The footsteps got closer to my room instead of stopping. A soft knock came from my door, and I opened it to see Leo standing in the doorway. His face looked tired and overworked. Mud was splattered across his skin from the stream he had been standing in.

"You've been looking into the rot in the forest, right?" Leo asked. We didn't know a lot about each other's research projects, but he had seen me give the samples to Professor Robinson last week.

"Yeah, I am. Why?"

"It's just that—"

Tap, tap, tap. Hearing what sounded like a tree branch

hitting the window in my bedroom, I leaned back, holding on to the doorframe to look. The curtains were closed, but I could still see an outline of a man standing outside my window, illuminated by the moonlight. What the...? Then I saw a flash of golden eyes and gasped.

You've got to be kidding me, I thought.

"Is everything okay?" Leo stood there waiting for me to give him the go-ahead to finish.

I couldn't give him the opportunity. Not when a certain shifter was outside my window.

"Can we talk about this later? It's getting kind of late," I said, keeping my door as closed as possible.

"Yeah, you're right." He dragged his hand through his hair. "Can we talk about it soon?"

"Sure, Leo. Another time." I placated him, ready to close my door and deal with what was lurking outside my window.

He mumbled something to himself as he turned around and walked toward his room. Jenny burst through the front door, and her eyes zeroed in on Leo. He ducked into his room before she could chase him down. Her posture dipped in defeat as she turned to head to the kitchen. I closed my door quickly before she could come into my room next.

Tap. Tap, tap, tap.

"Lyka. Open up." My heart skipped a beat, and my limbs stiffened.

I wanted to ignore him, but I didn't want to risk Jenny or Leo hearing and looking out their own windows to see a giant man standing outside of mine. Jenny might just invite him to her own window.

Pulling the curtains aside, I could see Everett's scruff-covered face. "What do you want?" Even though the window was closed, I knew he could still hear me.

"Let me in, Elise." I shook my head at him defiantly. "Fine.

I'll let myself in." Everett forcefully pushed up on the window pane, snapping the lock that was in place.

"Fine! Fine!" There was still a screen separating us, and I wasn't about to owe more damages to the university for an unhinged shifter breaking into my room. He relaxed his fist that had been about to punch through the screen as I carefully removed the screen frame and leaned it against the wall next to me.

Everett lifted his body through the window and landed with his feet on the floor of my room. His agility surprised me. He was large and could still fit his body through a window without a problem.

"You owe me for that lock," I said.

Everett shrugged as if it wasn't a big deal. "Not a problem. I'll replace the whole window if that's what it takes to get into your room."

Scoffing at him, I put my hands on my hips. The cool breeze from the open window alerted my nipples that I was wearing a thin tank top and shorts. Everett's eyes landed on them before I could cover them with my arms. He had only seen me in leggings and T-shirts. I felt practically naked in front of him.

"What do you want, Everett? Kidnapping and holding me hostage isn't enough? You need to add *breaking and entering* to your resume?"

He laughed quietly as he walked toward me. "I'm glad you found your nerve, Elise. I love when you talk dirty to me."

If attitude was what he wanted from me, then I had more than enough to give. I had too much attitude stored up from repressing it all my life.

"Are you always this dark and broody?" I asked. Everett was the king of mixed signals and sexual overtones. I wondered what signal he was sending me now, showing up at my window and breaking into my room.

"Only around you." Everett took the last step toward me and pulled my arms away from my chest. My nipples would not subside their protrusion, and I could feel Everett's gaze on them. He pulled me against his body, smashing my chest into his stomach. I was sure through his T-shirt he could feel the hard buds against his skin.

His head dipped to that familiar spot between my neck and shoulder as he breathed in. "I can't fucking stay away from you."

"And that makes you mad?" The thread between us was already taut, and I was losing my vision to the frosted glass forming around us.

"It makes me furious, Elise. I have never felt like this, and I don't know what I'm doing." His confession made me smile. How could an alpha wolf not know what they were doing? Something must've been wrong with him if he felt that way around me. I was nothing special. "Kleio told me this would happen."

The mention of Kleio and the thought that they were talking about me privately both warmed my heart and made me curious. "Kleio said what?"

"Nothing, Lyka. Nothing. You smell so good." His nose trailed up my neck and behind my ear, inhaling in my hair.

"Wonders, what a shower will do," I said.

"Oh, you're snippy, aren't you, Elise?"

"Only when I'm irritated."

"You don't smell irritated to me."

I gasped and pushed back from his hold. I suddenly felt cold and exposed. Crossing my arms across my chest again, I stared Everett down. He was dangerous, and his presence was addictive.

"Oh, you forgot I was a wolf, didn't you?" he said. "I can smell your need for me from a mile away."

"I don't need you, Everett. There are other things I need to do."

"Your mouth tells lies, but your scent tells the truth." Everett was practically steaming with sexual energy. It was hard not to be pulled into the current.

"What do you think all of this stuff is?" Gesturing to the plants that lined my desk next to the window and all the papers that littered my desk, I looked at him unamused. "I'm here to research. I don't need you. My thesis needs to be my priority. I'm far enough behind as it is."

Everett stopped his brooding and turned to look at my desk. He lifted one of the potted plants on the desk. "So not only do you save trees, but you also grow them?"

"Yeah." I laughed under my breath. "I do it all."

Everett took his time lifting the little pots and examining each closely. The number of plants that littered my room could intrigue some people. I had collected quite a few more to add to my collection, putting them in little pots of dirt.

"All of your plants are doing so well. They're so healthy." Everett seemed surprised. I guess when your forest was turning brown and dying, seeing healthy plants was unexpected.

"I've always had a green thumb," I said. "I had a large garden growing up."

Everett continued to examine the plants, lifting each pot and delicately touching the leaves.

I talked to fill the silence. "I'm most interested in medicinal plants, plants that can heal." He picked up a pot that held a flourishing plant of green leaves and white flowers. "That one's yarrow. That's what I used to stop the bleeding and heal your arm." I reached out to touch the leaves and found my fingers touching Everett's as he did the same. The sexual electricity in

Everett was still flowing, and my finger became a conduit, channeling the raw energy. I gasped at the shock and pulled my hand away.

Everett carefully set down the plant and stalked me as I backed up. The back of my knees hit the bed, and I fell onto my butt, sitting on the bed, looking up at him. His golden eyes were swirling. He placed one knee next to me and climbed fully onto the bed, placing his other leg on my other side. My face was against his abdomen, and I could smell the outdoors on his skin.

Placing his hands under my arms, he lifted me further onto the bed, dragging my legs through the bridge of his own, gently laying me down. Leaning over, Everett lowered a hand on either side of my head and dropped toward me, staring at my lips. My hands found his chest as I tried to keep a distance between our bodies. My legs wriggled, and my center burned with anticipation. Everett was right—my body didn't lie.

He easily broke through my hand barrier and planted a small kiss on my lips. This took me back. He usually filled my mouth with needy, rough kisses. What game was he playing? I'd gotten used to the uninhabited kisses. I needed the rush that came with Everett fully claiming my lips. My body came alive. I bucked my hips up to meet Everett's, and a low growl greeted me from deep within his chest.

"Is your body telling me the truth, Elise?" His voice was gravelly and strained. He needed the roughness too.

I didn't have words to answer him. I grabbed the bottom of his skull and pulled his face to mine. Our lips met softly until I traced my tongue along his closed lips. It was all the invitation Everett needed to proceed. The kiss was electric. Our lips and tongues were at war with each other, searching for some semblance of relief. Kissing did nothing but fuel the fire growing deep between my legs. I hadn't found release since I had gotten here. Wilder surely had done nothing to help me, and Everett left me feeling desperate every time we touched.

I wrapped my legs around his hips and lifted my center to his. I groaned at the feeling of his hardness, ready for me. The pressure against the nub between my legs was too much. Everett chuckled between my lips. He broke the kiss, getting into a kneeling position, and grabbed my hips. Lifting me up by my pelvic bone, he pulled my open center against his hard shaft, and I gasped at the sensation.

"I haven't been able to get rid of *this* since I kissed you at the bar last week." My eyes widened. "It's fucking miserable. Do you feel what you do to me?" He thrusted his clothed erection against my opening and started moving my hips up and down its length. My head fell back as I moaned at the sensation.

"Why don't you do something about it?" I was more than willing and wanting. Everett was being nothing more than a tease. He set my hips down and draped his body over mine. His nose trailed from between my breasts, up my neck and to my ear. I could feel the line he'd made even after his lips brushed my ear.

"Knowing you, Lyka, you would be anything but quiet," he said. "I won't share the noises that will come out of your mouth when I make you come with anyone. Those noises are for my ears only."

Luckily it was dark because I could feel my face turn a deep red. I wondered if he could smell that my roommates were home. Oh god, I hoped I hadn't woken them up. Jenny would have so many questions in the morning.

Everett stuck his nose in the spot between my neck and shoulder that had become one of my favorite parts of my body. Whispering quietly enough for only my ears, he spoke to me.

"I'll do something about it soon." He nuzzled the spot, inhaling deeply before he lifted himself off me.

I sat up on my elbows and gazed at his shadowy figure. Deep, rapid breaths filled the dark room.

He made his way to the window and started to climb out. "I need to get back to the pack. You're too tempting. You smell too good." In the shadow of his body, I could see him adjusting himself in his pants, trying to find a comfortable position. "Make sure you close your window after I leave. I don't want any other wolves to smell your desire."

I scoffed as he fully exited my window. "You're such a tease, Everett!"

What was he doing coming to see me, visiting me like *that* and then leaving me in a haze of need? I could hear him chuckling to himself as he walked away, back into the woods.

I closed my window loudly so he could hear the slam and flung myself back on my bed. Yet again, left unfulfilled.

CHAPTER TWENTY

THE NEXT MORNING, I woke up and got ready for my run. It was supposed to be a warm day, so I opted for a black sports bra and green running shorts. Throwing my hair up into a bun, I walked down the hall toward the kitchen. Leo's room was already empty. We would have to finish our conversation soon. He had never shown an interest in me or my work before, his focus only on Jenny and his research. His behavior last night had been strange.

Jenny waved quickly at me as I passed her room. I breathed a sigh of relief that no one had heard my guest last night. She certainly would have brought it up.

About a mile into my run, I was feeling good and ready to sweat out all my sexual frustration. Then out of the corner of my eye, I saw a large black wolf running parallel to me about twenty feet away.

I tripped over my own feet before catching myself on my hands and knees. I slowly lifted my head from the ground to see the black wolf sitting on his haunches with his tongue hanging out of his mouth, staring at me.

What did he want?

When I stood up, the wolf followed my lead, standing on four giant paws. I took a couple of steps forward, and the wolf did too, looking at me to take the lead.

I started off in a jog, keeping my eyes on the wolf jogging with me. He didn't get closer and kept my pace, running alongside me. It was like going for a run with a dog.

When I turned around after another mile, the wolf turned with me and began running alongside me back the way I'd come. He kept his distance, seeming to enjoy himself as his tongue hung out the side of his mouth in a steady pant.

At about a mile to my cabin, he let out a short bark, startling me. I stopped running and watched the wolf stop and stare at me with those gold eyes. He stared for a few seconds and then turned and ran back into the woods, leaving me to complete my run.

———

It was finally Thursday, and I was looking forward to meeting with Professor Robinson. I was hoping he would have some results from the rotted plant samples I had given him last week. Especially since I hadn't had a chance to talk more about it with Leo yet. Jenny was right. He'd been gone a lot the past two days, only coming home late at night to sleep. Maybe I could corner him when he was required to show up for Robinson's meeting.

It was raining outside, and I made the call to postpone my morning run to the afternoon. The clicking of my computer keys mimicked the rain outside my window, and the sounds put me in a daze.

I only woke from the meditative sounds when there was a knock on our front door. I looked at the clock on my computer and was stunned that the morning had gone by so quickly. Scrolling through my document, I saw that I had written a lot. Apparently all I'd needed was some rain pattering against my window to get work done.

I heard voices coming from the living room, ones I must've previously tuned out while I'd been working. Professor Robinson was here.

I quickly walked toward the living room, seeing Jenny and Leo with paperwork already in their hands.

"So nice of you to join us, Ms. Wilson," Professor Robinson said. "Jenny and Leo, you are dismissed." Robinson ran his fingers through his mustache, slightly curling the ends. Jenny and Leo scurried to their rooms, leaving me with the professor.

"Letter for you, Elise, and a package." Professor Robinson handed me a letter and a brown cardboard box that were addressed to me in my mother's handwriting. I set them on the table next to me to look at later.

Robinson handed me yet another envelope. "Your results from the samples you sent with me last week."

I snatched them from him and opened the manila envelope that contained them. I skimmed over the findings, and a heaviness came over me.

Robinson narrated the findings out loud: "We found nothing. I had my undergraduates run the samples, and then I ran them myself. It's common dust. A mixture of plant matter, human matter, and animal matter."

My stomach dropped. This didn't make sense. A plant that had once been alive had turned into nothing more than what someone would find in dust that collected on a shelf. "I don't even know what to say..."

"Have you been distracted, Elise? Focused on things other than your work?" I looked up at Professor Robinson, dumbstruck. "There have been rumors of you disappearing for days at a time."

A high-pitched gasp from the hallway caught my attention, and I looked over to see a flash of blonde hair disappear into Jenny's room.

"This isn't some vacation for you out here. You don't have time to be going out drinking, or whatever you young people do." Robinson looked at me with his eyebrows raised, waiting for an explanation.

I didn't have one. I had been absent from the cabin for days at a time, but not for the reasons he assumed. How did he know I wasn't always sleeping at the cabin? There wasn't any excuse that I could give him that would be remotely truthful.

"You'll want to check in with your supervising professor. I sent her an email once we found the results," he said. "She hasn't heard from you. You missed the second check-in call last week." My heart stopped beating, and my ears rang. I'd been with the shifters *again* when I was supposed to be making my check-in call. "We're both disappointed that you wasted our time running samples that you apparently collected from a bookshelf here in the cabin. We expected more from you."

My body went numb with shock. How could they not believe that I had found these plants in the forest? I would never lie about something like this, wasting everyone's time.

"I truly found this in the forest, about five miles from the cabin," I said. But I had no proof of where I'd taken the sample, no witnesses...other than Everett, and I wasn't about to mention him.

Robinson still had a look of disappointment and disbelief on his face. "Nothing more than household dust, Elise. The data doesn't lie," he said. "We could decide to put you on academic probation for this."

I froze as the word *probation* echoed loudly in my head.

"We don't take forged data lightly. One published paper with inaccurate or false information can stain an entire university." Professor Robinson gave me a glare that cut to my core.

The sound of shuffling feet came from the hallway that housed our bedrooms, and I knew Jenny and Leo were listening.

I turned back to the sheet of results. Something had to be wrong. A miscalculation or an uncalibrated instrument. I had misrepresented nothing. I stood there, dumbstruck. What the hell was going on?

The professor zipped up his bag. "Make good choices, Elise. I wouldn't want someone with promise like you to be tarnished for one misstep for the rest of their career."

I couldn't say anything to him. He had clearly already decided that I was a cheat and a drunk, spending my time here partying instead of researching. I stood with my hands crossed over my chest as he walked out the door. I was fuming. Hot bubbles popped in my chest, boiling.

"I know you're both listening!" I yelled into the quiet cabin after the front door slammed shut.

Leo and Jenny poked their heads out of their respective doors, guilty looks on their faces. Leo's cheeks were sunken in and his under eyes dark. He looked like he had gone days without more than a few hours of sleep.

"What the hell, Leo?" I slammed my hands on the table harder than I meant to. "Why didn't you say anything? Haven't you been seeing it too?"

"I'm sorry, Elise. I couldn't say anything to back you up," he said. "Something weird is happening in the woods, and I can't explain it. I have seen the rot, but if the samples came back from the lab as just dust, I don't know what to think. I can't make it make sense." Leo looked just as confused as I had been reading the lab report.

The boiling in my chest continued. "Who told Robinson I wasn't sleeping at the cabin?"

Jenny slowly raised her hand. "It was an accident. I didn't intend it to mean anything..."

"What did you do, Jenny?" My voice turned growly as I stalked closer.

"Nothing! I mean, I might have mentioned something about you spending time a lot of time with locals in the call to my professor, but I didn't say you were doing something you weren't supposed to." She was stumbling over her words, trying to explain herself as quickly as possible. "Just that you were probably getting a lot of good plant information from them."

The sheets of data left my hand and hit the floor with a smack. "I have so much riding on this scholarship. I don't have parents paying for my tuition." I narrowed my eyes at Jenny. "Or a bunch of previous publications to pad my CV like you, Leo." He looked down at his hands.

"This is it for me. This is all I have."

I turned to Leo. "What were you going to tell me about the rot the other night?" If he knew something that would explain the rot and clear my name with the university, I needed to know about it.

Leo nodded in agreement. "I just...noticed..." he began. But by the way he couldn't finish a thought and his stare was getting more disoriented by the second, I could tell he was exhausted.

I felt the urge to know what he needed to tell me as soon as possible, but Leo needed to be rested so he could tell me precisely what he knew about the rot. There could be no more mistakes or misunderstandings.

"You should go to bed and sleep until tomorrow morning," I said to Leo as less of a suggestion than as an order. "We can talk tomorrow." One day wouldn't make or break my standing with the university.

One problem down, I looked at our other roommate. "And Jenny, stop gossiping about me. I thought we were friends."

She looked down at her feet. "We are friends. I'm sorry, Elise. I shouldn't have said anything."

Sitting down in my chair at the table, I slumped over, tired from my outburst. Being angry took so much energy. "I'm sorry, you guys. It's just a lot to be accused of forging samples. I'm trying so hard, but I keep screwing up. This is so nerve-wracking."

Both Jenny and Leo looked at me with understanding. They didn't want to be in the position I was in.

"Let me make it up to you, Elise," Jenny said. "Come to No Bars with me tonight. I'll buy you a drink."

Leo caught my eye as his hunched-over form trudged back to his bedroom. I hoped he would get some sleep and look better in the morning.

"I promise I won't tell anyone you're going out," she insisted. "Never again."

"No way," I said.

"Please! I feel so bad."

"Nope."

"Just one drink? I promise—just one. And then we can leave."

Jenny was relentless. I couldn't lie to myself; I could use a drink after the accusations Robinson had thrown at me, and I was getting a little bit of cabin fever. Maybe I could even talk through some stuff with Jenny without giving too much away. If we had one drink and then came back, what could it hurt?

"Fine," I said.

Jenny clapped and bounced up and down at my response. I pushed back in my chair and announced I was going for a run. The rain had let up, and I needed some stress relief.

CHAPTER TWENTY-ONE

Thankful I had worn some trail-running shoes, I jogged along the gravel path made slippery by the rain earlier. A quick run to clear my head before I got to brainstorming how I was going to solve the situation with the university. I needed this escape first. My breath had evened out, and my legs felt warm and ready for some mileage. Every time I ran, I sensed something in the woods watching me, and today was not an exception.

Steady footsteps fell in step with mine from behind, and I whipped my body around to confront my follower. My hands squeezed into tight fists, ready to fight, and I regretted not looking into getting some mace like Jenny had suggested. My eyes landed on Everett in running shorts, a T-shirt, and a cheeky grin on his face.

"Why'd you stop?" he asked.

Only because you scared me, you idiot, I thought. I didn't want to let him know he had startled me.

"How long have you been following me?" I asked.

"Not long." His lips lifted in the amusement of his obvious lie.

"Well, good luck keeping up."

I turned and ran down the trail, happy I had already run about a mile and my body had warmed up. Everett's steady footsteps kept up with mine, and I couldn't hear any hard breathing behind me. He was in good shape if he could hold this pace. I, unfortunately, couldn't hold this pace for more than a mile, and I slowed down. So much for my taunting. Maybe all the running in his wolf form gave him an advantage. I could sense his presence behind me getting closer and closer as I slowed down to a jog.

The damn thread was back, and I could feel him reeling me in. Large hands reached out and gripped my waist, stopping my momentum and pulling my back against his chest. Both of us were breathing hard as I melded into him, once again a perfect fit. Our breaths found rhythm together, inhaling and exhaling. His heart pulsed against my back, beating erratically. My heart was doing the same, although I didn't know if he could feel it.

"Did you think you could run from me?" Everett's breath was hot against my ear. He seemed to enjoy a hunt. Maybe it was the wolf in him, or maybe it was just his nature. Everett could have had me several times in the last two weeks, but he was still playing with me. Like a wolf with a hare. "I'll always catch you."

He spun me around, and my forearms braced myself against his chest. Everett walked me backward toward a large maple tree. He pushed me against the tree with his body, reminding me how well we fit together. The exposed skin on the back of my body tensed at the feeling of rough bark. My breathing rate increased even though I wasn't running anymore. The smell of summer mixed with sweat filled my nose as I breathed steadily against his chest. The sports bra and shorts I wore left little to the imagination, and I wished I had one of my oversized T-shirts on to protect me from feeling all the muscles in his chest.

Sweat was dripping from Everett's body as he leaned over me, and a drop fell onto my chest. The droplet melded together with my own beads of perspiration and slipped between my breasts, disappearing under my sports bra. I looked up to find Everett's eyes following the same drip I was.

Probation. Distraction. The rot. The words again echoed in my head.

"I can't do this with you." It took so much will power to push him away. I wasn't able to push him far, my palms meeting muscle.

"Why not?" Everett filled the gap between our bodies again, pushing his against mine, caging me in with his arms by my head.

"There's too much at stake. I can't be...distracted."

"Do you find me distracting, Elise?" he asked.

Yes, in the best way possible. But...

"I could be kicked out of my program, Everett!" I ducked under his arm, leaving a space the size of my body between him and the tree. I stood with my arms straight by my sides, my fists clenched. As much as I wanted to, I couldn't do this with him.

Everett walked over and wrapped his hand around my upper arm, pulling me close to him. "What do you mean?" His voice sounded threatening.

"The sample of the rot I turned in for testing came back inconclusive," I explained. "I'm in trouble with my university. They think I falsified the sample."

"But you didn't. The rot is real." Everett played with my ponytail, letting the hairs slide through his fingers. I let him, needing the comfort, the intimacy.

"Of course it is—that's not the point," I said. "They don't

believe me. I need to find a way to prove that I wasn't lying. That's why I'm out here, running, trying to clear my head before I get back to work."

"I believe you." He moved his hand from my ponytail to the back of my neck, massaging the tense muscles.

"Of course you do. You saw the rot yourself..."

Everett put his fingers over my lips, silencing me. "I believe *in* you. I've seen what you can do, Elise. You're nothing short of amazing. The university would be stupid to let you go."

His fingers fell from my lips to the bottom of my chin. He lifted my head up so our eyes met. The swirling of gold eyes was again my downfall. I was so tired of resisting. I threw my arms around Everett's neck, lifting up my whole body so my face could reach his. Strong hands gripped under my backside as my legs wound around his waist. He pushed me harder against the tree as our noses touched, eyes staring at each other and lips opened, gulping in air.

"What is happening?" I asked.

"I found you, we ran together, and now you're having trouble controlling yourself." Everett's words were true yet annoyed me.

"Okay, says the man who's been following me on my runs," I said. "Is it really me who is having trouble controlling themselves?"

"Who says I've been following you before today?"

"I know it was you two days ago. Hard to miss a giant black wolf running with me." He smirked.

"My wolf wanted to spend some time with you and protect you on your run. I only agreed if he promised we would keep our distance. I didn't want to scare you."

"Your wolf?"

"My wolf is always in my head," Everett explained. "It's

like having another part of me. We can communicate. He likes to get out and run. He likes you."

"So, he's in there right now? Watching?" I looked into his eyes, trying to see the wolf inside his head.

Everett laughed. "Yep. And he's excited that I have you trapped against a tree. He's wagging his tail."

"You both have the same eyes." The golden color was like nothing I had seen before.

"We do. We also both like your scent." He leaned over and took a large inhale along my neck.

I pushed his face away, keeping my fingers on his cheeks and my thumbs along his bottom lip. "Ew, gross, Everett. I was just running. I'm all sweaty."

He shrugged. "Your sweat only strengthens your scent. Trust me—you always smell good, but you smell even better this way."

Everett turned his head and caught my thumb in his mouth. My eyes grew larger as I looked up to meet his. They caught mine, the thread pulling taut. I could feel my thumb roll between his teeth as he applied enough pressure for it to pinch, but not so much that it felt painful. His tongue flicked the tip of my thumb as he closed his lips around the base. The feeling of sharp teeth gave way to the pull of him sucking my thumb deeper into his mouth. I didn't know why this felt so good, but it did. Why was Everett always right?

I squeezed my legs against his waist and began slowly moving up and down his stomach. My running shorts were thin and not much fabric was between me and his bare abdomen. I quickly pulled my thumb out of his mouth and replaced it with my tongue, gliding across his teeth and feeling the sharp points of his canines.

Everett slid my body down a few inches and replaced his hands with his right thigh so that I straddled his leg. One of his hands wound around the back of my head to protect it from the bark of the tree, while the other felt my hardening nipples under my sports bra. He caught my purrs of want in his mouth, swallowing them until I could feel them vibrate deep within him.

I turned feral as his thigh provided the perfect hard surface to rub myself against. My arms found their way around his back, and I used them to guide myself back and forth in short push and pulls that had my body pulsing. The thread that was taut between us now pulled tight, deep between my legs, and threatened to snap at any moment.

My deep breaths turned short and shallow. I gripped my legs tight around Everett's thigh, bracing myself for what was coming. Sounds of release started leaving my lips when Everett dropped his leg that held me up and my feet shot out beneath me, catching me from falling into the dirt.

"What the hell, Everett!" My hands hit his chest as I pushed the rest of him away. I'd been so close, and he'd pulled away again. I didn't know how he was still playing a game of cat and mouse when I was so willing to get caught. Maybe *I* was the cat hunting for the mouse.

"I'm sorry. I got carried away," he said. "I won't have you coming for me for the first time against a tree. Maybe the eighth or ninth time, but not the first."

"I can't take it, Everett!" *Not in the tent, not in my bed, not in the woods!* "I have never been this needy before in my life." It was becoming too much. "Is there something wrong with me? Apparently I don't smell bad, so that can't be it."

"It needs to be perfect, Lyka. I'm not about to take you for the first time in a situation that is anything but perfect."

Everett was smoldering. I could tell he wanted this just as bad as I did, and it was killing him to have to walk away. But it didn't take away any of the frustration I was feeling. It was deep sexual frustration.

"You also made it clear you have work to do," he said. "I wouldn't want to be too much of a distraction."

Like he didn't already do just that. But I didn't want him to stop just yet.

"Who's Lyka? Why do you keep calling me that?" Now that we physically separated, I cooled down. The sweat that glistened on my skin grew cold, causing goose bumps to form on my arms and legs.

"That's what I like to call you," he explained, like it made perfect sense.

"It isn't some other girl you have me confused with?" Why was I suddenly feeling the pings of jealousy? We barely knew each other.

"No, I couldn't confuse you with anyone. You're my only Lyka."

Everett looked into my eyes intensely, making sure I absorbed all the words he was saying. Relief washed over me. At least I was the *only* girl he left unfulfilled.

He kissed me lightly on the cheek and turned around. "I'll let you get back to work saving the world."

Then he started jogging down the trail, leaving me more confused than ever. Tied to that damn thread, I was his personal yo-yo that he could push down and pull up at his leisure.

I ran as fast as I could all the way back to the cabin. I was done feeling this way. Everett had wound me up and refused to help me find relief.

I slammed the door shut to the cabin and stomped down the hallway, glancing in Leo's and Jenny's rooms. They were empty. The door to my room closed harder than I'd intended, making the walls rattle. Stupid Everett and his stupid games. I once again had lost control of myself and played right into his hand. Well, the control he had over me would soon be over.

I stripped out of my running shorts and threw them toward my closet where my laundry basket was. Not caring that I was sweaty, I flopped onto my bed. I was still vibrating with need from the woods. Running home hadn't removed any of the tension that was inside of me. The tension that had been building for the last weeks. It never went away. It just kept building, like one block on top of another. The tower was built so high it was wobbling. I needed the block tower to fall, and the only option was my hand. Maybe after I found relief, Everett's sexual atmosphere wouldn't affect me, and I could control myself around him.

I reached between my legs and found the sensitive spot I was searching for. It didn't take me long to find release. Moaning as I came down from the climax, I realized once again that Everett was right. I was loud. Damn it. Why was I thinking of him again? This little rendezvous in my bed was supposed to rid me of him.

Rolling over, I groaned. I still felt the tension between my legs. My hand had only knocked a couple of blocks off the tower. I knew if I encountered Everett again, I would add even more blocks, and I would find myself in the same situation I'd been in only a couple of minutes ago. What was wrong with me?

CHAPTER TWENTY-TWO

I took a shower and tried to cool off my insides, but that was unsuccessful. Wrapping a towel around myself, I walked back to my room. On my desk was the reminder of the meeting I'd had this morning with Professor Robinson.

Sinking into the desk chair, I laid my head against the cool wood top. This was what defeat looked like. I couldn't do anything right. Everett left me wanting, in the worst way possible. Who was I kidding? I enjoyed it, encouraged it.

I turned my face, letting my other cheek feel the chill of the desk. The more time I spent with Everett, the less time I had to conduct my research. Even thinking about him took me away from my work. I was distracted. Robinson knew that I had been away from the cabin. How long until he connected the dots and found out about the shifters? I couldn't be responsible for outing them.

The plastic bag of brown rot Everett had given me sat on my desk, inches away from my face. I picked it up and rubbed the outside of the plastic bag with my fingers. I'd held on to the rot Everett had found because I didn't know if he had followed the correct procedures when harvesting it, but that made me wonder—had I made a mistake when collecting my own sample? It had been after my first weekend with the shifters that I'd collected the sample I'd given Robinson. Had they already wedged themselves so far into my world that I'd unintentionally broken protocol?

But that couldn't be right. We'd learned proper collection techniques in Botany 101 during our first year on campus, so it was practically muscle memory for me. I knew what I was doing. I had collected that sample correctly. Something else wasn't adding up.

Did everyone notice that I was distracted? If Jenny was mentioning something to her professor and Robinson was concerned, I needed to take a step back and reevaluate my relationship with Everett. It wasn't working. I needed space from the way he made me feel when he was around me. It wasn't worth losing my scholarship over. The thought of moving back in with my parents made my stomach flip.

The small envelope with my mom's loopy handwriting was next to my computer. She'd told me before I'd left to let her know if I needed anything. Right now I needed my mom and whatever advice she could give me. I hadn't talked to her or my dad in a few weeks. A letter postdated a week ago didn't seem sufficient, especially with my dad's health. I needed to call them.

I stuck my head out of my room, looking to see if Jenny or Leo were around. I didn't see anyone, so I made a run for it, bounding down the hallway in my towel, grabbing the new phone and running back to my room, closing the door behind me. I punched in my mom's cell phone number. It rang only once before she answered.

"Hello?"

"It's me, Mom," I said.

"Ismet? Did you hear about my sculptures? Do you want to come view my pieces?" *What?*

"It's *me*, Mom, your daughter, Elise." I pronounced my words and spoke louder.

"Oh, Elise? Is that you?" I rolled my eyes. This was painful.

"Yes, it's me, Mom."

"How are you? I haven't heard from you in so long!"

"I know. I've been busy here."

"Oh, I've been busy too! So busy with my pieces. They're selling quick! With your father's medical bills adding up, it's so nice to have the extra money." *What?*

"What's going on, Mom? Is Dad, okay?"

"What's delicate?" *Oh my god. Help me.*

"Is *Dad* okay?" I asked again.

"Oh, Dad. He's fine now. He broke his femur."

"Why didn't you tell me?"

"I wrote you a letter." I looked at the unopened letter sitting on my desk. "Bessie's doing fine too. Don't worry about her."

I sighed. "I'm not worried about the cat."

"What bucket? You need a bucket?"

Was it the connection or my mother? Definitely my mother. There was no way I could bring up my issues with the university now. She would confuse *probation* with *vacation* and think I was coming home. They had enough going on at home. I would have to figure this out on my own.

"I've got to go, Mom," I said. "Take care of Dad. I'll be home when I can."

"Okay, dear. Thanks for calling!"

The line went static. This was so typical of my mom. Sandwiching important information between fluff, like how the cat was doing, and downplaying the seriousness of my father's illness. I needed to go see them soon and find out how serious my dad's injuries were. It wasn't in me to fully trust them after hiding their money and health problems from me for so long, but with the university breathing down my neck and the mystery of the rot, I didn't know when I could get away.

The package she'd sent me sat on the floor by my desk. I picked it up and carefully opened it. Inside was a sculpture of a wolf sitting on its haunches, its head tilted back, howling at the moon.

Disbelief shook me as I set it on my desk. What was going on? My mom always pulled from her surroundings for inspiration for her sculptures. Were they seeing wolves around their home too? Wolves seemed to be infiltrating all aspects of my life.

I heard the front door swing open, and the wolf researcher herself burst through the doorway. "Time for drinks!" she called out.

I left the letter on my desk. The wolf sculpture I moved to the windowsill next to my plants. I still didn't know what to do about that. My problems were those for tomorrow's Elise to solve. Tonight I needed to get out and blow off some steam. With a clear head, I'd be able to figure everything out tomorrow.

Even though this was supposed to be a chill, *blowing off some steam* night, Jenny asked for some time to get ready before we left. I sat on her bed watching her primp.

"Do you think your guy will be at the bar tonight?" Jenny asked, rubbing her lips together in her tabletop mirror.

"I don't have a guy."

She turned around and cocked her head sideways. "Of course you do. Who else have you spent the last two weekends with?"

I sighed, folding to her theory. "I hope he isn't there. He's a huge tease."

"Oh, well then, screw him. There are other cute guys.

Maybe you should cozy up to one of his friends. That would make him jealous. One guy with him last week was cute. He was big—well, they all are big, but he was especially large with black hair and tattoos." She motioned to her neck. Gavrill.

"I don't think so," I said with a snort. "How about no boys? I think I'll take the weekend off, maybe the rest of the summer off. I have enough experience with the men around here. They're all more trouble than they're worth."

My core pulsed, telling me I was a liar. Even thinking about Everett made my body warm. I was screwed. I just hoped he wouldn't be at the bar tonight, or I would find myself disappointed not being screwed in a different way.

Jenny finished her primping and announced that she was ready to go. Leo wasn't around, and I briefly wondered where he could be. With no Leo to drive us, I offered to drive. We drove the ten miles to No Bars and parked along the side of the building.

I followed Jenny into the bar. Once I saw Everett wasn't in the building, I could finally let out the breath I'd been holding. Exhaling loudly, I walked up to the counter with Jenny to order a drink. She slapped her credit card on the bar and exclaimed that she was opening a tab. We both ordered whiskey sours, and I thanked her for the drink.

Taking the first sip, I looked around the room and saw Kleio sitting at the table with Gavrill and Jack. She smiled and waved eagerly, motioning us to come over and join their table.

I walked over, with Jenny following close behind, whispering into my ear, "That's the cute friend. If you don't want him, I'm going for it."

"What about Leo?" I turned my head and asked her, a little surprised.

"What about Leo? He hasn't been around, and we haven't put labels on anything. It's open season."

Jenny finished whispering to me and made her way to sit down in the empty chair next to Gavrill. He looked annoyed at the intrusion but took a drink of his beer, pretending he was unbothered.

Kleio patted the seat next to her, and I sat down, placing my drink in front of me. "So...how's your week been? How's work? Have you seen Everett?" She bubbled with curiosity.

"I've run into Everett a couple of times. And his wolf once." I glanced at Jenny to make sure she couldn't hear our conversation. Jenny was so engrossed with talking *at* Gavrill that I was sure she wasn't listening.

"You met his wolf?" Kleio seemed taken aback. I hadn't thought it was a big deal, but maybe it was special to see someone's wolf in an instance where they weren't fighting and attacking?

"I didn't get close, but his wolf showed up when I was running, and he ran next to me."

"Oh, someone's got it bad." Her vague language left me with questions as she turned her head and patted Jack's arm as if he knew what she was talking about.

My heart skipped a beat when I saw Kleio's neck. She always wore her strawberry blonde hair down long past her shoulders, but today she had it braided and pulled back. Turning toward Jack had exposed two puncture marks between her neck and her shoulder. They were small but still clearly visible. The puncture wounds didn't seem infected, but they looked fresh enough that the skin looked irritated and red.

I grabbed her forearm and pulled her toward me, suddenly feeling defensive of her. Kleio turned to me and could tell I was desperate to talk to her. She met me in the bathroom, and I turned around, locking the door behind us.

"What's that on your neck, Kleio? Don't lie to me and try to cover up what Jack did."

"You saw?" Kleio's hand shot up to the puncture marks on her neck, and she rushed over to the mirror to examine them.

"Of course I saw the two red marks on your neck, Kleio! We need to tell Everett and let him take care of Jack."

"They are a little red today." She ran her hand over the holes in her neck, looking at them in the mirror and seeming strangely relaxed about the entire thing.

"Maybe you can stay at my cabin with me if you need to get out of the pack house. We can share a bed..."

"Take a breath, Elise." Kleio cut me off. "I always tried to wear my hair down around you so you wouldn't be able to see them."

"What are you talking about?" I asked.

"Everett didn't want you to see the marks," she said.

I took a step back. Everett knew about the marks on her neck? Why were they hiding them from me?

"I know you don't know a lot about Lycans," she explained. "Every Lycan has a mate, somewhere in this world. Someone who balances you—your counterpart. Jack is my mate, and yes, he did this to me."

I stared at her. "Kleio, even if he is your mate or boyfriend or whatever, he shouldn't hurt you."

"He did it to me because I asked him to."

My body seized with her confession. Who would ask for someone to make a deep mark on their body like that?

"There is no escaping your mate. The pull between you is too strong." Kleio walked forward and took my hands in hers. "Part of the mating process for Lycans is marking. There is sex, of course, but marking your mate solidifies the bond."

I looked closer at the two small holes along her shoulder and tried to picture what object could have made them. "How did Jack mark you?" I asked, even though I could guess the answer.

"With his teeth, of course." She flashed her sharp, elongated canines at me.

I shivered at the thought of someone—Everett—biting me on the neck. Surprisingly, the thought wasn't as appalling as I thought it would be. I flashed back to him grazing his fangs along my neck during the harsh kissing, body-consuming, turn-me-to-liquid make-out sessions that I had become accustomed to. His teeth dragging along my skin had done nothing but further turn me on.

"He bit you."

"Yeah, he did, and I bit him back." Kleio winked at me and turned away, heading for the door. "This is becoming too much like the birds-and-the-bees conversation someone has with their parents. Ask Everett all the questions you have—I'm sure he'd love to answer them."

I looked down at my feet, trying to process all this new information. Every time I hung out with Kleio, I learned something new that sent me for a loop. Her footsteps paused, and I lifted my head.

She turned around and walked back toward me, holding my hands again. "Thank you, Elise, for caring enough about me to say something. It means a lot." She squeezed my hands and walked out of the bathroom, heading back to the table.

The door shut, and I leaned against the sink, which dropped an inch, loosening itself from the wall. I quickly backed away with my hands in the air. Kleio hadn't been lying about the broken sink in the bathroom.

I shook my head, laughing to myself. My eyes glanced back at the mirror above the sink. I felt...different. Ever since I met the Cedar Moon Pack, my thoughts about friendship and family had changed. They were friends who supported each other and had each other's backs, even when one of them was in trouble. I had never experienced that before. Previously I'd had friends, probably more like acquaintances, but never had I felt that feeling of unwavering support. I liked Kleio, Gavrill, Jack, and even Kostas. They made me feel like I was a part of their pack.

Something had changed in the last two weeks, and I was starting to think it was me.

CHAPTER TWENTY-THREE

I washed my hands quickly and exited the bathroom. Stopping to look at our table, I saw Jenny was still talking to Gavrill and he was still sitting next to her. I wondered if he was even listening. Kleio had found her way back to Jack, and they sat as close as they could, whispering and cuddling each other. None other than the broody male I was trying to avoid occupied my seat. His dark, shaggy hair and broad shoulders gave him away. He was in a navy-blue T-shirt that heightened the color of the tattoos on his arms.

As if he sensed me, Everett turned around and slowly gazed up my body. He smiled at me as if he was being friendly. I knew it was nothing but a trick. Everett had left me against a tree in the woods today with nothing but excuses. I wasn't about to overlook his actions. I lost my focus when I saw brown round glasses on his face. They made him look even sexier, in an intellectual type of way. Of course he would do that.

I took a deep breath to center myself before I walked over to the table. He patted the seat next to him, and finding the bar had suddenly filled up in the ten minutes I'd been in the bathroom, I had no choice but to sit at the table.

"Nice specs." If I broke the ice and started the conversation, maybe I could take the reins and gain some control.

"They help me see clearly," he said.

"I should've guessed you had vision problems. Your lack of insight and all," I said.

Everett chuckled to himself and ran his hand over his scruffy beard. "When have I been lacking in insight, Elise?"

"Well, these"—I put my finger on the rims of his glasses—"must not work very well. I've been in front of you many times, and you still can't see what I want."

I looked away quickly after I spoke. Where was this banter coming from? I was falling into his trap again. Everett did something to me that made me lose all common sense around him.

He grabbed my fingers from the rim of his glasses and dragged them under his nose, inhaling deeply. I gasped, holding my breath at the sudden interruption of our conversation.

"What did you do, Lyka?" Everett kept my fingers to his nose and continued smelling deeply. The short hairs on his upper lip prickled my fingers.

"What are you talking about?" My fingers probably smelled like whiskey sour and the soap I had washed my hands with a couple of minutes ago in the bathroom.

"Did you pleasure yourself after our run in the woods?" His voice was low and husky. The black pupils surrounded by gold swirls dilated as he waited for an answer.

I tried to pull my hand back, but he kept smelling my fingers. He was enjoying himself. How could he know what I'd done? I had showered and washed my hands multiple times before he just picked them up and smelled them.

I panicked, trying to come up with an appropriate answer.

"I washed my hands." My voice was squeaky and timid, no louder than a whisper.

"Lyka, you forget how good you smell to me," he said. "*That smell won't leave your skin for days. I bet every wolf in here can smell what you did earlier.*"

My face flamed as I looked around the room.

"Are you that desperate for release that you had to use your hand?"

I looked back at Everett, shocked that he was asking me that. My eyes met his, and a wave of confidence came over me. I refused to take his teasing anymore. "Every time I'm with you, you touch me and kiss me and make me want more," I said. "Of course I'm desperate. You haven't helped me finish anything you've started."

Everett growled at my response. It was obviously not what he'd been expecting. We had caught the attention of our table, and Kleio smiled as big as the Cheshire Cat, pleased with what was happening between Everett and me. Jenny looked confused, and her mouth dropped open as Everett lifted me off the chair, cradling me with one of his arms under my shoulders and the other under my knees.

"I can fix that." His voice was confident and steady.

My legs squeezed together, trying to hold in the pressure that was building between them. He nodded at Gavrill and Jack before he stalked out of the bar with me in his arms.

I looked behind his shoulders. The shifters acted as if this was normal behavior. The only one just as shocked as me was Jenny. She stared at us with wide eyes and a gaping mouth.

CHAPTER TWENTY-FOUR

"Keys." Everett's one-word request had me scrambling for my car keys in my purse.

"Jenny. How will Jenny get home?" I couldn't just leave her.

"Gavrill will see that she gets home," he said. "Later. Much later."

Everett set me down next to my car and took the keys out of my hands. He opened the passenger door for me, and I slid into the seat, buckling my seat belt. As he walked around the car, Everett's shadow followed him. The shadow cast an ominous light around the car that sent shivers down my spine. We skidded out of the parking lot, sliding slightly on the gravel road.

I grabbed onto the door handle to steady myself and looked over at Everett. He looked calm and unbothered by his fast speeds.

"Don't you think you should slow down?" The speed the car was going would likely get him sent to jail for the night.

"I don't want to risk you changing your mind," he said.

The confession made my heart skip a beat and butterflies flap wildly in my stomach. Apparently my signals had not been strong enough for him to know that there was no way I would change my mind. I had imagined this happening so many times only to be let down. There was no way I was going to let him get away.

Everett made me into this wild and needy creature that was both meek and assertive. Not afraid to take what *she* wanted, but nervous enough to worry it wouldn't be good enough or it wasn't what *he* wanted. He had sent so many mixed signals to me that I felt chaotic.

We pulled up the driveway, and I jumped out of the car as he slid into park. He walked up behind me and threw me over his shoulder, carrying me the rest of the way into the cabin. I squeaked as the air rushed out of my lungs from the pressure of being held against his massive shoulder.

"Your fucking hand," Everett mumbled as he stomped down the hallway, still holding me like a sack of potatoes over his shoulder. He set me down on my feet carefully once we were in my room.

"It wasn't even that good," I confessed. It had barely taken the edge off, and after touching and talking with Everett, I was right back where I started.

"Of course it wasn't good," he said. "I'm the one who makes you feel good. I'm the one who will help you release the tension that's been driving you insane."

He walked closer to me and wrapped his hands around my back, pulling me close to him. My body hummed with anticipation. "I know how it feels, Elise. I've been feeling the same way."

He pulled my body against his, and I could feel every inch of his need against my stomach. We both groaned at the contact.

Fully clothed, it was still torture. His body leaned over, and his mouth found my ear, planting kisses, following the curve. Every touch of his lips made me feel over sensitized and sent slight shocks down my neck into my chest. I turned my head to meet his eyes. Our noses touched, both breathing deeply.

"Why did you make me wait?" I asked.

"I had to be sure. And I had to make sure everything was perfect for you." Everett looked into my eyes.

"Oh, I know—you don't like to share." I thought back to his previous comments in the tent last weekend.

"You're right, Elise; I won't share. Every shifter in the bar tonight could smell you." He took my hand and guided it between my legs. "Feel that?"

I nodded, my breathing turning shallow. My body pulsed at the lightest touch.

"That is mine. No one else's," he said. "I don't want any other male to even smell you."

My knees buckled at his words. He let go of my hand and grabbed me around the waist, supporting my weight. He was commanding and, in every sense, an alpha. Our eyes locked as I looked up at him.

"I'll forgive you this since you didn't know the proper procedures," he said. "We'll call it Lycan 101. You like learning, right?"

Academic talk in the bedroom? My mind was as mushy as my body, and I had lost all sense of self.

"We'll have to work on proper bathing techniques—since you must not know how to wash properly...maybe in the shower."

Hot steaming water, his slippery body touching mine. His breath was my breath, and his heartbeat was my own. I had gone limp with need. The pulsing between my legs had gotten so strong that one touch might push me over the edge. I was hot —too hot.

Lifting my shirt over my head, the fabric momentarily blinded me. Everett made a move, grabbing my waist and pulling my body toward his. I felt his mouth on my stomach below the sports bra I was wearing. The feeling of his lips touching my skin sent quivers all over my body.

Now I was cold. I needed to feel the warmth of his skin on mine. I finished removing my shirt and threw it onto the ground. Everett helped me out of my bra and started peeling down my leggings. He practically purred with delight when he discovered my lack of underwear. I was suddenly thankful for my dislike of wearing underwear under leggings. One less piece of fabric between me and him.

I stood there naked in front of Everett. Usually shy, I didn't feel that way in front of him. He looked at me as if I was both the most beautiful and delicious thing he had ever seen. His tongue came out of his mouth, licking his lips hungrily.

"This hardly seems fair." I motioned to his clothed body.

"I'm nothing but fair in the bedroom." Everett made quick work of taking his clothes off.

I wet my own lips hungrily as I grazed over his body. In only his briefs, he stood before me. The soft light of the lamp in the room set a glow around him that made him look almost angelic. The low growl that left his lips reminded me that there wasn't an angelic thought in his mind.

Grabbing the waistband of his underwear with his thumbs, he dragged them down, revealing his already fully erect shaft. The sight of it made me blush. He was a large man, and his manhood was in proportion with his body.

I moved around to turn off the lamp. Everett's hand touched the top of mine as I fumbled with the switch. "I want the light on."

I turned to face the naked man behind me. "Why?" Every other dalliance I'd been a part of had been in the dark. It hadn't even entered my mind to keep the light on.

"I want to see you." He wrapped his arms around my waist, pulling me close and cradling me to his body. We still fit together perfectly. "I want to see you writhe for me when I do this."

His hand snaked between our bodies, and his fingers slid between my folds. We both groaned at the sensation.

"And I want to see your face when I stretch you with my cock," he said.

I looked down between us at the impressive member. There wasn't a drop of moisture in my mouth, so I gulped some air.

"And I want to see your body tense when I come inside of you."

Everett pushed me onto the bed. He climbed beside me, lying on his side so I was curled next to him. His hands parted my knees, splaying them open and rendering me completely bare.

I turned to watch his face, tense with anticipation. Everett looked at me, asking for permission to touch me, and I guided his hand between my legs. There wasn't a question that this was what I wanted. He groaned as his fingers dipped between my slit and began sliding around, exploring my most sensitive area.

Our lips found each other's, nipping and biting playfully until his hand brushed against my clit and I yelped with an even amount of surprise and pleasure.

Everett chuckled against my lips in approval. "I love figuring out the puzzle to your pleasure, Lyka. I believe I just found the missing piece."

A moan left my lips as Everett put pressure on the nub,

slowly rubbing circles in the wetness. Wound up from all the times Everett had left me unfulfilled, it wasn't long before I could feel the tension building in my core. My breathing quickened and my legs tensed in readiness of release.

Everett quickly released the pressure of his fingers, and I cried out in frustration. Thoughts of him leaving me unsatisfied yet again ran through my mind, and I sat up, grabbing his arms to keep him close.

"Relax—just relax. I've got you." Everett's smooth tone eased me onto my back.

He resumed his slow teasing by easing a finger inside of me. I groaned, releasing the tension in my muscles and letting him take back control of my pleasure. His thumb found my clit again and began the slow circle of assaults that soon had my back arching. Between his finger making a *come hither* motion inside me and his thumb speeding up the rubbing against me, I moaned. The pressure was building. I felt myself getting closer and closer to the edge.

Everett's lips brushed against my ear. "You will only come with me. Promise me, Elise—your pleasure is mine tonight."

I lifted my hips, grinding them against his hand. My mind went blank, and a soft buzzing sound had replaced my hearing.

"Elise, I need you to promise." His fingers slowed, and I cried out in frustration. I would never touch myself another day in my life if this was what Everett could do with his fingers.

"I promise," I gasped out.

Everett picked up, rubbing me right where he left off. My legs began shaking as the orgasm took over my body. My eyes rolled back, and I moaned loudly against Everett's neck. He kept his fingers moving as I rode out the orgasm, extracting every last pulse.

I came down, opening my eyes against Everett's neck, trying to catch my breath.

"If you had turned the light off, I would have missed the performance." Everett picked up my chin and placed a light kiss against my lips.

"That was no performance," I said. I had never orgasmed as deeply before. There'd been no pretending or performing involved. I had lost control of my body in the most wonderful of ways.

It made me wonder what experience with women Everett had that he could make me feel like that. Any thoughts of other women left my mind when his muscled body climbed on top of me and settled his hips in the space between my legs. His hard erection pressed against my already tender nub, and I compulsorily trembled at the sensation.

Golden eyes met my green ones. The longing and need I could see was nothing but ravenous. Everett wanted me. He wanted to be inside of me. "Are you ready for the second act?"

"I'm on birth control, and I used a condom with—" My mouth got ahead of my brain. I shut up quickly. I grimaced, looking for Everett's reaction. His mouth turned down into a scowl, and the swirls in his eyes turned into cyclones, spinning angrily. Better to have the awkward conversation before than have an even more awkward conversation after.

He sat up and stared down at me. Was Everett mad I had brought it up? I had always been a safety-first type of person, but it could be a mood killer to some people. I should have started this conversation in the car before we'd taken our clothes off.

"Never mention another male in the bedroom again." His voice was deep and demanding. Such an alpha. Everett really didn't share. I guess I didn't want to share either. The thought of where he'd mastered his bedroom skills had gotten my blood boiling a few moments ago.

"Sorry—I won't do that again," I said. I looked for some sheet to cover my body.

Everett ran his hand through his hair and pulled the sheet back to the end of the bed, leaving me lying naked before him. "I had the pack doctor test me the moment I smelled you. There have been no others since."

I smiled at his response. He really had been thinking about me since he'd met me.

"Are you ready?" he asked.

I looked down between my legs at his impressive length. My nerves got the better of me as I imagined how far my body would have to stretch to take him.

Everett clicked his tongue at me, drawing my eyes back to his. "I'll go slow."

I nodded, lying back down on the bed.

"Tell me you want this, Elise. I will only continue if you tell me yes." Practically panting with need, Everett held his member in his hand, stroking it slowly up and down. He waited patiently for my answer.

I nodded again.

"I need to hear you say it." A small bead of liquid puddled on the tip of his cock. His abs tensed as if he was trying to hold it in.

Breathless myself, I whispered, "Yes, I want this."

On his knees between my legs, Everett parted my lips with one hand and guided the head of his erection into me. I could feel my walls stretching around him, submitting.

He stopped and took a deep breath, exhaling loudly. "Fuck, Lyka. I'm not even halfway in and you feel amazing." Inching his cock into me slowly, Everett looked like he was in pain. His face scrunched up and his muscles tensed.

"Am I hurting you?" I couldn't help but ask.

Everett chuckled at my question. "No, Elise. Nothing you

could do in the bedroom could hurt me. I'm trying to control myself. You feel too good. Too wet. Too tight." I tensed my walls involuntarily around Everett. He hissed at me. "Lyka...be careful. I want to last more than a couple of minutes."

I smirked at him. For once, I had the power. I lifted my hips to take the rest of him inside of me. He groaned, and I gasped as his tip hit the deepest part of me. I felt stuffed with him fully inside of me. I stiffened as my body adjusted to the stimulus. Slowly, my muscles that surrounded him relaxed, and we were both able to catch our breaths.

"I don't know how long I can last." Everett's ragged breaths met my ear as he leaned his body to cover mine.

Our bodies fit together perfectly. My breasts tucked into the nook beneath his pectoral muscles, and his hips fell perfectly in the space between my legs. Holding himself up with his elbows, Everett began slowly withdrawing his shaft before he quickly slammed back into me, filling me deeply again. What had started slowly, quickly hastened as Everett found a rhythm. His member filled me completely, rubbing against every part of my walls.

Between thrusts, he lifted my legs to his shoulders, standing in a tall kneeling position before me. My ankles locked between the muscles in his neck and his large trap muscles in his shoulders. The new angle had him hitting the rough spot at the top of my walls, making me see stars. I was moaning at the sensation, unable to control myself.

I arched my back, moving my body away, trying to escape the intense feeling. Everett grabbed my calves and slid my body across the bed toward his in one smooth motion, slamming deep into me again. I screamed this time, coming undone beneath him. The feeling surprised me. It was a deep, guttural feeling to come that quickly, without clitoral stimulation. It had never happened to me before. There was little buildup yet total release.

I lay there trembling with aftershocks as Everett picked me up and held me against his body, his hard cock still inside of me.

"Good girl." Everett smoothed my hair as he held me. "I love watching you."

I caught my breath and my vision cleared. Pushing away from his chest, I looked up at his face. He was smug with pride.

"My turn," Everett whispered into my ear. Laying me back down, he burrowed his scruffy face between my neck and shoulder. It was becoming one of my favorite spots for him to touch.

As he pumped in and out of me slowly, I grabbed onto his shoulders, anticipating his drives.

His lips brushed against my ear. "I won't last much longer." His thrusts increased in intensity, making me moan as his cock brushed against the sensitive spot he had just battered a minute ago.

"Why do you feel so good?" Everett asked between breaths. He got even harder as he continued to plunge in and out of me. Small pulses traveled down his cock, and I knew his release was imminent. He let out a deep growl, and I felt the whoosh of his come inside of me, coating my walls.

Before he lifted himself off my body, Everett whispered quietly into my ear, "Mine."

CHAPTER TWENTY-FIVE

I LAID my head against Everett's chest, listening as his pounding heart came back down to a steady rhythm. I used my fingertips to trace the tattoos that graced his chest. More thick swirls and loops. The patterns soothed my mind, which raced with thoughts about what Everett was thinking and feeling.

"Don't worry about me, Lyka. I'm nothing but fully satisfied."

It was like he'd read my thoughts. My head popped up from his warm chest, and I rested my chin on his pectoral muscles and looked at his face.

His eyes were closed, and the skin across his forehead was relaxed. "I'm sorry if that was shorter than you're used to. I'm trying to get used to how you feel. I find it very hard to control myself."

Giggling at his admission, I snuggled in closer. Everett had made sure I'd found my pleasure, but his own had been short lived. I hadn't given it a thought until he'd mentioned it. It felt good that I had that effect on him.

I changed the subject, not wanting to extend his embarrassment. "Why do you call me Lyka?" My question was one I had already asked, but this time I wanted a definition for the pet name he called me.

"I already told you—it's something I like to call you." Everett opened his eyes and brushed a stray piece of hair out of my face.

"Yeah, but I don't even know what it means. It could mean 'small, dumb female' for all I know."

"Oh, Lyka, you're not a small, dumb girl. Although you're kind of small. And for sure a female." His arms wrapped around me fully, and he rolled on top of me, bracing himself with his hands above me.

I swatted at his chest playfully, wanting an actual answer.

"*Lyka* means a wild, fierce wolf—something I've found you to be."

"I'm not a wolf."

"You don't need to be a wolf to capture the qualities of one." Everett bent his head down and nuzzled that spot between my neck and shoulders.

I couldn't help but purr at the feeling. His lips against my neck and his scruffy beard rubbing against my skin had my already sensitive areas inflamed once again. My hand shot to my neck, putting space between Everett's lips and my skin. He lifted his head and looked at me, puzzled.

"There isn't a...mark there, is there?" I asked. "I didn't feel anything, but Kleio said shifters like to bite their mates, and I saw her mark from Jack tonight and..." I was rambling in my panic. Having sex was fine, but now that I knew about marking, I wasn't sure I was ready for that.

Everett pulled my hand away from my neck and kissed my palm gently. "No, Elise, I didn't mark you."

His answer quelled my panic, but I also found myself

disappointed. The chemistry between Everett and me was undeniable. I couldn't get enough, and I had a hard time staying away from him. The thread between us had never been tighter, and I had a feeling I wouldn't be able to get it untied.

Kleio had told me that Lycans had mates—and if I wasn't his, if he wasn't feeling the same, I knew I would feel crushed.

"I can see the thoughts running through your mind, Elise. They need to stop. I've wanted you since I smelled you at No Bars and Wilder took you home." His body tensed at the memory. "You've been driving me crazy ever since. I can't stay away from you. Now that I've had you, all of you..." He looked down over my naked body lying underneath his. "You're mine."

My breathing stopped. My heart might have stopped too. "Am I your mate?"

The question was simple yet complicated. I wasn't sure which answer I preferred.

"Yes, you're my mate," he said. "I knew it from the moment I saw you, but I had to wait until you were ready." Everett lowered himself onto me. I could feel the warmth of his body envelop me. He planted a kiss on my lips that wasn't rough. It was soft. I moaned into his mouth. "I never thought I would find you. All this time waiting. I should have known that you would be the one to discover me."

"How do you know that it's me?" My question was breathy.

"That thread you spoke of before. The one that was pulling us together?" Everett looked deep into my eyes, remembering our first kiss.

I nodded, remembering as well.

"That's your mating bond reaching out to mine," he said. "I felt it too, my bond reaching to yours. The bonds know when they have met their mate, even before the individuals do." Everett nuzzled into my neck again.

There had been an undeniable pull between us from the

beginning. The thread, or the mating bond, had pulled me to him, even when I'd tried to fight it. I couldn't control it—I didn't want to control it. It was intoxicating.

"Being mated to an alpha is no simple task," Everett whispered into my ear, sending shivers down my neck.

Turning toward him, I licked his cheek with the tip of my tongue until I made it to his ear. "I'm more than up to the job," I whispered into his ear.

It was like something had snapped between us. I had accepted him, us for what we were. Mates.

He groaned, whipping his head around to find my neck, planting kisses along the side. Everett was mine. He wanted me, all of me, and I was more than willing to give. Wrapping my legs around his waist, I lifted my core up to meet his cock that had already recovered from a couple of minutes ago. He groaned at the wetness I dragged along his hard length.

"I want you to know, Elise," he said, his formal tone making me slow down, "I will not mark you until we're both ready. Marking a mate is a powerful ritual that will change your entire life. It links two people together forever and makes one's desire for their mate all-consuming. Once I mark you, there will be little you can do to stay away from me," he continued. "I want to make sure that this what you truly want before you make that sacrifice to me."

I was ready. I was ready now. My body was buzzing with longing underneath Everett's. Ready yet again for him.

"Impatient, my Lyka." Everett's smirk was aggravatingly sexy. "I'll give you what you need, but not that." His fingers brushed along the spot he claimed he would mark one day. "Not today."

I shivered at the anticipation of what his fangs would feel like piercing through my skin.

Everett snaked his hand between our bodies and scooped some of the liquid that was practically dripping out of my slit onto his fingers. He grabbed hold of his hard length and began smoothing the liquid up and down, coating himself. I looked down to watch what he was doing, only for my face to be brought back up to meet his gaze. His large hand cupped my jaw, keeping my head still.

"I want to watch your face as I claim you again now that you know you are my mate," he said.

I barely felt him at my entrance before he plunged into me, filling me completely. There was nothing that could stop the gasp that left my lips at the feeling of being stretched so quickly. It was uncomfortable at first, but once my body got over the shock of the stretch, I wiggled my hips, getting comfortable with him inside of me.

"Lyka, you're so ready for me again."

The wet noises that came from between my legs were something that would have made me embarrassed if not for Everett's genuine delight of them. I moaned his name as he slid in and out of me slowly. I needed more. I always needed more when it came to Everett.

"I shouldn't have stayed away from you for so long, Elise." Everett's breaths were becoming ragged, and his cock was getting even harder inside of me. He was already close to coming. "I'm going to have to fuck you every day to build up a tolerance for you so I can last longer than a couple of minutes."

"Yes." I whimpered as he continued pulling in and out of me methodically.

I could tell he was concentrating on not exploding too quickly. I felt powerful being able to make Everett feel this way. It was incredible that my body could make a man lose control like this. Maybe this was what all mates were like. If it was, I was ready for him to mark me immediately. I lifted my hips to meet his thrusts, and he growled with pleasure.

"Mate, you're going to come with me." He said it in his alpha voice, and I nearly came apart.

Mate. I was his mate, and he was mine. If the mating bond was the reason for all the tension between us, I felt happy that I had discovered how I could release it.

His fingers slid between us and found the sensitive nub between my legs. The muscle memory Everett had was impressive. He remembered exactly what to do to send me over the edge.

My back arched, my body meeting his thrusts that had become uninhabited. I saw stars as my eyes rolled to the back of my head. I might've been screaming? My hearing was momentarily inoperative.

Everett lost all sense of control and grabbed the top of the headboard with both hands, pounding himself into me until he found his release. A loud cracking noise filled the room, and I yelped as he pounded my body deep into the mattress that had abruptly sunken down several inches. His cock continued to pulse inside me as he carefully laid himself on top of me, moving his hands from the headboard back to the bed.

His head nuzzled between my neck and shoulder, teasingly dragging his fangs against my skin. I shuddered at the sensation.

Everett's voice mumbled against my neck. "Don't tell me you're ready to go again, Lyka. I don't know how much more of you I can handle tonight."

"I'm nothing but fully satisfied," I said. I couldn't help but smirk as I used his words from earlier.

Chuckling, Everett lay his body next to mine. "Good night, mate."

He wrapped a muscular arm around me and pulled me next to him so my back was flush with his front. I snuggled in against his warm skin.

The words felt unfamiliar against my lips the first time I said them: "Good night, mate."

CHAPTER TWENTY-SIX

THE SUNLIGHT HIT MY EYELIDS, casting a yellow glow beneath my closed eyes. My body was warm and covered. During the night, I had rolled into a divot in the middle of the mattress created by Everett's large body, and now I found myself cocooned between the wall of the mattress hollow and his warm chest. My muscles had never felt so relaxed. My brain had never been so relaxed. I wanted nothing more than to live forever in this state of meditation.

Breathing in the clean scent of outside air that seemed to radiate from Everett's chest almost sent me back into a deep slumber, had it not been for his arm pulling my waist closer to his. His hard erection pushed against my lower back, ready even after how busy it had been last night. I pushed back against it, sighing.

"See what my mate does to me?" Everett asked. He bent his head down to nuzzle my neck. "You make me insatiable."

I felt light kisses from Everett's soft lips make a line from my shoulder and up my neck to my ear. My head turned to face his, and I planted my own lips on to his. "How'd you sleep?"

The question was rhetorical, but I was genuinely curious. Personally, I had slept like a rock. It had probably been the deepest sleep I had in several years. Maybe it was the release of all the sexual tension that had been building between us, but I had slept great. I couldn't imagine Everett could say the same. My small bed at the cabin barely fit his hulking frame. I could only guess, due to the deep depression in the middle of the mattress, that we probably had broken the bed.

"I'm fully rested, Lyka." Everett pushed his pelvis into my back again to make a point. His morning erection pushed against my spine.

I tried to turn my body around to face him, but I found myself stuck in the bed, unable to move. It ended up being more of a full body wiggle than any rotation.

"Keep moving like that and I'll have you right here and now," he said.

My body froze at his threat. I was sore from last night, not used to a man of Everett's size, but the sore feeling wasn't a bad one. I rubbed my thighs together to test it, and the movement made me pulse between my legs. The soreness felt like a reward from the exertion of last night. I couldn't help it; my body was ready for him again.

"I can sense your desire, Elise. Didn't I tell you that would happen?" Larger than me, Everett could climb out of the mattress pit. I squeaked as my body rolled fully into the depression in his absence. Trapped in the mattress, the alpha easily found his way on top of me. "This bed might not make it through round three, but don't worry—mine at the pack house is much stronger and much bigger. Next time, when I have you on my bed, I will not be so gentle," he promised.

Gentle? Thinking back to last night and the current, sore state of my nether regions, I was curious what Everett was like when he was *rough* in bed.

"We've completed half of the mating process." Kneeling above me, Everett spread my legs apart with his hands, growling deeply at what he found between them. "I can feel you now." He palmed his cock in his hand and guided it to my entrance and inserted slowly. "Not just here..." I hissed at the feeling of him stretching me. There was pain, a dull pain that served as a reminder of the previous night. "But your emotions. I can feel everything." Everett paused. "Am I hurting you?"

"I'm just sore. I'm not used to someone of your...size," I said.

"It'll get better with time. It seems like we both have some things we need to get used to," he said through clenched teeth. "I told you I need more practice with you. Your tight walls do nothing but milk me. We both need to build up our tolerances to each other."

He pulled out and slowly thrust back in. The pain was less this time as my body adjusted. "Are you okay?" he asked gingerly, taking the time to brush a piece of hair off my face.

Smiling up at his concerned face, I crooned, "Practice makes perfect." It was all the permission he needed before he began steadily thrusting into me. Although longer than last night, it wasn't long before Everett began breathing heavily and whispering my name against my neck. I could feel him pulsing inside of me, filling me for the third time in the last twenty-four hours. These shifters were persistent.

"I'm improving, Lyka. I wasn't joking when I told you I need you every day," Everett said. "You're like a drug. I can only take so much of you, but slowly I'll build my tolerance to your tight walls, and soon I'll fuck you all night and day."

The quick sex didn't bother me. I was sore, and the fast sex had relieved some of the feeling. It was Everett's ability to talk so openly about our sex that threw me. Even having a mother like mine hadn't prepared me for his openness.

"Are all of you shifters so expletive?" I asked.

Everett lay down after pulling himself out of me. "What's expletive about sex? It's natural." He sounded just like my mother. I made a mental note to never introduce them.

"I guess I'm not used to it. I don't usually talk about sex with my partners," I said.

Propped up on an elbow, he played with my hair. "You don't talk about sex with your partners? Well, now you do. How do you expect to have good sex without talking? Oh, wait...have you never had good sex before?"

I scoffed and smacked his chest playfully. "Nope, never in my life."

"You're a terrible liar, Lyka." Everett leaned in and grabbed my chin. "You'll find *us shifters* to be very open and very good at sex. Another thing you'll have to get used to." He planted a kiss on my lips. I could smell his body again. Damn pheromones.

"I have to go," Everett said. "Today starts the last weekend of the tournament."

I groaned as I tried to roll over. Unable to move and still stuck in the mattress hole, I stuck my arms up, asking for help. He easily climbed out of the bed and lifted me up out of the depression.

We stood next to the bed, looking at the mattress. It looked like a hard-shell taco. Everett's massive body must have bent the mattress coils in such a way that there was no fixing it.

He smirked, catching my eyes. "Whoops."

"It's not even my bed!" I screeched.

I couldn't imagine how I would explain the state of the bed to Professor Robinson. I was already in enough trouble with him with the sneaking out and accusations of falsifying data. What had happened last night was the opposite of my strategy to fix everything with the university. But I couldn't deny the pull between us—it was too strong. Everett was a part of me now. By claiming me as his mate, he was also inheriting my problems. He had shown me that he was just invested in saving this forest as I was. We could be a team, two advocates saving the forest together. My heart warmed at the thought.

Everett stripped the sheets from the bed and handed them to me. Standing there with a mound of sheets in my arms, I watched as he easily flipped the mattress over. Now it looked like a small mountain, bowed instead of concave, but I could try to flatten it by putting my textbooks on top of it. I threw the sheets on top of the bare mattress to deal with later.

We quickly got dressed and opened the door to my room. The cabin was quiet. Jenny's room was still empty. I wondered what had happened between her and Gavrill. Leo's door was closed, and I grimaced, hoping he hadn't heard any of the activity in my room last night. Or this morning.

Before Everett opened the front door, he pulled me in for a deep kiss. It was like he was still starved for me. I kissed him back just as hungrily.

I watched him walk out the door. For a minute, I wondered how he was going to get home without a car, but then I remembered—he could run just as fast as a car in his wolf form. It wasn't a shock when he disappeared behind a tree, the black wolf with gold eyes appearing a moment later from behind the same tree. It looked back at me before it ran into the woods.

CHAPTER TWENTY-SEVEN

With Everett gone, I was ready to listen to what Leo had to say. Everett would be back Sunday after the tournament was over. I had all weekend to get some research done, and I couldn't waste any more time. My mantra sounded like a broken record in my head.

I walked back down the hall and knocked on Leo's door quietly at first, in case he was sleeping. The door wasn't latched closed, and it creaked open slowly. He was at his desk writing in his notebook, unaware that his door had opened. I put a foot in the room and called his name softly so as not to scare him. He whipped around in his chair, suddenly aware of my presence.

"Leo?"

"Elise! Sorry I didn't hear you." Leo looked lost. Dark bags hung under his eyes. "I'm so confused about this rot. I've been plotting where I found it on a map, and I can't figure out the pattern. Usually decay travels through waterways or underground in groundwater, but all the rot on Daniels' land is coming from a tree on his property. It makes no sense." He was visibly flustered. I had never seen him ramble like this before.

"Slow down, Leo. Show me what you have," I said, walking over to his desk. Leo moved aside from the map he was plotting on, and I leaned over the desk to look at it. Hand drawn by him, the map was very detailed. "Did you minor in cartography?"

Leo shook his head, unable to follow my jest. "Look, Elise. I've been meeting with the property owner, Charles Daniels, for the last week or so, and he's just as confused as I am," he said. "He asked if I knew anyone from the university who knew more about plant life and conservation science, and I told him you were already looking into the rot. He wants to meet you. It's all over his property, the rot. It's the worse around this giant oak tree here."

Leo pointed to a circle on the map that denoted the tree. He had carefully filled in the land where the rot had spread with a brown-colored pencil. Indeed, the rot was thickest surrounding the tree and thinned out farther away from the tree.

I took note on the map of where I had taken my samples from—about a mile away from the tree. I obviously needed to see the tree. I also wanted to know more about this Charles Daniels. I had never been one to stray from a challenge.

"This is good, Leo." I patted him on the back. "Can you bring me to the tree so I can get some samples? I think you're right that this is the source. All the rot seems to begin at this tree. It could be traveling along the root system."

Leo looked back at me with a skeptical face. Even I wasn't confident in that answer. I'd found rot a mile away from the tree. I didn't know of any oak tree whose roots stretched that far. Until I could investigate it myself, I couldn't imagine what I would find.

"We can go right now." He began packing up his backpack. "Daniels is always around. I'm sure he'll want to get your opinion."

I nodded and turned back to my room to retrieve my backpack. According to Leo's map, it would be at least a five-mile hike to the tree. I grabbed my trail shoes and a shirt to go with my leggings, then tied up my hair.

We set off on the trail with Leo leading the way. He seemed more relieved now that I was coming with him to see the tree firsthand. I almost felt bad that I had made him wait. The stress of his research must've been really getting to him.

His hair was untied, and it flew around his face as he looked down at his feet to avoid tripping on the rocky trail. I caught up with him, matching his brisk pace. The trail was wide enough for us to walk side by side, and I took advantage of the wide berth.

"So, what do you know about this Charles Daniels?" I was hesitant to talk to any other locals. My past run-ins with them had led to kidnapping and bloody tournaments. Leo had said he'd spent a lot of time researching this week on Charles Daniels's land, and it seemed like he hadn't experienced anything like I had yet, so maybe Daniels was just a regular guy.

"He came up to me about a week ago when I was knee deep in a pond on his property," Leo said. "I didn't know it was his property, and I apologized and offered to leave. He insisted I could stay as long as I looked at a tree on his property that was dying. I told him that wasn't my area of expertise, and he asked if I knew anyone who could help. I instantly thought of you and told him I knew someone. He wanted me to go get you that day, but I told him I wanted to see the tree first.

"When he brought me to the tree," Leo continued, "I knew

it was something that you would want to see. This past week, knowing you've been busy, I've been trying to figure out how the rot is spreading. I thought I could do it myself since most diseases can be traced to water, but I haven't been able to find any answers."

I looked at Leo's frustrated face with one of understanding. It was easy to remember all the times I had been there too, thick in the research, unable to find any solutions.

"Daniels has been getting impatient about wanting to meet you, since you're the expert," he said. "He'll be happy to see you."

A strange feeling came over me at the way Leo talked about Daniels. He seemed pushy and confused about how research worked. Solutions were hard to find. Often it took lots of data and analysis to find actual answers, and while I had some expertise, I was still just a grad student. There was no guarantee I would be able to do anything for him.

Nevertheless, I reached out and patted Leo's shoulder. "I'll do my best to help." He was tense but nodded in appreciation.

We came to the rocky avalanche across the trail, and I had flashbacks of Wilder telling me to turn around a couple weeks ago. Stupid Wilder and his stupid chivalrous act. He had just wanted to get into my pants. Warn the pretty girl that danger was ahead, and she'd fawn over you in gratitude. Too bad for me it had worked. Lesson learned.

Leo and I carefully climbed over the mess of rocks that littered the path. Thankful for my thicker trail shoes, I made my way across the rocks unscathed. Leo, although slower, followed behind, making his way over the rocks. He climbed over the rocks in a certain pattern that made me believe he had come this way many times before.

As we continued along the path, it became narrower, and we

had to walk single file. I let Leo lead the way, and our conversation diminished. The crunch of our footsteps and bird calls floating through the woods filled my ears as we got into a walking rhythm.

Miles went by as I flipped through the mental catalog of my research findings so far, which was pretty much nothing. My samples had brought back no results and had landed me in hot water with the university. Hoping that I would find something that could save my reputation kept me walking, one foot in front of another.

A few miles in, the ground surrounding the trail became littered with splotches of brown. Every fifty feet in, the rot became more and more prevalent. The spots of rot went from the size of a coffee mug to a basketball to a small car. Soon there was less green on the forest floor and more brown.

I stopped walking to squat down on the edge of the trail. Leo, hearing the loss of my footsteps behind him, stopped as well. My fingers reached out and brushed the brown foliage. Reacting as my samples had, the leaves crumbled beneath my fingertips and turned to a fine dust.

I looked up at Leo. "This is the worst I've seen."

He nodded and turned forward, continuing on the trail. I followed, interested in what I would find ahead.

The canopy of the giant oak tree blocked the sun from the sky with its thick branches and broad leaves. We weren't even to the trunk of the tree yet; I could see how large it was. The ground was completely brown. Each of my footsteps caused a mound of dust to poof over my shoes as the pressure of my footsteps pummeled the leaves beneath. Leo and I had to watch where we walked, dodging the giant tree's roots that weaved above and below the ground, making small bumps that were perfect to sprain an ankle on.

"This is it." Leo motioned to the trunk of the giant oak a

few feet ahead of us. I'd been so busy watching my footing, I hadn't seen it coming.

"Amazing." The tree must have been a couple hundred years old. Its bark was thick and strong, and its branches were large enough to support a complete set of swings. Any child would be lucky to have a tree like this in their backyard.

Walking forward, I dropped my backpack onto the ground near the tree, then ran my hand down the bumpy bark of the tree. It was so majestic that I felt the need to touch it. A tiny zap hit my hand as I laid it on the bark, and I jumped back, pulling my hand away quickly. I turned my hand to look at my palm, but there was no red mark, no inclination that it had injured me. Leo looked at me curiously and walked over to where I was standing.

"Hey there!" We both jumped at the loud voice and turned around, keeping our backs to the tree. A tall man with dark brown hair and a mischievous smile walked out from behind some trees. A baseball cap covered his head, thick black glasses outlined his eyes, and a long brown beard covered his chin, but I knew that face anywhere.

"Hey, Daniels. I brought my colleague, Elise, with me today. I think she can help me figure out what's going on with your property." Leo motioned to introduce us. I unfortunately didn't need any introducing.

"Charles Daniels? Is this what you're going by nowadays?" My blood was pumping.

"What, Elise? You aren't into a little role-play?" His smooth, deep voice now made me nauseous.

"Wilder! What are you doing out here?"

His presence and smug attitude had thrown me for a loop. After our initial encounter, he had been nothing but standoffish and quiet toward me, acting like nothing more than a grumpy teenager. Wilder stood before me, now a confident man. That made me nervous.

"I hoped he would bring you. I was told you're the expert in all things...nature." Wilder motioned to the surrounding trees. "It took some convincing, didn't it, Leo? Lots of late nights with you trying to figure out what was going on."

Leo stood still, taking in what he was saying.

"I was patient with you, let you figure out that you couldn't solve the mystery of what is happening in these woods," Wilder continued. "I knew you would eventually bring her."

Leo looked at me with wide eyes. "You two know each other?"

I gave him an annoyed look. He must have been too far down Jenny's throat that night to notice me and Wilder. Although I couldn't completely blame him—Wilder looked different. His long beard changed the shape of his face.

"Yeah, we unfortunately do," I said, looking at Wilder with disgust.

He walked toward us, strolling slowly as if he already had us trapped. "I don't remember it being so unfortunate. Maybe only unfortunate that we got so rudely interrupted in the morning."

Wilder's eyebrows lifted in anticipation of my reaction. I tried to back away, only to trip over a large root and run my back into the rough bark of the oak tree behind me. Electricity zapped at my back where I touched the tree. "Now that I have you here, Fumbles..." I gagged at the nickname. "I was wondering if you could look at my tree here. It's been causing all sorts of trouble in the forest."

I looked down at my feet and the brown dust that I had made with my footsteps. "I would need to take samples and bring them back to the university. Then I would have to compare data from..." I started.

"I don't have time for that!" Wilder roared loud enough that several birds flew away from their nearby perches. "Where's the stone?"

His question threatened me like I knew the answer. My silent shock was enough to further anger Wilder. "Where's the stone, Elise?" he said again. "I know you have it. I could smell it on you the first night we met."

My mind raced, trying to figure out what stone Wilder was referring to. I kept coming up blank.

"I'm a tracker, remember? The best in the pack. I can smell everything."

"I don't know what you're talking about, Wilder. I don't have any stones."

Unhinged, he stomped toward me, reaching into his waistband and pulling out a knife. His face reddened, and small beads of sweat popped out of his forehead.

I pressed myself further against the tree, wrapping the back of my body against it. The fear flowing through me numbed my back to the pricks of power coming from the tree. Wilder grabbed my chin with his entire hand and pulled my face up to meet his, inches apart. I could feel the icy blade of the knife resting against my throat, could see the angry veins protruding from his skin.

"Where is it?" he asked in a quiet voice then, and I wasn't sure which was scarier.

Unable to turn my head because of the knife at my neck, I couldn't see Leo standing next to me against the tree, but I could hear him. His voice started as a quiet monotone chant saying "*Stop*" over and over, like something an unsure child would do. "*Stop! Stop!*"

Wilder and I froze at his chants as they got louder.

"*Stop! Stop! Stop!*" Leo was always so relaxed and had such a passive personality that this type of confrontation had to be out of his comfort zone.

Time slowed. From what I could sense under Wilder's knife, Leo was standing against the tree next to me yelling one minute and the next, he wasn't.

I felt a breeze as he twisted off the tree and flung himself haphazardly across Wilder's back. His eyes met mine from across Wilder's shoulder, scared yet determined. The knife left my throat as Wilder used his arm to fling Leo easily off his back. With no weapon, Leo was unmatched against Wilder. He landed in a ball on the ground, hitting his head on one of the raised tree roots, then he groaned and rolled onto his back.

"Fucking idiot!" Wilder cursed as he turned away from me and stomped toward my roommate's limp body. Free of the knife, I shuffled away from the tree, trying to figure out an escape. Leo moaned as Wilder picked him up by the armpits.

"Leo!" I yelled, trying to gauge how conscious he was. He mumbled several jumbled words in response.

"Let him go, Wilder!"

As if my words meant nothing, he laughed. "I don't think I will. He served his purpose, bringing you here, away from your dear Everett's protection."

The thought of Everett made my heart pump faster. If only he were here right now.

"He just attacked me. And to think I was going to let him go home once I got the stone from you." Wilder let go of Leo's arms, letting him fall to his knees. Leo's body slumped over, but with quick reflexes, he caught his upper body with his hands. "No one attacks me. I am not weak. I am worthy."

Listening to Wilder spout off nonsense made my muscles tense. I walked toward where Leo's body lay hunched over on the ground.

"Stay back, Elise. Everyone will get what's coming for

them." The knife Wilder held in his hand reflected in the sunlight that peeked through the canopy of the trees.

I froze as he took a step over toward where Leo was and lifted his head up by his long hair. Leo groaned, still half-conscious from the hit to the head. With a practiced flick of the knife, bright red blood spilled from Leo's neck. It happened so fast I could do nothing but stand there, fully in shock. It wasn't until Wilder let go of his hair and let his lifeless body slump to the ground that I screamed.

CHAPTER TWENTY-EIGHT

Wilder killed Leo. Wilder killed Leo. Leo is dead. He's dead.

My mind raced with what I'd just seen. I could barely put thoughts into words, so I just screamed. With a bloody hand, Wilder grabbed my forearm and dragged me away from Leo's body that lay in a growing puddle of blood. My legs couldn't hold my weight as I relied on Wilder's arm to support me.

Unfazed by what he'd just done, Wilder spoke to me in a smug voice. "I tried to play nice. I asked you where the Lifestone was. All you had to do was give it to me, and your friend would have lived." I gasped, trying to listen to Wilder between the screams that left my throat. "Now someone else wants to talk to you. Maybe you'll listen to them."

I dry heaved as I dangled in his grasp. The iron smell of Leo's blood had reached my nose, and I did all I could to keep the contents of my stomach inside of me. The sound of rustling trees to my right gave way to two giant white paws that were in stark contrast to the brown floor of the forest. Either unaware or uncaring, the white wolf walked through the puddle of blood next to Leo's body, turning its paws a pink color.

"True Alpha." Wilder bent down to one knee, bringing me with him. He bent his neck to the side in submission. I struggled against his grip, but he held true.

The True Alpha shifted in front of us. Bent legs elongated, and giant paws contracted into human hands. A human face replaced the animal snout, and it looked nothing but pleased with what it saw. "Finally, Wilder, you obey me." The True Alpha's voice was low and grave.

"Of course, Alpha. I'm yours to command," he said.

I looked at Wilder in surprise. Since when did he answer to the True Alpha? He seemed like more of a loner type.

"She claims to not have the stone, but I don't believe her. I can smell it on her. I thought better than to search her before you arrived." Wilder pushed me forward, handing me over to the True Alpha, who grabbed my other forearm and pulled me close to him.

His grip was crushing, and I whimpered at the feeling. "So, you're the human who stole my son's heart." He took a deep sniff of my body, looking me up and down.

I was tired of being smelled. My fight instinct kicked in, and I raised my foot to kick him in the shin. I was too slow as a human, and the True Alpha easily dodged my attempt.

"Tsk, tsk. Is that the way you treat your father-in-law?" I paused at the revelation. "You think I didn't know you're my son's mate? I know my son very well, although he may not admit it. I tried to keep you away from him from the beginning." He eyed Wilder with a look of disgust.

"I'm sorry, True Alpha. I tried to make it up to you by bringing her here now. Everett is away at Camp, and..."

"He won't be for long. Not after you scared her by ending her little friend over there." The True Alpha motioned to Leo's dead body. "I expect Everett will be here shortly."

I looked between them. The tension between the two wolves was high.

"I tried to fix my mistake, True Alpha. I brought her here for you," Wilder groveled.

"If you had kept your dick in your pants like a good boy, I wouldn't be in this situation having to challenge my son over his mate," the True Alpha snapped. "You were supposed to bring her straight to me that night. Instead you had some fun with her—so much fun that you forgot your duty all together. She met Everett, and any chance of leaving my son out of this vanished."

My thoughts ran wild. Wilder had been instructed to bring me to the True Alpha the night we'd met at No Bars? Then Everett had found us the following morning when he'd come to bring Wilder to Camp. He'd ruined the True Alpha's plans to keep me from ever meeting Everett.

Out of all the things to be mad about, it was that he had tried to keep me from Everett that had my blood boiling. I pulled against the True Alpha's grip. He didn't even flinch at the movement.

A loud growl echoed through the woods as branches came crashing down off trees and the surrounding trees vibrated.

"Right on cue." The True Alpha looked irked as Everett's large black wolf ran into the clearing.

Quickly shifting, Everett stood before his father. I could tell from the look in his eyes that he was extremely unhappy that his father was holding me so close.

"Elise, are you okay?" he asked, scanning my body up and down, looking for injuries. I was sure I looked like a wreck. Red, bloodshot eyes and snot dripping down my face from crying and screaming.

"I'm fine," I assured him while pulling on his father's grip.

Satisfied with my answer, Everett stalked over to where we were standing, imposing his enormous figure over his father's. "Give me my mate, Father." His voice was authoritative and demanding. Any wolf in his pack would have handed me over before he had finished speaking.

The True Alpha was in a hierarchy all his own and pulsed in amusement at Everett's command. "I would gladly hand over your precious mate, my son, but she has something I need. And until she gives it to me, I will hold on to her." His answer was just as commanding.

"I don't have your stupid stone!" I yelled directly at the True Alpha, my voice hoarse from screaming earlier.

Everett looked between his father and me, confused.

"Oh, but you do, little wolf. I can smell it on you. Wilder here can too." The True Alpha motioned to Wilder, who nodded in agreement. Tracker. Jack had said the True Alpha was a tracker.

Everett set his sights on Wilder, seemingly just realizing that he was present. "What the fuck are you doing here, Wilder?"

He shifted his weight between his feet nervously before answering. "Following your father's commands."

Everett snarled in disgust. "You follow my commands. You're a member of my pack."

"A member of your pack only in tradition! You've never offered to help me! To help me become whole!" Wilder was spitting mad. The tension in this relationship clearly ran deep.

Everett calmed a bit and spoke like a concerned father would. "I can't help you get your fangs, Wilder. It was something you weren't born with. You have other skills that help the pack. Hands down, you're our best tracker. You don't need fangs to be a real wolf."

My heart thumped loudly as I listened to his kind words.

Wilder smiled knowingly, as if he had Everett bested. "Oh, but you forget. You're so wrapped up in your own she-wolf to realize that I can never be a real wolf without my fangs. I can never claim a mate." Everett seemed lost for words at Wilder's statement. "Your father offered to help me get in touch with others who can help me become whole if I brought Elise to him. I did it to have what you have—a chance at a mate. I won't ever apologize for that."

In a way, I felt for Wilder. Even after his second attempted kidnapping of me. I wouldn't want anyone to miss out on the chance of feeling what Everett and I felt when we were together. Maybe my heart was too soft.

But his confession met deaf ears with Everett. "Witches, Wilder? You're going to the witches for help?" He laughed deeply. "What a joke that is. My father fed you that garbage about the witches helping our kind. Let me guess, he said he would put in a good word for you? Set up a meeting?" Wilder's face turned red. "Let me tell you a little secret." Everett's voice lowered to a loud whisper. "My father doesn't know any witches. Our packs haven't seen one in a hundred years."

Wilder stumbled backward at the words. It was not the rebuttal he'd been expecting. He looked to the True Alpha for confirmation of Everett's words, and the True Alpha's silence said enough.

Gray fur sprouted from his shoulders and black claws grew from his fingernail beds as he shifted. His clothing fell beneath him as he fully transitioned, sitting on his haunches. Lifting his snout to the sky, Wilder let out a haunting howl that sent shivers down my back. I must have shaken physically because Everett's father tightened his grip. The sadness of the howl made its way deep into my bones, and I could feel the disappointment Wilder was feeling. Without a second glance, he retreated into the woods, picking up his pace as he fled.

"Why did you lie to him, Father?" Everett stalked over to his father and me. He held his broad shoulders high authoritatively. I guessed this wasn't the first disagreement he and his father had had. "You know as well as I do—we haven't had contact with the *witches* in decades." He snarled as he spoke, his canines pushing past his lips.

"Preying on the weakest member of my pack to do your dirty work..." Everett spat at his father's feet. "I always thought you were better than that."

The closer he walked toward us, the better I could see the dark gold of his eyes. The swirls that usually spun idly around his irises were still. Black claws peeked out of his clenched fists; he was ready to shift at any time.

"You're the one who keeps a wolf without fangs in your pack. Only as a favor to Beta Gavrill. It makes you weak, Everett," the True Alpha said. "A son of the True Alpha cannot be weak. You should thank me for weeding him out. The pack is better off without him."

The True Alpha's grip tightened on my arm as he spoke. He seemed unaware that his own claws were extending, piercing my skin. I could tell Everett was continuing to get angrier with every single word he spoke.

"Your ineptitude embarrasses me. The land I gifted to you is dying." The True Alpha motioned to the brown ground surrounding us with his free hand. "You have the Lifestone right under your nose." I shrieked as he pulled me forward and shook me in front of Everett. "Your land is dying, yet you do *nothing!*"

Everett's nostrils flared as he tried to keep his composure in front of his father.

"A weak leader," he said. "You're a weak leader who's done nothing to save your pack's land. I'm ashamed to call you my son."

Something snapped in Everett's composure. His claws fully lengthened, and black fur started spouting from his arms. Canines elongated in his mouth. He lunged at his father, careful to attack him away from where I was being held.

Laughing, the True Alpha batted him away with a white-clawed paw, having partially shifted. "You'll have to try harder than that."

Everett's voice was nothing but a growl. "I don't want to hurt you, Father. Just give me my mate." Crouched on all fours, he continued shifting. Large black paws held his body up, black shiny claws digging into the ground. His arms had black fur on them, as did the bottom half of his legs. He was shaking so hard with the effort to stay in his human form that it looked painful.

His father looked and sounded fully entertained. He hadn't seemed so enthused even at the opening of the Deca Tournament. "Oh, I think I will keep your little wolf. You see, I know what's best for the pack. I know we must make sacrifices."

My breathing stopped and my body froze at the last word.

"This little wolf is not what she seems." He lifted my body like I was a rag doll and held me dangling by my arm as I squirmed. A low growl emanated from Everett's throat. "I smelled her when she entered your land. An old breed. Not a lot of wolf blood flowing through her veins, yet it is still there."

"I've never smelled wolf in her." Everett came closer and took a deep breath through his nose, smelling me.

The True Alpha lowered me to the ground, and I stumbled, trying to find my footing. "Of course not. You're too intrigued by the *other* smells emitting from your mate." I gave him a disgusted look, and I once again tried to pull away. "But I can smell the small amount of wolf blood in her. I would guess there hasn't been a fully bred wolf in her family for generations. But there is wolf in her."

"I am not a wolf!" Screaming in frustration, I tried to pull away again. I didn't get anywhere, just received more cuts on my arm from his claws. Everett prowled closer, growling at his father.

"You can't help what you are, little wolf, but you can help me." The True Alpha tried a different tactic, speaking at me slowly, in a soft tone. "Give me the stone. I can smell it on you."

"I don't have the fucking stone!" My frustration was reaching an all-time high. Everyone asking me for the stone, the one thing that would save me, the one thing I didn't have.

"I've been searching for the stone for a hundred years," the True Alpha said. "Ever since the witches took the stone from the tree, the land has been dying. The balance between life and death is crumbling. I'm sure you've noticed the surrounding death? The void of new life?" He gestured around the forest.

Walking toward Everett, the True Alpha dragged me along behind him. "Why do you think I continue the Deca Tournament? I send our best wolves to our many pack forests to search for the stone." My body paused my struggle against the True Alpha, listening to his declaration. "I gave these lands to you, son. For you to rule and heal. Yet you did nothing, let the land continue to die around you. Soon there will be nothing left for you to rule."

"I was told the Lifestone was nothing more than legend. A scary bedtime story involving witches and the death of pack lands," Everett said. He had also gone still, listening to his father.

"Your mother did have a penchant for telling you stories. You ate them up as a pup. Too bad your mother was so soft. She made you soft—too soft to see what's right in front of you."

The talk of his mother had Everett shifting further. Two black ears popped up out of his head, his human ears sinking into his skull.

His father continued his discourse. "I knew the stone

would find its way back. The witches love finding new ways to trick us. This time putting the stone right under our noses, with you being too much in lust to find it. I'm sure Matilda is sitting back laughing, watching this circus."

His hand squeezed harder, plunging his nails deeper into my arm. I gasped as warm red liquid dripped down my arm and off my fingers, landing in a small puddle on the ground. "I'll save your land for you because I am a leader, one who puts his pack before anything else. Maybe this will be the tale you'll remember instead of the ones your mother told you."

The True Alpha turned to me. "One more chance, little wolf. Give me the stone, or I will go searching for it."

Glancing rapidly between Everett and his father, I looked for guidance. I didn't have a stone with me or anything else but the clothes on my body. I was wearing a sports bra, leggings, and a T-shirt.

"I don't have it." My eyes squeezed closed. I didn't want to see what was coming.

A sharp claw hooked the top of my shirt at the collarbone and made quick work, slicing it down my torso. The two halves of my shirt flapped away from my body, exposing my bare stomach and sports bra. Between my tight leggings and bra, there was nowhere else I could hide the stone. I opened my eyes, looking down at my bare torso. Using one hand, I tried to collect the two flaps of my shirt to cover myself.

The True Alpha chuckled at my attempts at modesty. "Not there. I wonder if you're hiding it lower..." He extended a claw toward the waistband of my leggings as I pulled myself as far away as I could, shrieking and flapping my arms like a wounded bird.

This was Everett's last straw. He shifted quickly into his full wolf and leapt at his father, looking terrifying. Long white teeth dripping with saliva and foam snapped close to the True Alpha's arm.

His father grabbed onto a chunk of black fur and threw Everett's wolf into a nearby tree. The movement took more effort than the first time he'd swatted at Everett. I was still in his clutches, being flung around with the momentum it took to drive Everett's wolf into a tree.

Everett let out a yelp as his head hit the tree. His body slumped over on the ground, unconscious.

"Everett!" I cried out, seeing his large, black furry body limp.

A tremor rocked my brain, and the world around me shook. I held my hand against my head, trying to stabilize myself. It felt like a warning. Maybe this was part of the mating bond that felt emotions and pain. My mate was lying unconscious on the ground, and I was having a physical reaction to his pain.

As I rebalanced myself, the True Alpha stood beside me, growling at his son. I took a moment to take stock of the situation before me. If Everett, who was an alpha wolf, couldn't take down his father, what chance did I have? There was no blood around Everett's head, and I hoped his lack of consciousness would only be temporary. I was on my own for now.

The True Alpha had a look of confusion on his face, his mouth set in a scowl. He looked up and down my body, trying to determine where I could have hidden the stone. His eyes followed the trail of blood that was still dripping out of my arm where his nails had embedded into my skin. With his other hand, he swiped a drop of blood off my fingers before it hit the ground. Bringing his fingers to his nose, he sniffed the blood before opening his mouth and rubbing it into his pink gums.

"I should have known. You have the power of the stone inside of you." He paced back and forth in the clearing, dragging me along with him. "That is why you could heal my son so quickly during the tournament."

I looked down at my body, looking for any sign of this Lifestone inside of me. I didn't feel any different. Healing and growing plants was just something I enjoyed, something I had learned to be good at. He must've been just as lost as Wilder. His eyes looked like Wilder's had—crazed and jumpy. I needed Everett to wake up.

I tried to channel my fear, though I didn't know what I was doing. Squinting at his body, I tried to send my fear to him mentally. Maybe sending my fear along the mating bond would wake him.

"You must have it hidden in a different location. Somewhere you can take the stone out and hold it, letting the power seep into your bloodstream. I will find it, little wolf. Don't you worry." The True Alpha held me at an arm's length away, staring at me knowingly. "You're just another clue in this scavenger hunt I'm on."

He dragged me toward the giant oak tree where the rot flowed from. I dug my heels into the ground the best I could to slow him, but it didn't work.

"Your blood will do for now. It will temporarily heal the forest until I can find the Lifestone and replace it." He threw me back against the oak tree.

Terrified, I watched as his index finger extended, sporting a long, sharp claw he clearly intended to bleed me with. Below my feet was a hole in the dirt at the trunk of the tree, and next to it was a black rock the size of a baseball.

"That's where you should aim." Everett's father pointed toward the empty hole where the missing Lifestone was supposed to rest. "There must be balance, Elise. I apologize, but sacrificing you is necessary to restore some stability."

I squirmed against the tree, throwing my body haphazardly

around in a last-ditch effort to escape. "Everett! Wake up!" I yelled. I only ended up tiring myself, cutting up my back against the hard bark of the tree.

"When he realizes that you have been sacrificed, he'll be upset with me. But he'll eventually thank me," the True Alpha said. "It's for the good of the pack."

I let out a guttural scream as the True Alpha manipulated my body so my blood would run into the empty hole when he cut me open. I wasn't willing to be sacrificed for some magical missing rock. His hand moved from my arm to around my neck, gripping it tightly. My arms dripped blood from the gashes that his had claws left. My airway constricted to where I could only draw in a thin stream of oxygen. He pushed the side of his hip against my pelvis, rendering me immobile. I grabbed his arm that was holding my neck with my hands, scratching and pulling. Anything to get him to release me.

"Keep squirming, little wolf. Your increased heartbeat will make the blood flow quicker." With his free hand, he took a single black claw and held it to the largest artery in my neck.

I could feel my blood pulsing underneath his finger. I squeezed my eyes shut, still scratching and grabbing at his arm.

A sharp pain traveled through my body as the claw sliced through my neck. Blood flowed freely out of the cut, pumping steadily out of my body and onto the ground. Every pulse of my heartbeat left me weaker and weaker. My ability to fight rapidly left me as I wilted.

"There you go, little wolf," he said. "Let me move you a little so we don't waste any of that precious liquid."

I felt my body being lifted and tilted so my head was closer to the ground, the flow of blood increasing with the new position of my body. My eyelids relaxed with the rest of my body, and surrendering to sleep became tempting. I could hear the dripping of my blood hit the red puddle that had accumulated in the hole next to the tree. I aimlessly wondered how much blood I had in my body. I was starting to feel cold.

"Sshhhh..." The True Alpha's whisper hit my ears.

I didn't even know that I'd been talking. My body was lifeless. My mind was empty. And I was gone.

My body hit the ground hard. The sound of my head hitting the forest floor echoed in my brain.

At least I would die where I was the most at peace.

CHAPTER TWENTY-NINE

"Lyka! Lyka! Don't you leave me. I fucking need you. Elise!"

Everett's voice was loud in my ear. He seemed so close yet so far away.

I tried to move my mouth to formulate a word, but either my brain or lips were not cooperating. I had lost too much blood.

"Open your eyes. Come on, mate. Open those eyes for me."

Sealed with cement, my eyelids refused to separate. I pulled and pulled, wishing they would open so I could see Everett's face one last time. I felt large fingers on either side of my eyelids, pulling them apart. The light was harsh against my corneas, and I winced at the discomfort.

My eyes were open, but it seemed as though I was looking through a telescope. Everett's face was so far away. Using the little energy I had, I lifted my hand to touch his face. He was much closer than my eyesight claimed, and I ended up slapping him on the cheek.

"You still have fight left in you." I could feel his rough fingers trace my cheek bone. "Don't waste your energy."

My vision widened. He was back in his human form, his face covered with blood. As I searched his face with my eyes for the cause of the bleeding, he read my mind. "Not my blood. My father's."

I relaxed in his arms, my body ready to let go. Never had I been this close to dying. I wasn't sure what it would feel like, crossing over, but I didn't have a choice. I would have to find out. Everett's face was pained as he looked at my own.

"I didn't want to have to do it this way." Everett continued to stroke my cheek. His fingers trailed along my jaw and down my neck to my collarbone. What little breath I had in my lungs left my body as he leaned his face close to mine. The click of his canine teeth popping from his gums made my body jolt. I could see the sharp white bones wet with saliva, Everett's tongue glossing over them.

He lowered his head to his favorite divot between my shoulder and my neck and inhaled sharply. "I wanted to wait until you were ready, but you have lost too much blood." His warm tongue coated my skin in a tender spot. He licked the spot, priming it for what was coming.

Feeling his warmth on the opposite side of my neck where his father had sliced me open to bleed out, my body shivered.

Everett's lips moved against the skin of my neck as he spoke. "This will hurt. I'll try to make it as quick as possible."

Pain was no longer something I feared. I had already felt all the blood leave my body. There was just numbness. I doubted I could feel much else.

"I'm sorry, Elise," he whispered. "I can't lose you."

The sound of his teeth puncturing my skin hit my ears before I felt them enter my body. There was a popping sound when his fangs pushed through my skin.

My body constricted, trying to combat the invasion. The pale skin surrounding the teeth screamed as his saliva hit my bloodstream, rushing through the veins and arteries throughout my body. My muscles tensed at the raw power that danced along my nerves.

I felt Everett holding my frame tightly against his, trying to manage the tremors that racked my body. There was pain. There was change.

I accepted it all.

EPILOGUE

Dafni

"THAT HUMAN GOT TOO CLOSE. She knows too much."

A whispered voice woke me.

My mother was here.

I knew better than to open my eyes. I knew that voice. I was better off pretending to sleep. My joints locked under the thin blanket covering me. I reminded myself to breathe evenly, naturally. Nothing good would come if she knew I was awake.

"The rot is growing. It can't come as a surprise that those in the woods are taking notice."

The familiar stirring of grandmother's wooden spoon hitting the sides of her cauldron were soothing. The sharp footsteps coming toward me were anything but.

"She'll let the shifters know everything she's discovered. If she hasn't already," my mother ranted. "After everything I've done. After everything I've created. I refuse to let an idiot human ruin everything." Her cadence increased, every click of her heel on the floor in time with the rapid beat of my heart.

"She won't be human for long," my grandmother mumbled from her place beside the cauldron. She had been working on a strengthening potion for the Coven when I'd gone to bed earlier. It wasn't uncommon that she stayed up late, tending to the potion, stirring it into submission under her careful tutelage.

"Do you have to throw it in my face, you hag?"

My mother's shriek was loud enough that I flinched beneath the blanket. My breathing stopped, all the air leaving my lungs.

Please don't notice me.

Please don't see me.

Please don't remember that I'm here.

"Hush, Matilda, the child's sleeping." My heart skipped a beat. The stir of my grandmother's wooden spoon continued, although quicker, the liquid sloshing against the sides of the cauldron.

"As if I wouldn't realize my child was in the room." The sound of her voice made my hands quiver. I clenched my fingersnails into my palms.

The point of her shoe poked me through the blanket and between two of my ribs. I held my tongue between my teeth, keeping my eyes closed. She would leave soon. She never stayed long. I just needed to pretend to sleep.

"You spoil her." I could feel her hot breath against my face. I opened my mouth, no longer able to stand the rancid stench entering my nose.

A finger pushed through my lips and ran along the gums under my upper lip, the pointed nail clacking along my teeth.

"There's nothing there yet," my grandmother said.

"That's what you said the last time. And the time before

that." Her finger left my mouth, her nail cutting the inside of my lip. The taste of iron immediately hit my tongue.

"Her poison will come. I'm sure of it." The handle of the wooden spoon hit the side of the cauldron, clanking against the metal. The floorboards creaked as they supported my grandmother's footsteps. "Leave her be. You promised me her first eighteen years."

A couple of heel clicks and a breeze let me know my mother had left my side. I let my eyelids open just enough to see the hazy scene before me. She and grandmother were toe-to-toe in the middle of the room, my grandmother standing her ground although she stood a full foot shorter.

"Don't make me regret giving her to you to raise instead of putting her in the Academy, where she belongs." Through the glow of the hearth, I could see drops of spit spewing from my mother's mouth as she spoke.

"You know Dafni's better off with me until she's grown."

"Dafni will corrode under you if you continue to coddle her."

"I raised you, didn't I?" Grandmother stood there for a moment before turning back to the hearth, slowly shuffling back to her potion.

My mother stood there for a moment, her silhouette that frequented my nightmares expanding and contracting with every heated breath. "Let me know if any dogs come sniffing around."

"You know I will," my grandmother said. "I will protect Dafni with my life."

A large exhale left Mother's silhouette, her long red hair catching her body's movement as she turned. I closed my eyes gently. My only defense was my supposed unconsciousness.

"Don't tell her I stopped by," she said. The clicking of her heels past the mound of furs I rested on and the slam of the screen door brought my heartbeat down to a manageable level.

Grandmother sighed, her stirring continuing. "You can stop pretending to sleep now, Dafni. You can't fool me."

I opened my eyes, staring at my grandmother in front of the flaming hearth. "I don't think I'll ever be able to stop pretending, Grandmother. Not in front of her."

She looked back down at her potion, getting lost in the swirling liquid.

"Then you'd better get better at pretending, Dafni. Your life depends on it."

THANK YOU

Did you enjoy getting *Entangled in the Woods?*

If you did, please leave a quick review on Amazon. Reviews are crucial to independent authors like me. Your review also helps other readers find books they love!

Thank you,

Evi James

ACKNOWLEDGMENTS

As a debut author, it's scary to have someone else read your work and give you feedback. Thank you to Abby and Kevin, who read it for the first time and didn't give me any weird looks about what came out of my brain and made its way onto paper.

Mandi, I don't know where to begin. You've been such a help to me through this entire process—I know a simple mention at the end of the book won't be enough to thank you, but I'll try. I opened your first edits of *Entangled* with only one eye open, scared you'd tell me it was crap and to scrap the whole thing. I was on cloud nine when I read your edits and realized that you *got* it. You understood what I was trying to accomplish with this book. I'm so glad my version of shifter romance didn't scare you away. You sprinkled your magical fairy dust on my writing, making it so much better than I could have on my own. I'm so fortunate to have clicked with an editor like you. Thank you.

ALSO BY EVI JAMES

The North Woods Series

Shadows in the Woods

Magic in the Woods

ABOUT THE AUTHOR

This is Evi's debut novel.

Evi lives with her husband, two daughters, and a clingy cat in Minnesota.

Website:

Evijamesauthor.com